First Edition: May 2018

Lulu Author. All rights reserved.
www.lulu.com
ISBN: 978-1-387-78621-3

Cover design by Missi Jay
Author photo by Johnny Stevens
Book design by Michael Campbell, MCWriting.com

# Dylan's Divide

• • •

a novel by
## Lane Rockford Orsak

Very special thanks to D.W. Griffin for inspiring the character of Dylan, and for your friendship.

C.M. Heck for illustrating what it means to truly have "heart and true grit," and for remembering the smile of a soldier. Gary Tso, Second Mesa, Arizona, for showing me the beauty, dignity, and importance of the Hopi culture and people.

Rory Stewart for writing "The Places In Between," and to Malalai Joya, for writing *A Woman Among Warlords,* both illustrating that the word truly is mightier than the sword.

Special thanks to Jim Thomsen, Bette Oliver, Laura Graham Hirschfeld, and Cathy Casey for making this a better story.

To Kuki for years of love and support.

# Contents

# Part One

• • •

"Pretty much anything that *you knew*, or *how you were* before you got here — you are going to leave it at the door."

— DRILL SERGEANT

2

# FOB Hamilton

*Summer, Afghanistan, 2012*

Another soldier and I are being deployed to Forward Operating Base Hamilton, the middle of hot fucking nowhere, Jaldak, Afghanistan, in the Zabul Province. We are traveling on a CH-47D supply and transport chopper, bringing bullets, Band-Aids, and a shit-ton of plastic bottled water, equally essential for both hydration and bathing. From my low-rank perspective, this war is about blowing shit up and putting it back together.

I spent my first five years in the Army back home, on the East Coast, learning how to fix complicated machines, and the last nine months of my deployment in Afghanistan buried on our base in Mazār-i-Sharīf, working on Mine-Resistant Ambush Protected trucks blown apart by IEDs, reading philosophy books, and hooking up with German girls in the I.S.A.F. Apparently, now they need guys with my skills in the more dangerous, remote operating bases. *Auf Wiedersehen,* ladies!

The other soldier traveling with me makes no effort to introduce himself. I find this utterly irksome, especially given the long, boring flight ahead. He has dark, intense eyes, high cheekbones, and seems pissed off at the world. He stares out across the mountain ranges mumbling what sounds to me like prayers in gibberish.

As I stare at the huge American flag mounted on the ceiling of the chopper, I wonder if he is an Afghan tribesman joining us as an interpreter. He sure as hell wasn't stationed back in Maryland, where I trained as a Power Generation Specialist. After a couple of hours of tedium, I hit him on the shoulder and extended my hand to shake his, and in a jovial manner ask, *"Como estas amigo?"* He just smirks and says, "I'm not Mexican!" and continues mumbling and looking off into the horizon.

About thirty minutes later, he stops mumbling, and turns to me, hand extended. "Mikey Sakiestewa, from Second Mesa, Arizona, how the fuck are you?" He smiles warmly. "Sorry man, I had to catch up with myself. It's been a long year, and this place seriously reminds me of back home. We Hopi pray a lot. Of course, we also like to grow corn, drink, fight, and fuck!"

All my disdain for the guy dissolves on the spot. He sure made up for lost time after his prayers. Apparently, he has been stationed in Iraq, and for the last year in the Korangal Valley in Afghanistan, which other guys refer to as The Valley of Death. He told Uncle Sam he would extend his deployment if he could transfer someplace with fewer daily 500-pound bomb explosions and less heavy fire from Taliban fighters. He says he stopped enjoying early morning mortar and grenades for breakfast and rushing to the wire in freezing weather in just his boxer shorts and OTV, which is his Outer Tactical Vest.

He tells me the President announced that the 33,000 troops presently in Afghanistan would be coming home over the next fifteen months, and we would all be out by 2015. The news gives me a feeling of invincibility and optimism, and I think, *We will find the bad guys, the Taliban, kick their asses, and in three months, I'll be out of this shit show, be back home in Austin, swimming naked in Lake Travis, attending the University of Texas by next summer! Life is good.*

As we near our new base near Jaldak, the pilot drops altitude and I can see the surrounding countryside: a dusty beige lunar landscape with contrasting expansive blue skies and the occasional fertile green valley. There are smatterings of medieval villages, with high brown mud and brick walls. The compounds are large enough to accommodate entire families, as well as a citrus orchard, mosque, or stables, all within the walls. It feels as if I have stepped back in time thousands of years.

Mikey and I are met as we come off the copter. The soldier gives us each a strong handshake. "Welcome to FOB Hamilton, gentlemen. I'm Corporal Steve Ramirez, but the animals here at FOB Ham call me Tacos." The L-T is up to his ass in paperwork and asked me to show you around. He said he will send your squad leader, Sergeant Reece, to get you later for a meet-and-greet."

"Why do they call you Tacos?" I ask Ramirez. The corporal responds, "Because when I got to my first FOB in the middle of the Iraqi desert, with camel spiders as big as my balls, which I know from being in the 'jack shack,' and having one crawl literally on my balls. They could hear my scream in Baghdad! Anyway, after eating MREs every day for six months, I lost it one day and climbed on top of a M1A1 tank in my tighty-whities, boots, and helmet, shouting at the top of my lungs, 'Who do I have to fuck around the place to get some tacos?'" Mikey and I both laugh and say, "Roger that!"

Mikey put his hand on Tacos's shoulder and says, "Well, amigo, my people, the Hopi Indians, have been making blue corn tortillas for centuries. If I see some corn around here I will make you a kickass taco, sir! Of course, we may have to 'commission' some local meat." Ramirez flashed a huge smile. "Now you're talking my language… *Tacos de cabra!*" I knew just enough Spanish to know Ramirez was talking about goats.

FOB Hamilton was named after the first fallen soldier, a young medic named David Hamilton. It is set up in the center of a confiscated compound known as a *Qalat,* selected for the tall, thick adobe walls and its strategic location on a hillside, far enough from the nearest village in the valley. The compound was once the residence of a powerful regional drug lord, and, most recently, as a Taliban arms stronghold. It is in close proximity to the Kabul-Kandahar Highway, or "Highway 1," that makes a huge semi-circle around the country, circumventing the Hindu Kush Mountains. Our base is thought to be instrumental in disrupting the Taliban and the warlords' arms and ammunition routes. It also allows us to intercept the opium exports to southern Pakistan, where it is converted into heroin and then shipped to America.

At the massive metal entrance door to our camp, I notice a hand-painted sign: WELCOME TO HELL. Once inside, I notice that about forty soldiers are housed in ten tents neatly arranged around a central sand-and-rock courtyard. In the center is an ingenious pool the guys constructed out of HESCO protective barriers and God knows what else. As I observed American ingenuity at its finest and all the effort the guys have made to make this hellish sandpit feel like home, I quietly christened our camp "The Haji Hilton."

The officers, medics, and briefing rooms are all in the old main house, and the ANA — Afghan National Army — guys reside on the second floor. The third floor appears to have a missing roof and the walls are riddled with bullet holes. Normally, when arriving at a new FOB, soldiers have to construct everything from the ground up: walls, tents, latrine area, ammo storage, mortar pit, and lookout towers. The most important area is where we store the massive stash of plastic water bottles that clean our dusty bodies and quench our constant thirst. It is tough work to set up a base. It could occupy several city blocks, or be simply four trucks parked in a square. I was fortunate that everything at FOB Hamilton is ready for me to get my proverbial war on.

On the way to show us where Mikey and I will bunk, Tacos babbles on about recent base events. He seems to have a real hard-on for Taliban skirmishes. He enthusiastically recalls what he thinks are "hilarious firefights" that almost get everyone killed: an ambush and a "daisy chain" of IEDs last week. Ultimately, he is sure the war is heading toward certain victory. "These people need our help, and they need to embrace democracy. We need to dig in and win this shit!"

He has an unapologetic attitude about winning at any cost.

"Man, these little Haji fuckers don't like to face us and fight. They try and blow up our convoys and triangulate ambushes from the surrounding mountains, or hide in the trees of an almond or pistachio grove. They love to attack us with RPGs in the morning and late at night. They are fierce fighters, but they make really stupid mistakes. They will attack us, and then all run into a small farmer's shed in an open field and think they are safe. They have an out-of-sight, out-of-danger mentality. Until we call in a bird, and we obliterate the little fuckers with a Hellfire missile."

Ramierz went on: "We let the Afghan Nationals do patrol duty during the day, mostly afternoon, and we take the night shift. We can't really trust that one of these guys doesn't have a cousin in the Taliban or that they have been offered twice what we pay them to leave a door open. If you know what I mean.

"These Haji dudes dig things that go boom! The fucking bigger the blast, the more excited they get. We can hear them on the Taliban radio intercept after they blow shit up chanting 'Allah Akbar.' Really gets 'em going! My God's got bigger bombs than your God's got, kinda shit."

When we arrive at our tent, the corporal enters quickly without announcement, and we hear him scream, *"Stand down, Kong!"* The command is immediately rebuffed by a crazy-sounding Alabama redneck yelling from the other side of the tent, "How the fuck am I suppose to cum with you fobbits making so much racket?"

I enter the tent and stand there in disbelief, staring at a soldier standing buck naked, wearing a beat-up straw cowboy hat, with an enormous cock, watching porn on his laptop, and masturbating openly in broad daylight. He seems to not have a care in the world.

Another soldier jumps off his bunk to greet us with a soulful, smooth, and deep voice. He looks at Mikey incredulously. "Oh, shit, if it isn't 'Tonto Sakowitz, the Hebrew Hopi!'"

Mikey lurches forward in what I think will be a fight and/or his court-martial, and he slams his finger in the face of a tall, solidly built, young black soldier, "Oh well, if it ain't 'Dope' you can't smoke. I thought those Haji fucks blew your ass up in Fallujah!"

Then Mikey turns to the naked soldier and screams, "King Kong! You swamp-fishing, oyster-loving, dirty-ass redneck, haven't you learned any manners in this United States Army? Don't you have the decency to go to the porno-potty like a normal soldier?"

The naked soldier sports a huge tattoo of a ferocious panther slinking down on his left arm, and bold letters across his chest spelling I-N-F-I-D-E-L. He starts laughing and tells Mikey, "First of all, it is too fucking hot for the jack shack. It is one hundred and thirty degrees in those stinky things. I know, 'cause I already passed out in one! Second, if the Lieutenant hadn't lost his fucking mind and posted the new DON'T SHAKE THE SHACK... IT IS A DERELICTION OF DUTY signs all over the Porta-Potties, making it a fucking crime to jerk off... how American is that? You can get blown up, shot, stabbed, and tortured, but for God's sake, *don't jerk off!*"

Mikey realizes, after about fifteen minutes of ruckus ranting by all parties, that he has failed to introduce me to the guys. I am unpacking my gear and stacking up my small library of books borrowed from the "honor library" back in Mazār-i-Sharīf under my bunk. The black soldier says, "Damn man, how many books did you bring? This is war, not Harvard, college baby!" That makes the others laugh.

He walks over to me, as if he is inspecting me. "Yes, sir, I know what I'm calling your blue-eyed, big-white-teeth, Hollywood-lookin' ass—Books!"

"My mama named me Dylan Griffith, but I like Books. So do you guys like to read?" I try to ask sincerely.

"Of course we read. Kong here reads *Hustler, Playboy,* and back issues of *Screw!*"

I smile and reach out with a book offering to Dope. "Here, I read this one on the way over to Afghanistan. I think you will like it! Sorry for the messy pages in the middle. A hot little Latina WAC gave me a hand job on my flight to Germany!"

"Man, you is as *nasty* as the Kong! *Autobiography of Malcolm X*—Even I know this cat—he is from Chicago! Thank you, Books. I appreciate this. Look here, Kong, Books done brought me a Christmas present in June."

"Sorry, Kong, I'm a little short on magazines!" I say playfully.

"Oh, it's cool, bro. My brother sends me this shit by the wheelbarrow-full. He thinks it's his contribution to the War on Terror."

Ramirez, realizing suddenly that he is supposed to be the man in charge, pipes up. "OK, Kong, you get cleaned up to meet the Lieutenant within the hour. See you men there. Oh, and Mikey, I'm gonna hold you to those cabrito tacos."

"Roger that," Mikey answers.

When Tacos is gone, Dope and Kong both say in unison, in creepy-sounding voices, "Uuuh Ohhhh, you are going to see Lieutenant Jack 'The Ripper' Breckovich."

The men start laughing, and I just stand back and watch them banter in amazement. Insults are flying, followed by more and more uproarious laughter at each volley. These guys all served together in Iraq, and went to boot camp back in Georgia at Fort Benning. It is obvious that they are no strangers to one another, or to war: they are loyal brothers by choice. For the next several months, it is going to be my job to kill the Taliban and protect my new brothers. I am overcome with anxiety for the first time since I joined the Army, by the enormity of that responsibility, and feel my first tinge of unprocessed, raw fear. As Dope says, "This shit is about to get real up in here!"

Within the hour, a man walks into our tent in his rainbow PT gear and no shirt. He is one impressive batch of pecs and biceps, with an elaborate, photo-realistic tattoo of the Garden of Eden on his chest: Adam standing alone eating an apple, with no Eve in sight, over his heart. In close proximity, a large serpent is spiraling down a tree.

Dope and Kong snap to attention, followed by Mikey and I, until we hear a very calm, "At ease men!" If I am correct, I hear a distinct southern Louisiana bayou accent, not Cajun but a distinct drawl.

"Gentlemen, welcome to Hamilton FOB. I am Staff Sergeant Reece Taylor, and some of the men call me Tiger. I am your squad leader and it is a pleasure to have you on our team. I'm asked by the Lieutenant to escort you to his office in ten minutes for a brief face-to-face to go over your mission. He wants the entire squad in attendance."

The squad responded with, "Yes G Sergeant!"

"Griffith, welcome aboard. I know this is your first tour of duty, and you're on a team with some serious soldiers. I expect you to get up to speed. What do the guys call you, or have they given you your team identity yet?"

"Sir, yes, sir. Books!"

"Let's hope you are as smart as your name, Private Griffith!"

"I am certain my *ass* is, sir!" I blurted out, unable to catch my response, a problem since grade school.

The sergeant smirks and salutes, flexing his huge bicep. "At ease, men. Movement at eleven hundred hours—sharp!"

Kong said, "Dude, you're begging to clean the Porta-Potties for days with that mouth of yours."

"I wouldn't try that shit with The Ripper. He might feed you to the Taliban," Dope says, laughing.

"A loving, family sort of guy?" I ask with a sly smile.

They both say in unison, "You'll see. Prepare to *embrace the suck!*"

For the next ten minutes, we exchange the usual questions and answers about our lives back home. I was able to piece together a picture of everyone's life story in about ten minutes. It's strange how that works in the military. I guess it is like being in jail. You know you aren't going anywhere anytime soon. You tend to look at a guy, and in a split second you try to determine if he is: a natural-born killer, smart, dumb, with heart, or what we call a "Blue Falcon": a buddy-fucker, inclined to screw the next guy. Everything gets distilled down to the simplest terms—is this contributing to my life or my death—and it's always determined by the guy standing beside you. In a firefight, no room for a buddy-fucker.

On the FOB, guys become masters of chitchat. We learn every good, bad, and stranger-than-fiction thing about the guys on our team. We learn who is brilliant and who is Neanderthal. It is simply amazing how much personal information Americans download in such a short time, but even more dazzling in the desert. I learn the following:

Michael "Mikey" Sakiestewa is twenty-three, a Hopi Native American from the Sun Forehead Clan, Second Mesa, Arizona. He is half Navajo on his father's side, which posed several potential problems, so he took his mother's family name. His father, who left the house when Mikey was five, served in Vietnam in the Special Forces and seems to love to drink, fight, and make love to women other than his wife. Mikey is good-looking, with piercing, intelligent dark eyes, and lighting-speed humor. He seems afraid of nothing, and talks incessantly, sharing political criticism and historical anecdotes.

He attended an elite private school in Arizona called the Orme School, an international selection of bright, rich children mostly from Southern California. He was the special little "Indian boy" who got an academic scholarship offered by the DuPont family, whose girl Sydney attended the school. They began to rethink their enthusiastic patronage when Mikey started dating Sydney in his junior year. Sydney was transferred to a boarding school in Europe the following year. Mikey was so angry that he quit and returned to the reservation, soon joining the Army.

Diego "Dope" Daniels, twenty-two, is from the Austin neighborhood in the South Side of Chicago. Of Chicago's seventy-seven communities, Austin is the largest and most dangerous. It was once a place to find the most elegant homes and now it is the best place to score the purest heroin in Chicago. The Vice Lords gang controls most of the heroin traffic, giving the area the name "Heroin Super Highway." Dope likes to say, "These Haji drug lords round here ain't got shit on me. My twelve-year-old brother got more game than these fools."

His father is one of the early founders of the Vice Lords, and his mother is a beautiful Latina from a rival gang, the Latin Kings. He went to a high school that ensured a stunted education, but he is by nature a super-curious guy, and is quick to identify foul play. He is filled with determination and moxie. He joined the service to get his brother and mother out of poverty and as far from the South Side as possible.

Connor "Kong" Macintyre, twenty-two, is from Point Aux Pins, Alabama. He is tough as nails, patriotic, and horny to the point of pathological. His parents own an oyster farm, where he grew up working in water up to his chest, moving heavy mesh bags of oysters, in a method called the "Australian longline," to keep the oysters off the gulf floor and away from predators.

His family has a military history that dates back to the American Revolution, and his greatest desire is to go to Army Ranger School and become an elite soldier like his father was in Vietnam. With that said, he seems to love pop music and eats more junk food than any human I have ever seen, and has zero body fat. He says, "Man, this dusty place makes me want to eat candy, fuck cheerleaders, and kill bad guys!"

• • •

At 1100 hours, Sergeant Reece pops his head in our tent and says, "Let's pop smoke!"

We jump up and spill out of the tent, making our way toward the main house. Several guys are clowning around in the pool after being on night watch. One guy is hanging on the side of the pool with his arms stretched out and is snoring, fast asleep.

In the main house, Headquarters, a large room is filled with four neat rows of folding chairs facing a whiteboard and a podium with the 1st Battalion, 24th Infantry Regiment flag boasting SEMPER PARATUS: Always Prepared. Mikey looks at Dope and says, "Man, they need to change this regiment name. You realize that the 24th Infantry Regiment was formed in 1869 so Buffalos Soldiers, afro-brothers like you, could come and try and kill Native American people!" Dope gives Mikey a glare. "Well, they obviously missed one!"

We joke around as the guys from our squad slowly fill the seats. Soon, Corporal Ramirez briskly enters the room barking "Attention!" We stand and salute, and I can't wait to have eyes on Jack the Ripper. Moments later, a tall, lanky man briskly cuts around the corner and stands at the podium as if he will call on someone in the audience to fistfight for fun. He stares at everyone in the room. His blue, beady eyes are intensified by his absence of hair and his arching eyebrows. He has a sardonic smirk of superiority. He seems particularly perturbed, and is obviously choosing the right moment to pounce.

"Good morning. For the new guys who don't know me yet, my name is First Lieutenant Jack Breckovich. Welcome to FOB Hamilton. Major Leeland Armstrong is called to Kabul to Strategic Command, and asked me to step in today. This will give me the opportunity to have a little heart-to-heart with you guys.

"What is all this boo-fucking-hoo going on around this FOB? I don't need this shit. You have about five seconds to *unfuck* yourself. I am going to break it down Barney-style for you little fobbits:

"*First point,* I'm a West Point graduate. I have a chemical engineering degree and I am an Army Ranger. Oh, What's that? You went to college, too? Oh, I know you did. I'm sure that semester and a half at Bumfuck County College really taught you a lot. However, not enough to stop you guys from losing your Camelbak. The difference between you and me is you don't get your ass chewed out by the battalion commander when some private loses a fucking Camelbak; I do. A goddamn canteen! You think I want that kind of shit to cost so much? You think that I want to be responsible for every screw, nail, and rubber band that makes an MTOE? No, I don't. So, keep your shit with you, and don't lose it.

"Next point. Intel confirms enemy movement of arms on Highway 1 between Jaldak and Shahjoy. It is our belief that the Taliban are using those small village hamlets to hide arms and to move opium to exporters in Southern Pakistan and east to Iran. Effective oh-three hundred hours, your convoy squad will patrol this area everyday until otherwise informed. The ISAF Romanian units will support your team: Second Infantry Battalion 'Calugareni' and 495th Infantry Battalion, Captain

Stefan Soverth. They are located north of Qalat-e-Gilzay at FOB Dracula. I shit you not—FOB Dracula! They fly blue, gold, and red patch with Romanian Army, and wear MP on their sleeves. Over the radio, they will respond to Drac-one-two-three, et cetera. I don't want any good-initiative, bad-judgment calls from you Hollywood Fuck Puppets. You will remain courteous and professional at all times.

"If you are a 'double-digit midget,' and you think just because you are going home soon you will just sit on your ass and jerk off on FOB Hamilton all day—think again! We are in this war to win it, not babysit these farmer's poppy fields and eat Pringles your mama sent you.

"To win this war, we must achieve our objectives: defeat terrorists. Suppress opium production. Access the region's natural resources. Prevent the rise of regional hegemony: that means Russia and China. Contain Iran.

"To achieve those goals, *you have to be achievers,* like Patton, MacArthur, or Colin Motherfucking Powell. You know what they had in common? They're all hard-ass, eat-up-a-private and spit 'em out, democracy-savin', enemy-killin' sons-a-bitches. Oh yeah, all of them! What? You gonna try and say something, or just salute me? I suggest you do the latter. Now get out there and win their motherfucking hearts and minds!"

"Sir, yes sir!" We stand and answer in unison. Half the guys are pumped up, and half are mumbling under their breath, "What a *psycho fuck.*"

Mikey turns to me and with a big smile whispers, "The Ripper strikes me as someone who smells little girl's bicycle seats back in Manhattan!"

I love Mikey more by the second.

# Hearts and Minds

AFTER OUR MEETING with The Ripper, we spill into the courtyard, and the base is buzzing with activity. There are guys splashing in the pool and another group playing with the ANA guys in a less brutal version of Buzkashi, the Afghan national sport. If ever there was a perfect metaphor for the conflict in this country, Buzkashi is it. The tribal leaders ride on horseback and try to grab a disemboweled goat carcass and drop it in the winner's circle. It is a brutal display of macho manhandling. However, in the FOB Hamilton version, the men are on one another's shoulders as if they are mounted on a stallion, and they are trying to grab a big stuffed Miss Piggy doll, and drop it in a winner's circle drawn with white flour "requisitioned" from the kitchen.

Ramirez trots over and tells me and Mikey that we are to follow Dope and Kong in the convoy and rendezvous with the Romanian troops at FOB Dracula in Qalat.

We make our way to the loading area and our convoy trucks are ready to go. Dope and Kong are in front of us in a Cougar 4x4 MRAP, mounted with a .50-caliber machine gun. Of course, Kong is the gunner. I am to drive the Buffalo MRAP and Mikey is my gunner. Our truck is the big daddy of all trucks. It is 26.9 feet long, eight feet wide, and allows for an additional twelve passengers. It can travel three hundred miles and reach a cruising speed of sixty-five mph. Our trucks both have V-shaped hulls and mesh, specially designed to redirect blast, out and away, from IED blasts, and also for passenger transport and route clearance. It is equipped with a hydraulically powered articulated "claw." If you are blown up, stranded, or sliding off an Afghan mountain, I'm your guy.

Just as we exit the FOB, I hear Dope on the radio saying, "Hooker Two, this is Hooker One, you copy? Over!" I start laughing and respond, "Hooker One, this is Hooker Two, ready to *turn tricks* with the Taliban. Over!" As we briskly make our way down a goat trail to the Kandahar-Ghazni Highway, I can see Kong on the .50-cal acting crazy and sending me the hook-'em horns hand signals with his long tongue fully extended, like he is a member of the band KISS. God only knows what Mikey is doing up top.

It takes about thirty minutes to reach the town of Qalat-e-Gilzay. I can see the ancient fortress built by Alexander the Great over two thousand years ago, on his push to India. Today it struggles for life, while overlooking a magnificent valley.

As we arrive at the outskirts of Qalat-e-Gilzay, Mikey can't take the heat and dust, and joins me inside the cab. We laugh and exchange observations about this strange new land. Mikey insists that it looks exactly like New Mexico, and parts of Arizona. "These folks live like my folks — it is unbelievable. Feels just like home. We Hopi also live in an ancient culture, with a new culture trying to destroy it."

Mikey points to Alexander's old fortress in the offing and says, "Wow, that is amazing. Truly, the graveyard of the empires."

"Why is that?" I naively ask.

"That is what they call Afghanistan because so many empires have tried to invade her unsuccessfully. These poor bastards have been invaded by the Persians, Greeks, Arab caliphates, Mongols, the Mughal Empire, Sikhs, British — twice — Russians, and now Dylan, Mikey, the United States of America military, and the International Security Assistance Force: fifty-nine of our buddy countries, with four hundred military bases to provide 'security' for these nice agrarian folks."

"Why are we here again?" I ask, laughing nervously.

"Oil, black gold, Texas Tea is one reason. Our CIA helped the Shah of Iran take power, and Iran and Saudi Arabia were called the 'twin towers.' They kept the political stability in the region. My grandfather met the Shah of Iran on the Hopi res back home!"

"Man, have you been smoking peyote?"

"No, I can show you a picture of the Shah of Iran standing on our patio looking like a Parisian fashion model, watching the Kachina dancers."

"The what?"

"I'll get into the Kachinas later."

"Man, I thought we came to Afghanistan in 2001 to kill Osama Bin Laden and Al Qaeda, the guys—they say—are responsible for the attacking the Twin Towers?" I ask sincerely.

Mikey laughs hysterically, "Dude, these guys are Saudi Arabian, not even from Afghanistan, but they were hiding here in the northern mountains near Pakistan. The Pakistan government gave them shelter. Saudi Arabia and Pakistan are both Sunni countries and have a long history of mutual support."

"But, our Navy SEAL, Team Six, killed Bin Laden in Pakistan. The bad guys are dead. Can we go home now?"

"Well, not so fast, Books. We still need to accomplish our objectives: a 'democratic' government in Afghanistan, flex our geopolitical muscles, and to try and 'stabilize' the region. Oh, and in the process, we have found a shit-ton of natural resources worth a fortune: vast mineral wealth, rare metals, oil and gas, mineral wealth, emeralds, and of course, Afghanistan is the world's largest supplier of opium. I assume we don't want that to go to the bad guys."

"Do people still smoke opium?"

"Buddy boy, opium is the base for heroin. You have been watching too many Chinese Kung Fu movies. Global drug trafficking is about a four-hundred-billion-dollar industry, not to mention opium that makes billions of dollars for our U.S. pharmaceutical industry. And, isn't it interesting that we are here getting blown to bits, and this year CNPC—China's National Petroleum Company—is awarded a contract to create three oil fields along the Amu Darya River in the northern Afghanistan, and India is given a ten billion dollar lease for iron mining in Central Afghanistan."

Mikey smiles. "You see, our lofty, God-loving democracy rhetoric comes with an equally high interest in capturing wealth. Is that *for the good of the nation,* or simply for the few who enjoy the profits? Tricky business, that!"

He is really wound up now. "As long as you, and the average Joe, are given the idea of the possibility of advancement, the system stays sexy, 'the American Dream.' That is how our President was elected, on the idea of hope! When our entire economic system was about to implode. When the house of cards crumbles, all that love, compassion, and loving thy neighbor as yourself shit goes out the proverbial window. And that is why I am a Hopi, my friend, until I die."

"What does being Hopi have to do with it?"

"Hopi is not our race. Hopi is our *way of life.* A path. One has to learn and grow for a lifetime to understand the way of the Hopi. We have been around fourteen thousand years in Arizona, not to mention still live in the oldest city in America, over eleven hundred years of continuous occupation, and the average Joe has never fucking heard of it."

"What?"

"Yep, Oraibi. It's beautiful. Someday, if I make it out of the sandbox, I will invite you to visit me there, Books."

"Wow, that would be amazing. Thank you!"

Mikey stares out the window, and starts mumbling prayers again. After a few minutes, he gives a heavy sigh and reaches for a plastic water bottle in the back.

"Mikey, if the Afghan people of this country hate the Taliban and want democracy so badly, why are we needed? Why don't they just have elections and we can get on down the road?"

"This is very tricky. First of all, Afghanistan is a nation of fiercely independent tribes. There are about thirteen different ethnic groups. The largest tribe is where we are stationed, the Pashtun: about forty percent of the population, and they speak a dialect of Persian, *Pashto*. Pashtuns that are living in Pakistan are now called Pakistani Pashtuns, basically the same folks. Also, to add to the complexity, within tribes, there are sub-tribes."

"So, we like to see Pakistan as our ally, and they are the same people as the ones we are fighting?"

"Yep."

"In Afghanistan, there are other ethnic tribes. The second largest ethnic group is in the North, the Tajik, along with the Hazara and the Uzbek. They speak *Dari*, more like the Persian language spoken by their Iranian neighbors to the west. Almost all people living in Afghanistan are Muslim, in religion, but there are two different branches."

Mikey is interrupted by the radio squawking, "Hooker Two, this is Hooker One, you copy? Over!"

"Roger that Hooker One. Over."

"Man, we need to pull over for two mikes. Break. Kong's dong has had an accident. Over."

"Roger that."

Mike starts laughing, "That dude is going to get his dong blown off before the end of this conflict."

"What's up with that?" I ask, truly dismayed by Kong's fascination with his penis. He was like a four-year-old warrior porn star.

Mikey says, "That boy is complicated." Yeah, complicated like this fucking country, and the crazy politics.

As Kong is finishing cleaning up his mess in the other truck, I sit for a moment and realize that I am sweating profusely from the intensity of the heat. Soon, the guys take off ahead of us bellowing dust, and I can't see the road in front of me. After it clears, and I am quickly back on the road, I ask Mikey, "So before the we rolled in, I know the Russians invaded, right?"

Mikey flashes me an ironic grin, "Before the Russians invaded in 1979, Afghanistan had a Shah, or king. His name was Mohammed Zahir Shah. He tried to modernize Afghanistan. He believed women should be educated and work. He didn't believe in cloaking them like stored furniture. When he went to Italy for an eye surgery in 1973, his cousin overthrew the government."

I slip in, "That brings a new meaning entirely to the expression of 'being blindsided!'"

"Or in his case, surgically fucked by his cousin. Anyway, as the story unfolds, the Russians invaded in 1979. After the Russians left in 1989, leaving a political cluster fuck, a violent Mujahedeen commander put in place a radical Islamist government. This began a brutal civil war among the Afghan people.

"In the midst of the conflict, the brutally strict Taliban gained control of the nation and ruled from 1996 to 2001, until we invaded. Karzai was put in power by the United States. His half-brother is thought to be a warlord involved in the opium trade. Many of the Afghan tribes do not trust him and view his government as merely puppets for foreign interest.

"So, that's where we enter the shit show? Dude, can you get me a water bottle please? This fucking heat is killing me."

I had to pause Mikey for a moment. I want to know what he was telling me, but it is just so exhausting trying to keep up with all this shit.

Mikey hands me the bottle. For just a moment, I see a man walking over the barren, rocky landscape with such purpose. We are trained to scope anyone for possible danger. His arms are gathered behind his back as if they are bound with rope, or a philosophy professor on his way to class. He wears a brown turban, long tunic, loose pants, and a long black vest. He has a full gray beard. His dusty, black leather shoes are worn with no socks. We are miles from any sign of humanity. Our eyes lock, and he turns his gaze ahead. I feel his disdain and repulsion, followed by my feeling of isolation as a stranger in a strange land. The moment is poetic and painful. Mikey is oblivious to how deeply this impacts me, as he continues to "explain" the story of why we are here.

"The United States enters the show with the Taliban regrouping its leadership across the border in Pakistan, headed by Mullah Mohammed Omar. Of course, Pakistan is at odds with India and they have nuclear weapons, and we are at odds with Iran, who we are trying to prevent from gaining nuclear weapons, and we invaded their Shia neighbor, Iraq! And that, my friend, is the political shit storm that constitutes the stage for our new hit Broadway musical, *Operation Enduring Freedom!*"

Mikey draws in a deep, long breath, and I break in.

"Man, there are many countries on the planet, like North Korea, that have corrupt, despotic leaders in power and we don't try to go in and overthrow their government and create a democracy."

"Democracy in Afghanistan? That is a fucking joke!" Mikey shoots back. "They have no strong central government, regional warlords and drug lords compete for power, and they have a national economy based on black-market opium sales, thanks to the British who used to trade them tea for opium, and the United States who now buys the majority of their opium. We give the Afghanistans the idea of security, freedom, and democracy, and they give us an excuse to invade, ensuring someone is making billions in profits, giving the American taxpayer the bill, and tell the American public we are chasing the *bad guy*. Look at my people, you guys have tried to convert us for two hundred and thirty-five years, and we still aren't buying your shit!"

"Dude, you guys call me Books, but I'm going to start calling you Wiki. You are like fucking Wikipedia! So why are you here, Mikey?" I'm slightly bewildered by the intensity of our conversation, and horrified by my ignorance on the politics of a war, especially given that I am smack dab in the middle of the morass.

"Because I don't want terrorists in my country, or any other country. There are some very bad dudes out there. Did you know that after the World Trade Center attack on September 11, 2001, the old Hopi warriors got on their horses and rode out to meet the enemy? Everyone agrees the Taliban are illiterate thugs that believe in a system of law that is archaic, and will not improve the lives of the Afghanistan citizens, but from someone, such as myself, who lives in a culture that is fourteen thousand years old and has watched—and continues to watch—foreign invaders with agendas fuck us out of our natural resources in the name of progress and democracy... this is a tough pill to swallow, my friend! As we say in my language, *Koyaanisqatsi*: life out of balance."

"Shit man, looks like you and I have a lot to talk about, brother!"

"My grandfather, Willy, Junior, used to say, 'Before you make any decision, consider its effect on the next seven generations.'"

"Wise man. I'd like to meet him someday," I say.

Mikey pauses, looking out onto the expansive vistas and welcoming the chance to absorb everything around us. The little villages outside of town have little wobbly roadside vendor stalls spilling into the narrow crowded streets. Small boys sell nuts and fruits in front of the various shop stalls. A market offers slaughtered goats, carpets, and traditional men's clothing like the ubiquitous *khet partug,* or "pajamas," that the Pashto men wear with turbans and scarves.

"Books, I recently heard an Afghan warlord, the real unofficial power base of the country, while serving as an elected member of Parliament, in control of four provinces, say on national television, 'The U.S. is like a blind man walking on a roof: sooner or later, he will fall off.'"

As we enter the city, I try to connect with my surroundings. As a kid, I grew up poor. I took a bath using a bucket of tap water, eating pork and beans out of a can for dinner, and not having money for school supplies. But this is different. It appears as if these people only have the clothes on their back. Many of these people have never seen a school classroom, much less a computer, or a department store.

I don't see a single person who appears dangerous, or threatening, but each man's eyes appear chary, distrusting and weary. There are groups of young male children playing and working. So many kids everywhere. *Why are they not all in school?* Then I learn, the region struggles to find teachers, because the Taliban loves to execute educators who don't share their views.

As we enter, the urban area driving becomes crazy. There are no shoulders and everyone is in competition for control of the road. I pass funny small three-wheel trucks named "Rangers" filled with entire families and large, colorfully decorated "Jingle trucks" transporting produce to market. I dodge old men on donkeys. I avoid numerous motorcycles with colorful hand-knotted wool rugs fashioned as seat cushions, as they zip around me. I narrowly miss hitting bicyclists and pedestrians who litter the roadways, donkey carts, and cars driving into oncoming traffic. There are no posted speed limits, street signs, or traffic signals. The street chaos is a microcosmic symbol of how life really functions in Afghanistan—every man for himself!

I spot delicious prepared foods for sale on the street. I haven't enjoyed homemade food in a while and I want to stop so badly and buy something to eat, but I don't speak the language well, have no Afghani currency with me, and it is against orders to stop the convoy to try local delicacies. The fresh naan bread is driving me crazy, but I'm trying to keep up with Dope and Kong, who are now a considerable distance ahead.

Outside of Qalat we turn west and head toward another fortress on the hillside: FOB Dracula. The watchtowers are manned with .50-caliber machine guns. We stop in front, and the doors slowly open. It occurs to me that I have never met a Romanian and have no idea what they look like. A tall, slender guard with dark brown eyes and hair walks up to the window of Hooker-1, checks Dope's identification, and waves him into the compound. He signals for me to follow. As we enter, I am struck by the architectural similarity to our FOB. The Romanian soldiers are enjoying their lunch outside, under a makeshift patio cover.

A short, affable soldier introduces himself as Anton and repeatedly apologizes, "Excuse me bad English!" We introduce ourselves by our nicknames, which they seem to find hilarious. Anton kindly invites us to have lunch with his squad. Of course, we accept and before we know it, we are all laughing, trying to communicate, and eating a home-cooked Romanian meal: sour meatball soup, followed by chicken paprika with tomato and garlic sauce over rice.

The other guys at the table are Vali, who looks Middle Eastern; Costin, a gentle giant; and Dracul, a tall thin guy with dark eyes. They all seem cool. The Romanians don't really speak English beyond present-tense simple sentences, with the occasional trumped-up adjectives like *incredible, fantastic, or amazing!* They say things like, "I love McDonald's hamburger —*fantastic!*" The next guy will offer, "I like Apple iPad computer —*incredible!*"

Of course, as with all conversations in the Army, eventually sexual savagery wins out. Leave it to Kong to immediately go for the porn gold medal!

"Hey, Dracul, are the Romanian porn girls hot?"

"Very hot. I am liking Romanian porn star Dayanna Kill. But, I am also liking Internet American porn girls — Incredible! Do American girlfriend like to fack like in movie show — *a pula* in every hole?"

As the ambassador of all things sexual in the United States of America, Kong responds for the squad.

"You bet your vampire ass they do! Do your vampire bitches like to do double anal?"

Seeing the incoming sexual RPG (ridiculous porn grenade) about to explode, I try to steer the conversation to something more erudite. I tell them that we don't really know anything about their culture. What are some things Romanians have brought to the world? Costin proudly announces, "We bring the world insulin," which he pronounces in three syllables: *"een-sue-lean."* Dope blurts out, "Man, you people did not bring the world Chinese food!"

Anton chirps up and says with tremendous pride, "OK, OK. We bring the world the fountain pen." Mikey leans in and fires off a pun, "So is it safe to say that your culture has *written* a very unique page in history?" Anton is obviously frustrated by our lack of appreciation for giving the world the fountain pen and adds, "OK, OK. We have heaviest building in the world!" We Americans burst out laughing, almost falling off the picnic benches and the Romanians just sit expressionless with a growing sense of displeasure. Realizing the futility of truly communicating about anything of significant cultural relevance, Kong continues with more universally appreciated topics and inquires about the Romanians' mothers, sisters, schoolteachers, girlfriends, and female livestock.

Kong continues to push Dracul about his name. Kong insists that he is Dracula's illegitimate son from the castle's vampire cleaning maid. Dracul insists his name is not derived from Dracula, the vampire, but instead means "devil or dragon," but Kong keeps pushing him on it, saying, "Man, you little devil, you know you are the grandson of the most famous vampire in the entire world!" Dracul tries to retaliate by saying, "Yes, but you are not *King* Kong!" He makes a lewd gesture to accompany his remark. Kong tells him to go fuck himself. Dracul, now agitated, gives him a lesson in Romanian expletives: *"Du-te in pula mea!"* (Basically, "fuck you!")

Kong's reactions get crazier, and so do the insults, each man digging into what appears to be an endless reservoir of testosterone. The escalating jocular jabs cause both squads to laugh more, and more uproariously, drawing an impressive crowd of onlookers. And finally, the crescendo: Dracul, realizing that he could not be trampled on in his own country's operating base, in front of God and country, stands on the bench, half-crazed, pulls out his cock and screams to Kong in a hoarse, guttural command, *"Sugi pula!"*

At first, the other Romanian soldiers have the look I have seen one thousand times in the Army, wondering: *Have they gone too far? Did he just cross the line? Are they going to kill one another?*

Kong just smiles, jumps on top of the table and pulls out his favorite toy, which causes all of the Romanians to drop their mouths in astonishment as Kong screams, "Sugi and pull-a ON THIS, you vampire motherfucker!"

All of the fun quickly comes to an abrupt halt when their commander walks over and loudly inquires if they will think it is funny when a Taliban sniper shoots off Dracul's and the American's *pula?* Of course, this makes everyone cry with laughter, including the commander. He introduces himself as Captain Soverth, and we all stand, and give him a crisp salute, as Kong frantically tries to stow away his show-stopping *pula.*

In very good English the captain welcomes us to FOB Dracula, adding, "And, no, we don't want to suck your blood!" He reiterates our mission in a more serious tone, and encourages us to make contact with the villages north, and get back to our base before dark. He reminds us that we are simply trying to have a *presence* and gather intel. We are not to kick down doors or search villagers. "Remember, as your leaders say, 'Hearts and minds,' gentlemen!" With that, we all get in our trucks and head northwest down a small, dusty goat road toward the mountains.

The Romanian guys are driving in between us in a Humvee with mounted M240Gs.

When we leave the compound, it is the first time that I feel like I am entering the war. But now I don't feel alone, with our Romanian brothers, which gives our mission a strange sense of excitement.

As we bump down the narrow, dusty road, Dope says, "Hooker One to Hooker Two, over…"

"Hooker One, this is Hooker Two, over!"

Then we hear, "Hooker One…" the call is interrupted by "Drac One over."

"Copy you, Drac One. This is Hooker One. Go ahead."

"You see guy in black man-dress in the field on left, over?"

"Copy that, we have eyes on the man in black. Over."

"He is Taliban scout. We see him many times. Over."

"Copy that, Drac One. Should we stop and have a chat?"

"Chat? What is chat? Over."

"Drac One, never mind. Let's go on to Patkheyl village. Over."

"Copy that, Hooker One."

The convoy continues charging down the goat trail, causing a cloud of dust to fly high above us. After about ten minutes, Dope slams on his brakes, causing everyone to panic and slide sideways to a stop. Without using radio contact, he continues again at full speed. Mikey says, "Probably hit something."

"Hooker Two, this is Hooker One. You can let Tacos know that we are having BBQ *cabrito* tacos tonight, due to an unfortunate accident! Over."

"Hooker One, this is Hooker Two. Be on the lookout for corn. Over."

"Roger that, Hooker Two, gonna be Taco Tuesday on the FOB. Over."

"Hooker One, this is Drac One. Over."

"Drac One, Hooker One. Go ahead."

"What is Taco Tuesday? Over."

"Drac One. No time to explain! Over."

"It must be very special day and *exciting*. Over."

"Roger that."

Mikey says, "Man, we hit Navajo goats for sport all the time back on the rez."

"Where do you live exactly in Arizona, on a reservation?" I ask, trying to take my mind off the fact that we can get blown to bits at any moment from an IED blast or heavy DShK machine-gun fire from the mountain ranges to our west.

"I live on the Hopi Reservation, on the Second Mesa," he says with pride.

"Man, I have to be honest with you, Mikey, I don't know shit about Native Americans."

He starts laughing and asks, "You mean you didn't watch Western movies as a kid — 'How kimosabe!' You're not afraid I'm going to scalp you in your sleep?"

I laugh and say, "Not so much."

As we pull into the village of Patkheyl, my stomach begins to feel tight. No one is in sight, just a few compounds surrounded by thick mud walls, with several small fields of newly planted corn and a beautiful almond orchard toward the mountains. The tiny village square displays three enormous Himalayan ash trees casting very needed shade over an ancient water well. There are no visible commercial signs, shops, or vendors.

As the convoy begins to slow, the loud static blast of the radio startles me. "Hooker One, this is Drac One. Over."

I can't distinguish who is communicating, but the Romanian accent is so strong, his pronunciation is, *"Húker Wan, this is Drac One."*

"Drac One, this is Hooker One. Over."

"Húker Wan, We vill stop for peeing and water from well. OK? Over."

"Roger that, Drac One. Over."

Mikey took this as an opportunity to go on one of his political diatribes.

"Apparently, the Romanian government doesn't feel the same need to send their troops to war with a shit-ton of plastic water bottles like Dick Cheney's buddies at KBR. Did you read in the news about KBR, allegedly using open fire pits to burn human corpses, medical supplies and waste, paints, solvents, asbestos, items containing pesticides, animal carcasses, tires, lithium batteries, Styrofoam, wood, rubber, large amounts of plastics, and even entire trucks." Mikey laughs and says, "So, you see, *war is bad for your health!* This warning should be put on cigarette packages, milk cartons, and billboards across America."

Our vehicle is too large to park in the tiny village square, so I drive several blocks outside and park off the road slightly in a cornfield. I am happy to get out of the truck and stretch my legs. The air is cooler and fresher than back at the FOB, and the rustling of the leaves in the breeze enhances the seductive quiet. Mikey points to a small corn stalk in the field and says, "Where there is baby corn, there is a mama! Tacos tonight, buddy boy."

We follow a narrow mountain stream into the village square. When we reach the other guys, who are laughing and joking around, one of the Romanians goes over to the well and throws a large old wooden bucket down into the well, and as it descends, it makes horribly loud scraping sounds until it finally splashes at the bottom. He pulls up the heavy bucket of water and rests it on the side of the opening.

As he lowers his face enthusiastically to drink, we hear the blood-curdling scream of a young girl yelling—*wadrega!* Stop!

The Romanian throws his head back and we all instinctively point our guns at the exasperated young lady, ready to shoot to kill. She stops dead in her tracks and raises her hands high above her head. She catches her breath and says, *"Salaam Alikum."*

The young girl is adorable and obviously small for her age. Even in this moment of upset, her big, bright shining eyes exude a charm and imaginative quality suggesting that a magical kingdom lives within. Her dress is multi-patterned: A long scarf covers her thick, mahogany hair. It is turquoise, gold, and black, with a complex pattern of flowers, and she wears a small black vest over a gold and rust paisley tunic, with black and white polka-dot leggings. Her small toes stick out of her clean leather sandals. She appears dressed to attend an important occasion.

Vali steps forward, as the Romanian squad commander, and the only one of us that speaks Pashto, and says *"Salaam Alikum, Koor ke khairyat dae? Sehat de kha de?"* ("Peace be with you! How is your family? Are you well?")

She is quiet and obviously still afraid. Vali asks gently, *"Staa num tsa dhe?"* (What is your name?). The girl smiles, perhaps because of Vali's funny, heavy Romanian accent, or perhaps realizing that we are not truly a threat—she would not be raped as she would be if we were Taliban fighters with a thirteen-year-old girl alone—and she responds proudly, *"Shahzada."*

She excitedly explains in Pashto that the well has been poisoned for years. The warlord Mansur Khan, sent his men to poison us and threaten the village elders because her father would not grow opium, nor support the Taliban leadership in the region.

I don't know why, but of the twelve armed soldiers standing with machine guns aiming at her, Shahzada changes her gaze to look at me and with her sweet voice says, "I've been wanting to meet a real American!" My mouth drops. She speaks with a crisp British accent. "Do you find me strange?" she chirps with a big smile, reacting to my obvious dismay.

Costin interrupts by anxiously asking Vali something in Romanian. Vali turns to Shahzada. *"Bakhena ghwaarum, tashnab cherta di?"* Shahzada giggles and points, indicating that Costin should find a nice tree in the orchard to use as a toilet. This causes us all to laugh, completely breaking the previous tension.

"So you want to meet a real American?" I ask sweetly. She nods coquettishly. I pull Mikey by the arm in front of me. "This, is a *real American!* He is from the Hopi tribe."

Her eyes open widely and she excitedly asks, "You are a *real Indian?*"

Mikey begins to chuckle nervously, embarrassed to be put on display, and grabs me and pulls me closer, and spits out, "Actually, I am not from India!"

One of the large compound doors opens and an older man with an impeccably groomed beard, wearing all black with a rhubarb-red colored turban and a beautiful red patterned scarf, approaches the group. Two large young men flank him on either side. He speaks to his daughter sweetly in Pashto and she obediently scampers through the door without saying goodbye. The man solemnly greets us with *"Eid Mubarak, Salaam Alikum."* He introduces himself as Ahmad Khan, and informs us that he is the girl's father and the leader of this village. Vali graciously introduces us ceremonially and respectfully. The man insists that we enter his home for the festivities. Vali says that her father insists that his daughter, Shahzada, makes the finest naan in all of Zabul province.

Vali informs us that we have interrupted Ahmad Khan's family from *Eid al-Fitr* prayers, and given the unique circumstances of our visit, the family wishes to extend their home for our comfort and to include us in their feast. He adds that *Pashtunwali* dictates that it will be unimaginably rude not to accept their offer of *Melmastia*.

Vali tries to explain to us the significance of *Pashtunwali*, the way of the Pashtuns, and the importance of the religious celebration. Apparently, *Eid al-Fitr* marks the end of Ramadan, after a month of fasting to commemorate the revelation of the Quran to Muhammad.

In spite of having had lunch with the Romanians not long ago, we accept graciously and enter the compound. We are guided to a large room. We must remove our boots before entering, which proves to be quite a spectacle, as Kong loses his balance and crashes to the floor, startling Ahmad Khan's special guests. Our host shows us where to sit: on cushions on top of a huge Persian rug, with a sheet of plastic spread over the floor serving as an enormous placemat. We sit in a large circle. The women don't sit with us and seem to be busy serving the men.

The family and friends are so warm and welcoming, I almost can't believe it is happening in the middle of a war zone. Shahzada's sister, Jamileh, serves us all tea, while her father speaks boldly to Vali about the problems in their village: lack of clean water, the weak economy, the falling prices of corn and almonds, the Taliban's archaic and violent practices among villagers, the brutish tactics of the drug lords, and the ineffectual central government run by "the idiot" in Kabul, as Khan referred to the country's president.

Much laughter is shared over the hilarity of our awkward manners and uncertainty of which hand to use to eat. Shahzada's brother, Bahman, jokes in Pashto about using the left hand in the communal bowl and her father gives him a sharp glance. Dope politely asks for a fork, which causes much laughter. I watch carefully to see how the village men eat the food before I begin. They roll rice into a ball effortlessly. Finally I give it a go and fill my mouth with delicious, scented rice that falls from my mouth in every direction. Sincere inquiries follow, in Pashto: "Do you like it, my friend? Is it delicious?" I just smile and give them a thumbs-up, which seems to amuse them.

We are served a feast. I imagine this meal is as important to them as Thanksgiving is for any American family. They serve *Perakai* (flatbread filled with vegetables and lentils, served with a mint yogurt), *Kofta Kebab* (skewered lamb kebabs), *Kabuli Pulao* (rice cooked with meat, topped with fried raisins, slivered carrots, and pistachios), *Shor-Nakhod* (a beautiful green chickpea and potato salad), followed by *Cake wa Kolcha* (a sweet corn cake), and *Jalebi* (looks like orange sugary pretzels).

My favorite item by far is the homemade hot flatbread that Shahzada prepares in the tandoor oven. It is amazing. She also offers it with fresh honey, harvested from her family's hives nearby in their almond orchard. She explains that bees are proven to help increase crop production, and honey tastes delightful on hot naan bread. At thirteen, she has her own little business selling the flatbread to local area farmers and the occasional passerby. Locals refer to her as the "Princess of Naan" because her name, Shahzada, in Pashto, means "princess."

Poor Vali has to act as both Ambassador of Romania and interpreter for the United States of America. We are so lucky to have him. He explains to the village men that he is from Northern Dobruja, Romania, where the very small percentage of Muslims live in his country. He is Sunni, as are the Pashtuns. Shahzada also translates whenever she can, without being overtly involved, which might be considered rude to her father and his guests.

(Mikey tells me later that the reason our squad is without the all-important "Terp," or local interpreter, is because Lieutenant Breckovich took the last guy out into the middle of nowhere and put a bullet in his head for lying to him about critical Taliban intel, a lie that caused our guys to be ambushed and killed. He made the guy's death look like an accident.)

Kong doesn't say a word, but eats more food than I've ever seen a human consume at one time, which seems to delight Ahmad Khan's humble, lovely wife. Every time she brings him more, he just smiles and says, "Ma'am, I love your cooking and thank you from the bottom of my heart!" She doesn't speak English, but she understands that he is pleased, and her eyes light up and she smiles as if she understands every word. Some of the guests stare at Dope, the first African-American man they have seen in their life. One of the guests asks him if he can dance like singer Michael Jackson. Dope laughs and says, "Sure I can. I will teach you all how to moonwalk after dinner!" This delights the guests, who insist that dancing in this manner would prove impossible.

After we eat, Shahzada sits beside me. This is normally unthinkable, but her father encourages her to interact and learn about other cultures and languages. She instantly puts a spell on me with her carefree charm and innocence. Somehow, I feel very protective of her. She reminds me of my little sister, Gabby. She excitedly tells me about her friend, Teacher Amelia, who comes from Oxfordshire, England. Amelia works with I.L.C. (International Learning Care) and runs a small rural school in the neighboring village of Chachub. I just know that we are going to be the best of friends.

Shahzada is so innocent, yet so sure of herself. I am brought to unexpected tears watching her interact with her father and mother during the meal, and her family friends and relatives, who obviously adore her. Every unresolved emotional discord of my childhood rushes through me in contrast to the lovely family before me, and I have a disturbing and unexpected flashback from when I was fifteen:

My younger brother and I are in our living room, watching television, and our unremarkable stepfather, Malcolm Dunlap, comes home drunk. He slams into the room mumbling obscenities, and stands in front of the television. "What are you little useless faggots doing up? Don't you have school tomorrow?" He then pulls out his cock and grabs it aggressively. "This is what a real man's cock looks like. Your mother couldn't even feel your father's cock. That is why you are dickless little faggots." Malcolm would stumble back to my little sister's room and get in her bed. *Someday I will kill that motherfucker.*

After everyone finishes eating, some of the guys begin to feel a little uneasy about the time. It will soon be getting dark and we need to get back to the FOB. Vali and Ahmad Khan are in the midst of a passionate conversation about the prospects for "good Muslims" in the world among a growing population of fanatics. Shahzada senses the tension, and whispers into her father's ear. Ahmad Khan pauses and apologizes to his guests, and claps his hands together to call for entertainment.

Ahmed Khan's wife brings him a beautiful instrument to play, the *Rubab*. It is like a western guitar married to an Indian sitar. The long, dark brown wooden neck is elaborately inlaid with mother-of-pearl, and adorned with an assortment of small, festive multi-colored wool balls dangling from the neck. The bottom of the rubab is stretched goat membrane, with two curves indented just before the neck, somewhat like a violin, but more severe and sculptural. Bahman will play the *Tabla* drums, and Jamilah will perform a traditional folk dance.

After Ahmad Khan positions the instrument as one would play a guitar, he gently plucks the strings of the rubab and the sound reminds me of a banjo, yet with a warmer tonal quality.

The finger picking and strumming evoke a sense of mystery and beauty: ancient caravans, starry nights, and veiled dancers, with the air perfumed in scents of musk and sandalwood. We are all spellbound.

Bahman plays the tabla drums, creating undulating bass notes, brought on by his palms, and lively, complex rhythms accented by his quick, darting fingers. An unstoppable energy lifts me up and transports me to another dimension, place, and time. I feel intoxicated. I close my eyes and surrender to this moment, to the family, and to the Afghan culture. I am in love with life—on its own terms.

The sun is beginning to set and a golden light floods the room. Jamileh enters dramatically, wearing a long orange veil with golden lace and a bright flowing pink skirt; she is barefoot and walking precisely to the beat of the tabla drums. She holds her veil over her face to effect a flirtatious attraction with her eyes, looking downward, and then playfully turns her head away from the men after everyone has taken in her beauty. Her eyes are deep brown and accentuated with eyeliner to command more attention.

She dramatically drops two concealed scarves and begins to dance with abandon, throwing them in the direction of the men and closing her eyes, turning ever faster, as if in a state of ecstasy. The men clap and cheer as she turns like a top until the tabla builds to a climatic crescendo, and suddenly, abruptly stops in an instant.

Shahzada enters in a fancy red sequin top and sheer genie pants, with her mid-section exposed. She assumes a pose like a flamenco dancer, and waits. Her father gives her a big smile and digs into the strings of the rubab, and the tabla plays a driving rhythm: 1-2-3-4, *bang-bang-stop*-1-2-3-4, *bang-bang-stop*.

Shahzada begins to roll her stomach and move her hips hypnotically with such precision and ease that the men are immediately captivated. She uses her arms, gazes, and hands to enhance her seduction, with the knowledge and skill of a mature woman. Her small body moves perfectly in time to the music. I can't stop thinking how strange it is for an innocent 13-year-old girl to be able to put a spell on a room of men. It is overwhelmingly sensual, which makes it all the more uncomfortable and perplexing.

As Bahman builds the rhythm of the tabla to a feverish pitch, we are jarred by the sound of a large explosion in the courtyard. Ahmad Khan throws the rubab to the side and rushes to the window. Within seconds, another blast hits his shed in the courtyard and then we hear what sounds like firecrackers popping. Bullets ricochet on the stucco walls near the room we occupy. By that time, Mikey, Dope, and Kong were already out the door and in the courtyard, running to take strategic positions. Vali told Ahmad Khan to stay with his family, and the rest of us rush out to join the other guys.

His son, Bahman, pulls my arm to follow him, and takes me up a series of stairs, so we are able to see outside the compound from a grain tower filled with corn and bags of almonds. I don't know if it was because it was my first action in combat, or my crazy adrenaline rush, but all I can think about is if Mikey will make fresh, homemade corn tortillas and goat tacos for the corporal. As we rush up the stairs, I notice an area filled with clear plastic bags with something dark brown and rust colored, not almonds. *Is that opium?* Before I can ask Bahman, I hear Vali over the radio, "Drac-One to Hooker-One. Over."

"Drac-One, this is Hooker-One. Go ahead. Over."

"By the water well is the man in the black dress from earlier. Over."

"Copy that. I have eyes on him. Can you identify a weapon? Over."

"Negative. Over."

"Hold your fire, unless you can positively see a weapon. Over."
"Copy that!"

From our vantage point high above the compound, it was clear that the man is up to no good, but isn't armed. He is talking into a cell phone. Bahman makes a strange guttural sound of disgust and rummages through the hay on the floor. He pulls up an old military-style rifle that I've never seen before. He leans against an old wooden timber in the tower and quietly breathes, then whispers, "Insh'allah," and squeezes the trigger. The bullet hits the man in black in the forehead. He is the first man that I've witnessed killed in action. Bahman smiles, understanding my dismay, makes a sound of disgust, and says, "Mansur Khan." He spits on the ground.

Everything is silent, except a goat bleating anxiously in the courtyard. It appears that the Taliban is sending a message to Ahmad Khan for having infidels in his home. Kong contacts our FOB command and the Lieutenant's order is for us to return to base immediately. We return to the living room in the home, where Ahmad Khan and his wife and guests are involved in an intense conversation. I imagine they are discussing the repercussions of having us in their home, and for killing a local Taliban agent. We quickly say our good-byes by offering a disjointed assortment of handshakes, bowing, and Kong offering awkward hugs to Ahmad Khan's wife to show our gratitude for their kindness.

Shahzada runs up to me and flashes a big smile. "Please come back and see me. I will make you bread and we can speak about many things!" I respond warmly, *"You can count on it!"* She looks puzzled, so I rephrased, "Of course I will!" Her eyes light up and she says something sweetly in Pashto, and then skips over to the other guys to say goodbye.

When Mikey and I walk out, Kong and Dope are already in their truck behind the Romanians' Humvee. Dope is fully loaded and ready. The Romanians are piling in their Humvee, and we still have to walk a couple of blocks to where we parked in the cornfield. I am nervous. It's getting dark and there are so many places from which the Taliban can strategically attack us. Mikey says, "Don't worry, they aren't going to hit us like this. Shit, I forgot to get some dried corn for Tacos to make fresh tortillas!" Mikey tells me to stay put, and he will run back quickly and ask the family for some corn. It feels really creepy sitting there alone waiting. I had the strangest thought. *I wonder if I will ever have a family?* It seems like an eternity for him to return with a bag full of corn. He jumps in. "Man, those people remind me of my grandparents who raised me. We Hopi have so much in common with these people."

As we speed through the town center, we see Ahmad Khan's family dropping the lifeless, bloody body of the man in black into the well. The scene awakens me to the reality that we are truly in a theater of war, and not just attending a family celebration.

I get on the radio to touch base with the guys:

"Hooker-One, this is Hooker-Two. Over."

"Go ahead, this is Hooker-One. Over."

"We are Oscar Mike about two klicks behind. Over."

"Roger that, Hooker-Two. Stay Frosty! Over."

I'm driving fast, the truck is rattling on the rough, dusty road, and I'm stressing out. Mikey senses my anxiety and tries to distract me by holding up an ear of corn in his hand. He pulls back the husk to inspect the quality.

"You know, Books, in my culture, the cultivation of corn is *everything* to our people. The actual process of farming on our dry, dusty soil is the very way that we are able to remain a spiritual people and united for over fourteen thousand years. All of our prayers, our very reason for being, are tied to that process, and our connection to Mother Earth."

I find it nearly impossible to hear what Mikey is saying. He is talking about his tribe's existential cultural relationship to Mother Earth and I am trying to prevent us from being killed. It occurs to me that war makes every man a storyteller: we feel we must try to make sense of the senseless. As long as we are talking, we are still alive. Somehow this realization makes Mikey's diatribes feel more endearing than off-putting.

A motorcycle with two riders races up from behind and tears past us. In spite of the dust it kicks up, I can see two young men on it. One is concealing something and waving his arms wildly, and the other is holding a cell phone.

Mikey says, "Fuck, that can't be good!"

Mikey gets on the radio. "Hooker-One, this is Hooker-Two. Over."

"Go ahead, this is Hooker-One."

"We have two young dudes on a motorcycle going fast in your direction, and possibly armed. Over."

"Drac-One. This is Hooker-One. Over."

"This is Drac-One. Over."

"Did you copy that?"

"Yes, we copy. We have eyes on motorcycle. We take care of them… *Oh Cacat!*"

Just as we reach the area where we first saw the man in black on the road earlier, the Romanian Humvee explodes in a massive ball of fire. The IED blast is followed by two more explosions, which light up the sky. My stomach is in my throat. Mikey screams for me to stop the fucking truck. "Those fuckers used a daisy chain. If I hadn't gone back for that corn, those Haji fucks would be dead-checking us right now, buddy."

I am in a state of shock. If we hadn't slowed down, thanks to the two guys on the motorcycle, all three bombs would have taken out all three trucks. Mikey is up top on the machine-gun turret, and I wait to receive orders from our team leader, Dope.

Mikey fires into the surrounding fields in case we are not alone, and the radio begins to chatter:

"B.C. Hamilton, this is Hooker-One. Romanian squad has been hit by IED. Break. All are angels. Two unfriendlies on the motorcycle lit up. Over."

"Hooker-One, this is B.C. Hamilton. Pop smoke, return to base on the double. Over."

"Base Command, Hooker-One, roger that, sir. We are Oscar Mike."

"Hooker-Two, this is Hooker-One. I am sorry to inform Drac-One, all angels. Over."

"Copy that Hooker-One. Charlie Foxtrot." I use our term for *cluster fuck*. "Over."

"Charlie Foxtrot for sure. Are you good for Oscar Mike? Over."

"Roger that. Oscar Mike."

When Mikey and I arrive, the Romanian unit's Humvee is in flames and the horrifying silhouettes of our new friends' charred bodies are still visible in the vehicle. I open the truck door and throw up everything in my stomach, which just minutes before I ate without a care in the world, and with a sincere appreciation and love for the fine people of Afghanistan.

• • •

When we get back to the FOB, Reece and Ramirez meet us, and they don't look pleased. Dope tries to soften things by pulling the roadkill goat out of the truck and telling Ramirez that Mikey has the corn for tortillas in the other truck for Taco Tuesday! Ramirez flashes a smirk. "No time for tacos, my brother. The Lieutenant wants to meet your team on the double."

It occurs to me that I am more afraid of The Ripper than any of the Taliban fighters.

use, the lieutenant is barking at another squad
grooming standards and the repeated abuses of
:ed anti-Jack Shack legislation. "Tell your men
he *clown punching* in the God damn porta-potties
or I'm going to have them removed, and all you fucktards will
have to go outside the wire and jerk off with the Taliban shooting at you!"

As we wait for the Lieutenant, I can't stop thinking about
Shahzada and her family. I'm worried that we have put their lives
in danger. I relive how cool it was for Ahmad Khan to invite us
into his home and treat us so well. I can only imagine the shit
he has had to deal with over his lifetime. I have no idea if I will
ever be able to see that family again.

Once The Ripper finishes grilling the squad leader about his
men's facial hair and naughty pleasures, he shifts to us. He
unknowingly scratches his groin with agitation, loudly sucks
in air, and points his rigid index finger at us as if he will use it
to poke our eyes out.

"So, what do I tell Major Armstrong when he inquires how
these men were charbroiled on a fucking goat trail in the middle
of nowhere, because you insane, retarded fucks decide to stop
and have dinner and a movie with the locals? If you had followed
orders and returned by sunset, this horrible shit wouldn't have
happened. What in God's name possessed you to do this? Dope,
you are the team leader, explain this to me."

"Sir, yes sir," Dope says. "Hearts and minds, sir. We had an
opportunity to enter a local village chieftain's home and gather
intel in the area. We learned that the villagers are scarce on
water and have difficulty economically, further that the Taliban
is definitely in the area, as they attacked us while in their home.
A regional drug lord is out for the village because they won't
convert their corn crops to poppy fields, sir!"

"Is that right, Private Daniels? Hearts and fucking minds! You geniuses killed three of our local informants. The so-called 'guy in black' is Abdul Ali and has been on the U.S. payroll since we invaded in 2001. The two on the motorcycle that Kong lit up were his cousins—also on our payroll!"

"With respect, sir, why didn't you brief us on this before our mission?"

"Well, Private, if you had followed the fucking ROE and your orders, nobody would be dead. Did you see weapons on any of our informants?"

"Sir, no sir!"

"Then what gave you the initiative to take them out?"

"Sir, at Ahmad Khan's home, we were under small-arms fire and mortar attacks. Later, the Romanians were hit by an IED. We saw two young men flying toward us on a motorcycle and we received word they may be armed."

"No, you received word that they have something concealed. The guy on the back was concealing his laptop that *we gave him* for our Intel purposes. The two men on the motorcycle were trying to warn you about the IED that they discovered when you were first arriving. Abdul Ali was waiting outside Ahmad Khan's house to try and get your attention to warn you."

"So they weren't part of the Taliban guys shooting at us?"

"Apparently not, Private!"

"Sergeant Reece and Corporal Ramirez, this will mean you rejoining your team on the convoy, to keep this *special* band of brothers from getting in further trouble. I want you to continue patrolling the area for Taliban arms and drug trafficking. Restrict your 'hearts and minds' to being courteous drivers. And the next time you clowns decide you want to have a dinner party, you better think about the food you will feast on in Fort Leavenworth federal prison. Is that clear?"

"Sir, yes, sir!"

I didn't want to tell the Lieutenant that the Romanians told us that the man in black was Taliban, and I was the only one among us that witnessed Ahmad Khan's son, Bahman, killing the man in black. I was afraid it might bring harm to him and his family. The others couldn't have known, given the chaos and incoming fire.

# The Symposium

BACK IN OUR TENT, the Sergeant pops his head in and tells us to take the night off from our watch duty and to relax, so we can leave the FOB for patrol by 0600 hours. This is good news. We all seem a bit off-kilter after our unexpected participation, and attack, with the villagers, in addition to losing our new Romanian brothers.

Dope is really down, but acting like he isn't. Kong, who shot the guys on the motorcycle, seems less cocky than usual, and throws himself on his bunk and mindlessly stares. I didn't know how to feel. It is the first day on the job, and I'm already exhausted from the intensity. Mikey seems particularly energetic, which I find strange. He is using his pocketknife to begin carving an odd-looking piece of wood, a root, that is bent and curved.

Whenever I am upset, I like to read. I lie on my bunk and grab my copy of the *Bhagavad-Gita* (Song of the Lord), and read about Prince Arjuna on the battlefield. Arjuna is so distraught over the idea of another battle that he collapses, overwhelmed with anguish. He must turn to a higher power, Krishna—the Hindu God of compassion.

Arjuna: *The very thought of war itself gives me grief, and I feel dejected, therefore, I will not fight.*

Krishna: *You grieve for those who should not be grieved for, and yet seemingly speak like a wise man: but the wise man does not grieve for the living, or the dead.*

Arjuna: *Wherever I look, I see nothing but evil and unpleasant omens in the upcoming battle.*

Krishna: *A karma-yogi does not care about omens. He is unattached to everything because he neither rejoices when meeting pleasant circumstances, nor does he feel dejected if he encounters unpleasant events.*

Arjuna: *In this battle, I do not foresee any good resulting from the slaughter of my friends and relatives.*

Krishna: *There is nothing more welcoming to a warrior than a righteous war, One's own duty, though devoid of merit, is preferable to the duty of another, because even death in the performance of one's duty brings happiness.*

Arjuna: *But I do not covet victory, kingdom, or even luxuries. And of what use will this kingdom, luxuries or even life be to us, if we kill all the friends of our childhood.*

Krishna: *A Karma-yogi should fight while treating victory and defeat alike. Gain and loss are alike, pain and pleasure alike, and fighting, thus, he does not incur sin.*

Arjuna: *Those for whose sake we seek kingdom and pleasure: teachers, uncles, sons, nephews, grand uncles, and other relatives… they all stand here today on the battlefield staking their lives, property and wealth."*

Krishna: *Dedicating all actions to me and with your mind fixed on me, freed from the feelings of hope and sadness, and cured of mental fever. Arjun, you must fight. Because he who has given up all desires and has become free from the feelings of "I" and "mine" eventually attains peace.*

I was really getting into the idea of being free from the feelings of "I" and "mine," but Dope interrupts everyone's silence and pulls out a big bottle of clear alcohol with a whole purple plum submerged on the bottom.

Kong looks over. "What the fuck is that?"

"*Tuica!* One of the Romanians gave it to me at FOB Dracula."

"You let one of those vampire ladies suck your big black *pula* and you hid that from us?" Kong blurts out.

"No, fool, one of the guys gave it to me as your prize for winning the King Dong contest. It's the national drink of Romania!"

"Dude, what exactly is inside that bottle? It looks like Dracula's fermented balls!" Mikey says, making a creepy vampire noise.

"This fine beverage, my friends, is made from twice distilled Romanian plums. Who will join me for a shot?" Dope asks in a triumphant tone.

"Hell yeah, I'm in! That shit will *fuck-you-up*. My pop used to make a homemade brandy with Alabama wild berries," Kong enthusiastically offers, having snapped out of his funk.

"Kong, get your Dixie cups!" Dope says, lifting the bottle.

"Mikey, you in?"

"Have you ever known an Indian to stand down from a fight, fuck, or fine shot of plum brandy? You know I'm in, brother!" Mikey does something hilarious with his eyes, making them overly large and intense like a cartoon character.

"Hell yeah! I'm in, to the end." I say, somewhat surprised by how excited I feel about drinking with these guys.

Kong jumps up and gets everyone a plastic Dixie cup from the supply his mother sent him with a giant bottle of Listerine mouthwash, so he would remember to gargle before he goes to bed. A small example of the weird shit sent to us from back home to offer comfort while we are fighting a war.

After Kong pours everyone a shot, Dope says, "Let's begin with a small prayer of remembrance for our departed Romanian brothers. Lord, we ask that you welcome our friends into your loving arms. We express our gratitude for having one another to protect and safeguard in this strange land, and we ask you to use this plum shit for the benefit of our 'hearts and minds.' Amen!"

We all lift our cups, say, "To FOB Dracula" and shoot the cup of Tuica brandy, only to soon realize it has a mule-kick as strong as tequila. We all cough and whistle in unison. The second shot was much smoother. The third shot was delicious. By the fourth shot, we all love the "plum shit," as it is now lovingly referred.

Mikey sits back on his bunk and resumes carving. Kong walks over, looks at the long curved cottonwood root, grabs his crotch, and asks, "Hey Mikey, are you carving a Hopi cock statue in honor of my victory? Do you need a model?" We howl with laughter like a pack of coyotes.

"No, Kong, I am carving a dildo to send to your bucktooth, redneck mother back in Alabama!" Mikey spits back.

"That's good, man. When she is through using it on your dad's ass, I will send it to your mother to hang on her wall as one of your Kachina dolls!" Kong fires back.

"What is a Kachina doll?" I ask with some trepidation.

Mikey begins to explain, "A *katsintithu* doll, usually referred to by the white man as a Kachina doll... which, I think, gives them a kind of tragic 'Little Miss Sunshine' persona, especially given how important they are *spiritually* in our culture."

Kong, still determined to mess with Mikey, jumps in. "Dolls are important in your culture? Man, that explains a lot about you!"

"I wouldn't expect a coastal Anglo-Saxon Southern Baptist swamp monkey to understand the complexity of my culture's connection to nature, and all of the mystical nuances of the spirit world..." Mikey says in a tone that is sub-textually messaging, *Look, redneck, I went to an elite, private boarding school, so don't mistake me for your pathetic stereotype of the disenfranchised, uneducated and drunk Indian.*

Kong continues to prod. *"Your culture.* That's the problem with *you people.* You are *Americans,* just like the rest of us! Why can't you just accept that and get on down the road, son?" Kong says, as if he is ordering bacon and eggs, and that is the only thing one could eat in the morning for breakfast.

"Well, you see, Kong, the first problem is the *'you are an American like the rest of us'* part. I am a Hopi first, whose land and people have been invaded twice, and then amalgamated into your culture by the United States federal government, and therefore I am called an *'American'* by reasons of extortion.

"I aspire to become Hopi! You see, Hopi is a level of spiritual attainment, development, and knowledge that in my culture takes a lifetime to achieve. It is not simply a name to identify where we live on the map."

"Well, excuse me, Grasshopper! I don't want to get in the way of your fucking enlightenment." Kong dramatically bellows.

"What does Hopi mean?" I ask, trying to calm Kong down.

"We call ourselves *Hopituh-Shi-nu-mu.* Non-Indians say it means the 'peaceful people.' Actually, it means something more like *people who seek balance.* Of course, when you are in balance, you tend to be more peaceful. Perhaps that would explain why *your culture* is always at war—*out of balance.* The United States has 800 military bases and is performing military operations currently in seventy countries and territories abroad. You really think you guys are really in balance with the rest of the world?"

"Well, man, I got excellent balance. You should've seen me catch the winning pass in my high school playoffs. I flew above two big-ass black guards from Selma trying to kill me, and I caught the pass and landed with perfect balance!"

"I don't think he means that kind of 'balance,' *you fucktard!"* Dope says, throwing a fast, hard jab to Kong's arm.

Kong makes a wimpering noise. "Damn, Dope, white people bruise!"

Mikey continues to talk, refusing to get sucked into Kong's childish antics. "To be an 'American' means that you must be born on the continental United States, nothing more, nothing less."

Dope, stands, salutes, and begins to recite the Pledge of Allegiance as Mikey talks.

"Bourgeois Americans tend to act as if the entire population is in agreement on what constitutes an American: someone who is 'fair,' propagates the fairy tale of 'democracy,' and believes the western Christian idea of God. That is funny because President George W. Bush, after losing the popular vote of the American people in his election, a self-proclaimed Christian, invaded Iraq and Afghanistan. So who gave this Christian, a follower of Christ—the embodiment of compassion and love—the authority and power to invade these nations?"

Dope says, "Come on, Mikey, tell it like it is! Preach that shit!"

"Was it the will of the people? Did the American people have all of the facts, sufficient to even formulate a reasonable opinion? A democracy—by definition and theory—is a government by the people, with rule of the majority. Was that honored? Is that honored today?"

Dope lifts his voice. "Rule of the *majority,* son!"

"Instead, a *minority* rules, an *electoral college*—a governmental body that few truly seem to understand—put him in office. Who are these people? Who do they work for? What do they represent? Do they represent the will of the majority? Is it an even playing field in all fifty states? Americans, like you, Kong, are too fucking busy taking selfies, jacking off to the Internet, and buying affordable dream homes and other bullshit to care or understand that their own government is manufacturing the illusion of democracy."

Dope, sensing the escalating tension, starts dancing like a teenage girl and singing a pop song, "Call Me Maybe." It is clear that they are not going to stop. Mikey is on a roll.

Kong leans into Mikey's face. "Are you telling me that America is not a democracy, you little red-skinned Communist fucker? Are you telling me you would rather be a fucking Haji bastard terrorizing your own people? Or some sorry fucker in Somalia watching his wife get raped in front of him before they cut his balls off and stuff them down his throat!"

"That is precisely what I am telling you, Alabama! We are not a true democracy and there are really sick, dangerous, and fucked-up people all over this planet, really bad guys, including in our own country, government, and communities. Because you 'Americans' live in an illusion of a false sense of greatness! Your model is the same as Alexander the Great—conquer for the glory of acquisition. Ours, the Hopi, is the greatness of the life within and our connection to nature, and the amazing interconnectivity. You acknowledge the words, but you don't live, or understand, them as a lifestyle.

"On your question about would I rather be a Haji bastard? The answer is no. I also wanted to kill the guys that blew up the World Trade Center. I too want to get the truly bad guys, and protect my family."

"Then, what the fuck are you going on about, you rabid Hopi dog?" Kong roars, unable to stand still.

Dope and I try again to lighten the mood, singing, "Hey, I just met you, and this is *crazy*, but here's my number, so call me maybe!" Nothing seemed to help. Mikey looks like he is re-negotiating a failed peace treaty, and Kong looks like he's trying to convince a virgin it's a good idea to go to his fishing camp to spend the night stargazing.

"Look man, I can explain it to you, but I can't understand for you!" Mikey says, growing increasingly more agitated.

"I feel like I am trying to explain the bowl to the gold fish," Mikey says, ignoring Dope and me. "Let me break it down Barney style, Kong. The shit that the Spanish and your British ancestors did to my people would freak your little redneck brain right fucking out of existence if it happened to you, today in America.

"Imagine today if Russia invaded and occupied the United States. Imagine for a moment that they are seeking rich natural resources. In the process, they rape women and young girls, and enslave men, cut off their right feet so they can't run. There is even a report of a man covered with tar and set ablaze for praying in a Christian church.

"They make some men walk four hundred miles and carry timber back to your communities to build Russian Orthodox churches. They destroy your Catholic and protestant churches, temples, mosques, and synagogues and build their own churches, first destroying yours and filling them with virgin sand, and then razing them and building over their foundations. They regard you as barbarians. They don't speak English and expect you to learn Russian. At first, you don't kill them. You try to understand them and to get along."

"Man, I'd kick some Commie fucking ass!" Kong blurts out.

"Well, after years of abuses you revolt and drive them off your lands. You are again 'Americans.' You return to your way of life with individual rights and freedoms.

"Three hundred years later, China invades America, to provide more land and resources for their expansion. Initially, you don't fight, as you believe in democratic process and legislation to resolve conflict. You are allowed to remain on our land, but you are now living on land designated as 'Chinese Federal Land.' Many years later, the Chinese discover coal, oil and gas, and uranium in our sacred national parks, including Yellowstone and the Grand Canyon. They make citizens move: forced re-location in order to extract our natural resources.

"Instead of Americans being the richest people in the world, you become some of the poorest. They send you to Beijing for school and make you speak Chinese. They punish you for praying to Jesus Christ. Further, they have dumped toxic waste on our land that will take seventy thousand years to recover. They have drained, in thirty years, our water supply of our natural aquifers that can't rejuvenate in order to transport coal sludge to produce power for big cities in China, not for our people's use.

"This is our story, motherfucker — the Hopi story," Mikey growls. "How would you and your family fucking feel if that was your history? So as you can see, Kong, I don't get very excited about being an American, just as I am sure the Afghan people and culture don't throw their arms around their invaders, who kill their civilians and superimpose a 'democratic' government, because we are selling the idea of 'democratic hope' to help these poor people. Interestingly Kong, I have yet to meet a person who wasn't attracted to something that was working!"

Kong is overwhelmed by the complexity of Mikey's passionate diatribe, and lifts his hands high above his head and stretches.

"Dude, you have serious fucking Indian issues. Damn, man, you are one pissed-off redskin. Dope, I think we need to bring out the extra-chill-shit herb, the full-fucking-metal-jacket Kandahar Gold from your secret stash!" Kong says, as if getting Mikey stoned will help relieve his post-cultural-genocide blues.

Mikey, realizing the futility of sharing anything further with Kong, says, "Finally, Hano the village idiot has a good idea!"

While the guys pass around the joint, everyone takes a moment to enjoy the détente.

I try to lighten the intensity of the mood by asking Mikey again about what he is carving. "So what is a Kachina?"

"Oh, not more Indian shit, Man!" Kong blurts out like a spoiled child.

Mikey flashes a defiant glare at Kong and says, "We call them *Katsina.* You call them Kachina. They act as messengers between humans and the spirit world. We use them to teach our children about the many different spiritual beings. Think of them as, say, saints in Catholicism. There are like three hundred and fifty of them. The Hopi believe that for six months of the year the Katsina spirits live among us in the Hopi villages to help the people. We carve them using cottonwood root. It is strong like our children. I carve this to ask the spirits to help protect our team. At the base I will carve corn, which symbolizes my spiritual connection to Mother Earth, and to symbolize my growth, or my path to becoming Hopi.

"The next figure is *Koshare or Hano,* the clown, which will be Kong. He intentionally disrupts and behaves in an over-the-top way to show our people how overdoing anything is bad, not only for the individual, but for the entire tribe."

"Fuck you man, I'm not a clown… I'm a warrior fucktard!" Kong says, as he throws a paper wad across the tent and hits him in the head.

"Next, *Chakwaina,* the Black Ogre, representing Dope, which reminds us of dangerous outside forces in the world, like the thugs back in Chicago."

"See, there you go again, racial profiling. Why am I the black ogre? Why not Kong, as the Great White Porn Ogre?" Dope says, laughing uncontrollably.

"Last, but not least, the eagle, representing Books, who brings our prayers to God. Books, of course, having been damn near a minister will get this honor."

"Yeah, man. Seems like several lifetimes ago. It was when I was in college doing missionary work." I say, cryptically.

"Well, go on, preacher. No maybe about it! Have you accepted Jesus Christ as your personal savior, or not?" Kong asks, as if in the backwoods of Alabama at a Baptist tent revival, in his patented black-or-white philosophical position: it's either this, or it's that! I tended to subscribe to the one hundred-shades-of-gray manner of thinking.

"Kong, historically, I accepted Jesus Christ as the ultimate symbol of compassion and love: two things that I still think are essential for human beings to embrace and live by. In Basic they wouldn't let us have any books, unless it was a 'religious' book."

Dope says, "I know that's right!"

Kong follows with, "Me too, couldn't have a single fucking sex magazine!"

"So, I brought the Bible, the Quran, the Book of Mormon, an Alan Watts book on Zen Buddhism, and the Bhagavad Gita. I am currently finishing that one. I must say, after reading all of them, it is changing my perspective radically."

I hope my answer will satisfy Kong, I am getting really stoned and don't have much bandwidth to get into the more esoteric corners of my beliefs. That seems to satisfy him for the moment, and we continue to all get fucked up and laugh some more.

After a while, Kong takes an enormous drag off the joint. "Come here, Preacher Boy, let me give you a supercharge." He inverts it, and sticks it in his mouth and blows. The marijuana smoke charges into my mouth as I inhale quickly, reaching full lung capacity, and I choke back up the smoke, coughing like a bellowing smokestack, and laughing, with my eyes watering.

"Let's have some more plum shit!" Kong suggests as he pours the last of the plum brandy into the Dixie cups. After we make another toast to all the men throughout history who have tried to make a difference by fighting a war, Kong continues to push me. "So man, do you believe Jesus is our lord and savior, or not?" His tenacity is annoying me. I'm sure for him it is as simple as, "Do you like to fuck teenage cheerleaders, or not—that simple, yes or no?"

I try to give him an honest answer without going too deep. "For me, Kong, that question is as complicated as asking me if mankind is really advancing. For example, humans invented the cell phone to aid in connectivity, stay in touch with friends and family, and the Taliban uses them to detonate and blow up a child—in the name of God. Is that advancing?

"Do you really think that God, the same monotheist God that both Christians, and the Muslims, profess to believe in—the highest expression of compassion and love—wants to blow up an innocent child?

"An American might argue, 'Ah, but you see *their God* isn't our brand of Jesus Christ, the *true God*. Well, that's funny. Our presidents, all Christians, like to say, 'God bless America' and profess their faith, yet they order more airstrikes, drone strikes, and send more troops that kill innocent civilians—collateral damage—throughout the Middle East, as if they are on the winning side of God and truth. So, we would have to deduce that the real God, the American God, is OK with killing innocent people. I recently read that 1,462 innocent Afghan civilians were killed in the first six months of this year. The bureaucratic fucks, far removed from the reality of what those bloody, torn apart bodies actually look like lying on the ground, simply refer to them as 'collateral damage.'

"I haven't forgotten your question, Kong," I say, waving away the joint as it's passed to me again. "I do believe that within all humans is the capability of tremendous spiritual growth and development, as well as physical, emotional and intellectual achievement. Where you focus your attention and energy, whether it is for spiritual attainment, or sexual excellence... so there will be results! It is as simple as cause and effect. If any person focuses on being angry, and violent, one kind of result will manifest and occur. If the same person focuses on being compassionate, and loving, a very different result will occur.

You get to decide how you use your thoughts and energy, every day, every second. You don't have to believe me. It's scientific. Do your own study. One day focus on being hateful and violent and the next day focus on love, and let me know which yields you more happiness. Buddhism does a wonderful job trying to explain this."

Kong, now stoned, is determined to hear me answer his question and forcefully blurts out, "Do you fucking believe in God, or not?"

"Do I believe that you can sit in some wooden church in the middle of Alabama and think that by simply accepting Jesus Christ as your personal savior, one is immune from needing an education in personal responsibility, both emotionally and spiritually? Hell, no! Do I think that person will then know how to be responsible in a marriage—hell, no! Do I think that same person is somehow superior, and/or more entitled than other humans on the planet with different religious practices—hell, no! That person does not get to rape women, kill other Americans, lie, cheat, and steal. That person is equally as nauseating to me as some of the men we fight here in Afghanistan, who think that just because they kneel on a carpet five times per day and call themselves Muslim, that empowers them to rape women, marry thirteen-year-old girls, stone women to death, prevent them from being educated, rape young boys, and run around the planet killing so-called infidels."

All the guys look at me seriously, as if I am becoming a real drag on the party fun.

"Damn, Books, we got you all worked up! What the fuck is wrong with humans?" Dope shakes his head. "We seem to lift ourselves out of grimy sludge, only to ooze down the sewer, time and again. Man, I grew up in the projects and my mama dragged my ass to church every Sunday. That gave her the strength she needed to raise two boys and keep us away from gangs and violence. There is something wonderful about bringing people together in the name of love, regardless what you call it! Am I right?"

Mikey stood up to stretch and take a break from carving. "In America, I think the problem is education! It's *how people are educated*—as a culture, individually, and spiritually. My culture has lasted fourteen thousand years and your culture, if you count the pre-independence occupation in Virginia, a whopping four hundred years, and to my eyes you appear to be accelerating toward a self-created shit storm of self-indulgent youth who think they are too cool to communicate, don't know how to move their ass to make things happen, and don't have a fucking clue about where they fit in the world. They think that the world is theirs for the taking and they are entitled to everything they want, and everyone should find them attractive, interesting, and sexually desirable."

"What's wrong with that?" Kong says, trying to break the intensity of the mood. "You think that the Native American kids are any different, Mikey? I've seen them on a television show, talking about how they are doing drugs and drinking, not going to school, and all these suicides…"

"For us Hopi, we are unique amongst the Native American tribes. We don't follow other people's laws and cultures because the divine law we follow never changes. The problem is the violent cultural indoctrination from the internet, television and movies in America are challenging our ancient way of life. Look at Ahmed Khan and his family. They are a tribal people. They have tried to live peaceful, spiritual, agrarian lives for centuries and they continue to have invaders threaten their cultural norms and religious practices.

"You see, when our people entered the fourth world, from the *Sipapuni*—the place of emergence—in the Grand Canyon, we agreed to live by instructions of *Maasaw,* the Creator or Caretaker of Earth."

Kong got in Mikey's face, "Oh shit, here we go again… More Indian shit about how you guys are more tuned into nature." Mikey ignores him and looks at me. "Can't you just break this shit down Barney-style, Tonto?"

"This is Barney-style, Kong. If you want to learn something, you have to have the fucking patience to listen. Everything can't be given to you in two-clicks. This isn't your teen porn site of the day, Sport. One has to study your entire life to understand the complexities of our philosophy."

"Go on Mikey, I am really interested," I say, much to the others chagrin.

"Anyway, when our people arrived to this world, we went out in all the four directions. The Bear Clan, the oldest clan, was the first to return and settle in Oraibi, on the First Mesa in northeastern Arizona. When other clans arrived, they saw how well the people lived in harmony and peace. They wanted to live among us. The Bear Clan chief would ask what they had to offer our people spiritually. The chief of the new clan would give a presentation. If he was boastful, or had nothing real to contribute, they were not accepted and asked to leave."

"Someone should ask you to leave!" Kong blurts out.

Mikey ignores him.

"If the clan brought something good spiritually, they would be allowed to stay. The *difference* for us is that we honor the individual religious practices of *each clan* that we accepted to join us. It's as if the United States said, OK guys, we are glad you are here to make *your* life great, and we realize that you all come from different experiences, and bring different spiritual beliefs—so we want to honor that—and we create a spiritual calendar year to ensure that *everyone* will be represented. In January, we will be going to the Kiva and practice our rituals, as we Hopi were the first to arrive, then the Protestants will be our February religion, and we will go to church and try and have a direct connection to Jesus, and in March we will go to the cathedral and celebrate Catholic mass, and in April we will go to the synagogue and pray as Jews and honor the Torah. In May, we will chant as Buddhists, et cetera."

"That sounds fucking crazy to me!" Kong says, standing up and pacing around the tent.

"Well, unlike you, Kong, our forefathers realized that *no one man should be too big, or too important, and one spiritual practice is not more important than another.* This simple realization assures peace, and an egalitarian harmony. Now, if our children think that they are gangbanging rappers who can sell drugs, and not work in the cornfields, or go to their clan's kiva to worship... We are becoming a divided tribe, facing possible cultural death, thanks to the old U.S. of A."

"Yeah," Dope responds, now very stoned. "One thing about American kids I don't understand as a black man, are those white kids who try to sound black. They flash gang signs, listen to gangsta rap, and dress like they are Compton gangbangers. They seem to be trying to absorb the depth of feeling of the urban black experience, because those kids *know* who the fuck they are, and what they have to do to survive. Those white kids seem so fucking lost... that's one of the reasons why they join the Army! Am I right?"

"Yeah, you are right about that!" I say.

"And of course," Dope continues, "some black families jump on the white man's corporate economic hamster wheel and now they feel the same cultural divide in their communities as the Native Americans... it's about education and economics, man.

"Did you know that in 1920, there were only ten thousand African-American people, one in one thousand, in this entire country that had a college diploma?" Dope says. "My grandpa used to say that it was about as easy for a black man to finish college as it was for him to play shortstop for the Boston Red

Sox! Now, almost five million African-American people have college degrees, and our own President is black! Education is key… am I right?"

"We as Hopi accept poverty, because we want to be free from corporate economic co-dependency. But, the very thing that makes us free is that which kills us. It's the same with the Afghan people. You can't just kick the doors down and shoot people if they don't want to change. You must talk to the elders, and if they want to meet you, they will invite you in. Don't tell them what you are going to do. Ask them what they want. Respect is critical in our culture, and this one. You experienced how people responded to Ahmad Khan tonight. They respect him as a community elder and chief. There is so much about this culture that I relate to and understand."

"This shit is exhausting me. I didn't join the military to have a fucking philosophy course all fucking night! I came here to kill the fucking bad guys. Jesus, where is the plum shit when you need it!" Kong says, looking around his bunk, as if he had another bottle. "If anyone needs me, I will be in the Jack Shack, getting my *happy philosophy* worked out with Miss Alabama, in the great USA." Kong puts on his straw cowboy hat and heads out of the tent.

"I would hardly call this discussion an honors philosophy course. More like philosophical Pop-Tarts!" I say, laughing.

Mikey, without skipping a beat, adds, "Man I would kill for a strawberry-jam Socrates with vanilla frosting and sprinkles right now!"

"Or even a Blueberry Camus Cinnamon sticky bun!"

We all break out laughing, desperately needing something to be funny.

"But seriously, I agree with you, Dope! Education is key," I say, trying to negotiate with myself just how much I should tell these guys I've just met about myself.

Dope walks over to Mikey. "Ain't this some shit, I gotta come all the way to a country where half my country doesn't even know where Afghanistan is, to get the so-called bad guys, and shoot at these illiterate farmers that hate me and don't want me here. And all I'm trying to do is get my mother and brother free from poverty, in my own fuckin' country, where *my own black people* want to shoot me for twenty dollars for the fucking drugs they are growing here. Can't find jobs or go to college easily, can't afford healthcare, and white people are worrying about these Afghan girls getting to school and building hospitals for them. That is some bullshit there, son. Am I right, Mikey?"

"Preaching to the Indian choir!" Mikey says, laughing.

I decide to share. "In my case, both my mom and dad were poor, uneducated — strung out on drugs — and in and out of rehab and prison. I was introduced to the state child protective services when I was one year old, and got passed around like a Frisbee. I lived with various families and finally with my aunt for one year until I was five, when my Mom brought me to Texas.

"We drove from Northern California through the southwestern part of the United States. As a child, I was fascinated with the desert, and the magical landscapes of Arizona and New Mexico. I always thought some day I would return there."

Mikey pipes up and says, "Yes, you will my brother!"

"Anyway, my mom hooked up with my stepfather, Malcolm Dunlap, a real piece of work! He fancied himself a self-styled preacher and wrote scripture all over the walls of our shitty rental house in Marble Falls, Texas. He was a real macho fucker and liked to get drunk and stoned, and continuously tormented my brother and me. After that abuse, he went and got in bed with my younger sister, Gabby. She soon stopped appearing happy, smiling, or being her usual talkative self. It was as if Malcolm had turned her joy off, in an instant. In fact, Shahzada reminds me of Gabby before that: so cute, spunky, and smart.

"Anyway, I knew I was going to hurt Malcolm, it was only a matter of time, so I threw myself into Christian youth groups at school, and our church. I was told that if I turned my life over to the care and love of Jesus Christ, and had sufficient faith, God could change Malcolm Dunlap's satanic behavior. Besides, I didn't want to burn in hell for my own sins! I wanted to do the right thing, walk on the righteous path with God.

"I became best friends with a kid from our church, and the Neilson family kindly adopted me, and I was able to live with them until I graduated high school. Mr. Neilson was cool and taught me how to work on my old white Chevy pickup truck. It was better than my home life, but I always felt like a visitor in my new home. I got jobs on neighboring farms to save money for school, and was able to get a grant to attend Abilene Christian College."

Mikey laughs and says in a cowboy accent, "Man, that sounds like Redneck Harvard!"

"Yes, sir! I studied philosophy and religious studies, and I was a youth minister for kids from underprivileged backgrounds. Then the money ran out for school my junior year. My buddy back home had joined the Army and told me about the G.I. Bill that would pay for college and I thought, cool, I'll join, do my time and go back to school and continue preaching. It never occurred to me that they would actually deploy me to Afghanistan!"

"Yeah, buddy, I understand things like poverty, drugs, and a shitty family life," Dope says.

"And for the record, you are not the only one in this tent with that background... Well, there is "Kong", Connor Kenneth Macintyre IV. He and his rich redneck family have been in Alabama since they hung niggas like me from trees—am I right, Mikey? They own the largest oyster farm in Point Aux Pins, southern Alabama, since 1892, with thousands of acres of land! Am I right, Mikey?"

"Yep!" Mikey says lazily, clearly stoned and unimpressed with Kong's family pedigree.

"Why did he join the Army?" I ask.

"The men in his family have fought in every war since the American Revolution. His father was a highly decorated Army Ranger. That's his goal. He has applied to Ranger School, but they put a hold on his application until he finishes this tour of duty."

"Why did you join, Dope?" I ask, not expecting a sincere answer.

"Economics and security, the same reason these small villagers are mixed up with the Taliban. I *also* understand these people. Well, certainly the drug lords! When you are poor and disenfranchised with no good education, infrastructure, or jobs, you are vulnerable to these crazy motherfuckers that just care about themselves and making money, and the entire game shifts — on a dime — from 'we' to 'me.'"

Before Dope could continue, the tent flap opens, and to our surprise it is Sergeant Reece, still in his workout shorts and no shirt. Dope quickly snaps to attention. Mikey and I jump up from our stoned slumber, and try to look alert and on the double.

"At ease, men. Just wanted to stop by and make sure my new guys are ready for our day tomorrow?"

"Sir, yes, sir!"

"Do I smell marijuana in this tent, Team Leader Daniels?"

"Sir, no, sir. You smell the patchouli oil on my pillowcase, sir. My girlfriend sent it to me to remind me of her beautiful, fine ass and legs, sir!"

Reece gives a Cheshire-cat grin. "Great. I'll see you men at oh-six hundred hours. Better try and get some rest, going to be a long day tomorrow and Intel is sending reports of enemy movement in the area northwest of Qalat. We need to visit Ahmad Khan's village and see what's happening since you were attacked. Right, sleep well, see you in the morning."

After the sergeant leaves, Dope relaxes. "Man, that is one smooth white man! His voice is so calm I feel like I want him to read me a bedtime story."

"I bet he would do more than that in bed with you, Dope!" Mikey says, taunting him like a devilish child.

"What the hell are you talking about?"

"Well, he sure wears gym shorts and no shirts a lot!"

"Yeah, because it is about two hundred fucking degrees *hot* in this place! I thought you Hopi people like to run around naked wearing a washcloth."

Before Mikey can respond to Dope, a loud explosion hits our courtyard. I almost jumped out of my skin. Dope tenses up. *"Puta Madre,* that mortar fire is close. Haji is getting better at aiming!"

He walks over and looks out our tent. "Our boys are shooting illumination flares!"

We could hear return fire on the 50-caliber machine guns. Then total silence. Kong comes flying into the tent huffing and puffing, laughing to the point of being histrionic, after his sprint across the courtyard.

*"Oh My God,* there I was, in the throes of dreamy hot loving relations with my girl Bianca, my favorite Alabama State cheerleader, and a fucking mortar blasted in front of my Jack Shack. It rattled my cage so hard it almost gave me a heart attack! I've never lost my hard-on *in my life*—until tonight! This is historic shit!"

We all laugh hysterically, and decide we better turn in for the night, with the exception of Kong. He has to go back to visit his dreamy cheerleader and finish some unsettled business.

# Dead Goats and Melons

THE TEAM AND I are hanging around the trucks complaining about the foul coffee and waiting for Corporal Tacos and Sergeant Reece to join us. Apparently, the Ripper wants to speak with them first thing this morning. After listening to Kong talk about all the crazy things he has done with his imaginary fantasy cheerleader last night, Dope looks over my shoulder and quickly calls attention to the approaching Lieutenant, Sergeant, Corporal, and an ANA Terp, all walking briskly toward us.

"At ease, gentlemen!" Lt. Breckovitch says, looking at us strangely. "Looks like you *fucktards* found a way out of the wire and went to Studio 54 last night for dancing and drinks. You have a big job to do, gentlemen, and I expect you to be bright-eyed and fucking bushy-tailed. Is that clear?"

"Sir, yes, sir!"

"I've had some troubling news this morning from our Command in Kabul. Apparently, our illustrious ANA Commanders and some local police commanders are engaging in sexual activities that are starting to piss off a lot of people up the ranks. Recently, one of the Afghan militia commanders raped a fourteen-year-old girl who he spotted working in the fields. Our Captain Davis complained to the provincial police chief, and he levied a punishment — one day in jail — and then *she* was forced to marry the psycho.

"In other happy news, another commander murdered his twelve-year-old daughter in a so-called honor killing for having kissed a boy.

"Captain Davis also informs me that it is common practice for Afghan 'men of power and position' to illustrate that fact and display their swagger by using boys nine to fifteen years old as *bacha bazi* for 'boy play.' I assume that I needn't have to explain the details.

"So as you can see, men, we are not in Kansas anymore! We are told by Command to stay out of any such matters we might encounter. They are referring to this as a 'cultural difference,' and we are instructed to turn the other way."

The Lieutenant tightens his facial features, makes a deep and obvious sigh, looks down sharply, and spits on the ground.

"On a happier note, our brothers, the Army Rangers in the Seventy-Fifth Airborne, paid a visit to Mohammad Karam Khan last night, the chieftain of the village Basukheyl, about thirty mikes north of Patkheyl. There was an unexpectedly large cache of weapons, shipment of drugs, and Taliban fighters. They fought all night, but I don't have to tell you who came out on top! Remember, we are never, never going to quit this fight; they can't make enough IEDs to defeat us."

Kong excitedly blurts out, "Hoo-ah!" By instinct, we all follow.

"Needless to say, we are on Threatcon Charlie, and I need you guys to stay frosty out there. Staff Sergeant Reece and Corporal Ramirez, I want you to join these guys today and head to Patkheyl and see what you can see, and learn what you can about the enemy movement in the area. Stay safe and report back to me."

Kong interrupted. "Sir, what about the Romanians?"

"Son, I think it would be better for us to manage this one alone!"

"Yes, Sir, Lima Charlie!" Reece steps in front of Kong who gives him a crisp salute. The lieutenant gives a quick salute back, turns and heads toward the main house with a sense of determination and purpose.

The Sergeant looks around and at us. "OK, Deuce Four, I want Dope, Kong, and Ali in front, Tacos and Mikey in the Humvee. Books and I will follow. Let's head out."

I feel a little nervous about driving with the Sergeant in my truck today. I don't know why. Perhaps because of his rank or maybe because he is older than I am. He seems so calm and quiet, and I'm not sure what to talk about for the hours ahead with just the two of us. He doesn't strike me as the kind of guy that likes to chitchat.

When the Sergeant sits, he starts looking at something on the ceiling of the truck with puzzlement. I ask him, "Is everything OK, sir?"

"Oh yeah, I'm just admiring Kong's artwork."

"How do you know it's Kong's, sir?"

I reach over and look up, and someone has drawn with a Sharpie marker a stick figure of a woman that looks like a caricature of Dolly Parton: with ringlets of long hair and enormous breasts with the caption, I LUV BUUBIES! I start laughing and the Sergeant cracks up too. He just shakes his head. "That Alabama boy is mental!"

I look at him with an ironic smirk. "You think?"

He smiles. "The theatre of war is an enigmatic and intriguing bed partner!"

As we head out, I feel more relaxed about hanging with him. Hooker-One is losing me on the Kandahar Highway about two clicks ahead of me.

"Excuse me, sir, for punching the gas, but I need to catch up with the others."

Just as I say that, Hooker-One is blaring on the intercom.

"Hooker-Three, this is Hooker-One. Do you copy? Over."

"Hooker-One. This is Hooker-Three. Read you, Lima Charlie! Over."

"Can you please bring your vehicle up to formation? Break. Picnics are not advised at this time. Over."

"Roger that Hooker-One. Just finished the carved turkey and dressing, green-bean casserole, and apple pie. Break. Actually, The Sergeant and I are busy admiring Private Kong's art installation in the truck. Over."

"Hooker-Three, this is Hooker-Two. You mean to tell me I am transporting a famous artist, 'Picasso Kong'?"

"Hooker-Two, that is affirmative. Over."

As the Sergeant and I caught up to the convoy, I was thinking about what the Lieutenant told us about the kids being abused in Afghanistan. It gave me an upset feeling in my stomach. I was no stranger to abusive adults, but something about the blatant and raw injustice, the cultural acceptability of it made it worse for me. I find it difficult to be present. As I'm driving, I run over some trash on the road. This is never a good idea in the Middle East, especially in a theatre of war. The Sergeant notices my careless mistake and pensiveness. "Dylan, are you OK?"

I imagine my feelings are so transparent that my face flushes red in embarrassment. His eyes search mine for understanding. I am unfamiliar with men asking me about how I feel, much less if I am OK, or that anyone might actually give a shit. After a lifetime of trying to survive emotionally, I was far more skilled in reading others' feelings, registering their needs, and giving them what they needed. I just assumed that I would be fine. *I would tough it out.*

I look at him from the corner of my eye and realize his sincerity. Without really analyzing it, I just blurt, "Yeah, Sarge, thank you for asking! Just feeling a little wobbly."

"Do you want me to drive?"

"No, sir, I'm just thinking about the Lieutenant's comments this morning about the abused children, sir!"

"I understand. That shit it is very upsetting."

"Especially for me, sir, I came from a family with nine kids and two fathers. I was the oldest. As a result of my parents never being home, I had to do a lot of parenting. I guess you could say that I was more of a parent than our real parents. Also, there was a lot of sexual abuse in my family and that stuff gets me really angry."

"I understand. I had a similar experience. I wasn't from a large family. In fact, it was just myself, and my father growing up. My mom left my father when I was about five. She just couldn't take his shit anymore. He was a Ranger, and served in Vietnam.

"When my father got home, he tried to cope with his PTSD by drinking. They didn't call it PTSD back then. My grandmother just said, 'He was *changed* by the war.' She ought to know, my grandfather served in World War Two. They didn't really go into details. There was no place for him to talk about his feelings. He was expected to just suck it up and deal with it — like a *man!*

"My family is from outside of New Orleans, basically in the swamps, from Terrebonne Parish, Cocodrie, Louisiana. They are from several generations of inland-bay, shallow-water shrimpers. My dad tried to go back out on the boat and dragged me out there with him. He got so fucked up all the time that he just stopped working, sat home, or disappeared for a couple of days. He made my life a living hell. He would make me scrambled eggs for breakfast and he would drink Jack Daniel's. For dinner, I made him whatever I could and then he kicked my ass before bed for no reason. My grandmother tried to protect me by enrolling me in a private Catholic school in Houma, which proved to be very ironic.

"Especially, when entering fifth grade, and Father LeBlanc, my school's head priest, asked me to be his altar boy, and to help him with Mass on Sundays. That was a big deal back then. A big honor! My grandmother was so proud of me. Father LeBlanc showered me with love and affection, which I was starved for, and didn't understand. I didn't realize what was happening really when he touched me. I thought it was because he was so

close to God, and if God was the embodiment of love, I trusted
that Father LeBlanc was just executing the will of God, in a
strange way. I was so desperate for someone to love me. When
I entered sixth grade, Father LeBlanc's behavior changed for
the worse. He no longer touched me lovingly. I was so angry
with my father. I couldn't say anything to him about the Father
because I knew he would kill him and I didn't even know how
to talk about any of it. I was embarrassed and afraid that I was
going to hell.

"When I actually *rolled into a living hell*—Baghdad, Iraq—with
my battalion, and saw the charbroiled remains of men, blown-
apart buildings, and felt the whizzing bullets of the snipers,
mortar blasts, and RPG fire, I finally had a long-overdue epiphany. I understood my father—*his pain*—for the first time, and
right in the middle of a mother fucking battle I broke down
crying, because for the first time I could feel compassion and
love for that miserable, drunk bastard."

I stare ahead and listen to the road noise of the truck. My
feelings are stuck in my throat. I want to say something, and
I can tell that he wants to say more, but I am afraid I won't be
able to keep it together with my own shit. I am saved by Dope's
chatter on the radio.

"Hooker-Three, this is Hooker-One. Over."

"Hooker-One, this is Hooker-Three. Go ahead."

"Whiskey Tango Foxtrot. There is an ocean of goats blocking
the road, and a jingle truck flipped on its side throwing fruit
everywhere. Over."

"Hooker-One, Roger, Roger that, do not approach until we
get there. Gunners, stay frosty. Over."

"Roger, Roger that Hooker-Three."

When we arrive at the scene of the accident, my perverse
brain begins to see this as a Hollywood sitcom. The colorful
jingle truck was hissing and smoking on its side, and the goats

are bleating nervously, seeing several of their flock dead from the truck impact. Large orange Afghan melons are strewn across the barren landscape, and the jingle driver is screaming obscenities at the old goat herder, who is blasting Dope about the fact that the jingle truck has hit and killed several of his sheep.

Ali, our interpreter, is trying to calm everyone down, but the insults are only getting louder. Meanwhile, trucks and cars are stacking up on both sides of the highway, honking their horns and shouting out the windows. In short, it is a total Charlie Foxtrot!

The Sergeant is determined to step in and quickly resolve the squabble. The truck driver is screaming and cursing at the old man for crossing such a large flock of sheep on a national highway. The old man insists it wasn't his fault that he had to slam on his brakes, because the idiot American driver was going too fast, and therefore hit him from behind.

Both are demanding compensation. The Sergeant brings two Afghan Claim Forms and hands them to the men and asks the Terp to ensure they understand it. Even though the form is also in Pashto, the illiteracy rate in Afghanistan is about 70 percent.

Atop the form in bold are these words: DEPARTMENT OF THE ARMY 48TH INFANTRY BRIGADE COMBAT TEAM, CAMP PHOENIX, KABUL, AFGHANISTAN. It begins:

*I am sorry we had an accident. Due to the orders of my military commander, I am not allowed to stay. It you wish to submit a claim for any damages resulting from this accident, please take this paper to the front gate of Camp Phoenix and ask for the claims JAG or paralegal.*

**There is no guarantee of payment for your claim. If the United States Government Personnel did not cause the accident, your claim will be denied.**

As the men continue to argue and insist on being paid in cash today, the Sergeant orders me to use my "helmet wrecker" to get the jingle truck back upright. This is precisely what I have trained for, and finally feel useful in my war effort. In little time, the hissing gypsy truck is off its side and standing upright. A band of small children have gathered to watch the carnage. For them, this level of entertainment might as well be a front row seat at Cirque du Soliel. The others on my team are carrying armfuls of melons to clear the road. Two men from the crowd approach the pandemonium; one is wearing a long white *perahan* with black vest and turban. The older of the two sports a bright red-orange beard dyed with henna. Even though it is intended to emulate the Prophet Mohammad, who apparently also used henna, it gives him a stylish, postmodern-hipster look. His tunic is lapis blue and his turban is mixed muted colors of blue, sage green and lavender. His eyes are piercing and intense, and seem to convey that he has lived many lives and seen many deaths.

I hear Kong, obviously agitated by the mounting tension, and growing onlookers, cock the .50-cal on the truck, aim the gun directly at the approaching men, and he screams *"Imshi"* several times. The men keep coming toward us. Now he screams even louder, "Stop, motherfuckers, or I'll blow your fucking heads off—*you understand that?*" He fires two shots above their heads that causes everyone to scatter, including the goats. The two men stop, but remain calm. The man with the black turban says, "As-Saalam-Alaikum," and then in perfect English continues, "Excuse us my friend, we are religious men trying to reach our mosque, and wish you no harm. You see, *Imshi*, as you have used it, I understood to mean the command form, *Yalla imshi*, or 'Come on, walk!' or 'Let's go! Move along.' I see now, in this context, you mean, 'Go—away from here!'"

Before Kong can respond, the Sergeant moves forward and extends his hand. "Salaam Alaikum, gentlemen. Excuse us, we didn't mean to startle you. As you can see we are in the middle of trying to resolve a serious problem."

"Yes, that is precisely why I have come to offer my assistance in this matter," the younger man says, bowing his head slightly as a sign of humility. "I am Mullah Akhtar Mansur and this is my father. As you are visitors in my country, may I offer a possible solution?"

"Well, sir, I am certainly open to any advice for conflict resolution!" Reece says sincerely.

"You see, gentlemen, the truck driver is from a different tribe than the goat herder. The truck driver is *Sarbani,* from the largest Pashtun tribe, and the goat herder is from a small *Hazara* tribe. Lately, there have been many problems amongst the two tribes. Also, the driver is a Sunni Muslim, and the herder is a Shia Muslim. This is the first point of conflict.

"Further, the herder lives with his entire extended family and must support twenty people. If you do not pay him for his three goats your truck struck, this could mean his children will not eat meat this winter. The American Army in Kabul will most likely not pay for his goats.

"In addition, the driver has damage to his truck, and his cargo. He will lose money from the time lost driving to market, damage to his cargo, and with the injuries to his vehicle you have ensured that his family will not eat anything this winter unless it is repaired."

"I understand the severity, sir, and I would appreciate your recommendation," the Sergeant says, as if he was speaking with a high-ranking officer.

"First, you must tow the damaged truck to Qalat for immediate repairs. Second, you must help him get his melons to the market. Third, give him fifty dollars today so he can have his truck repaired. He can wait on the Army payment for the body damage.

"As for the herder, my daughter will marry soon, and this evening we will have a special celebration to honor her. We can buy the three goats today for a fair price, and the old man will be happy, *but* remaining is the question of restoring his honor. The truck driver has spoken down to him and this must be resolved."

"These are fantastic and insightful suggestions, sir! Can you please explain your proposal to these gentlemen, and see if they are in agreement?" The Sergeant is obviously thrilled to have an exit strategy that will not delay our squad further.

The Mullah gently explains the reparation agreement and both the driver and the herder seem to accept the terms initially. The driver, however, is concerned about *badal* being served according to the *Pashtunwali,* their moral code, and felt that fifty dollars was insulting. After much haggling, he settles on one hundred dollars.

The herder is pleased to have the unexpected income and to contribute his goats to the Mullah's daughter's happy occasion, as there were so few to celebrate these days, but felt like he deserves some money to restore his honor, and for the time that was lost in his workday. After much back and forth, he agrees that fifty would cover the damage.

The Sergeant thanks the Mullah profusely for helping to resolve the "difficult situation." As the Mullah's men gather the dead goats for transport, the Mullah takes the Sergeant's hand tightly, smiles, and gently, as if speaking to an inexperienced boy, says, "Remember this, my young friend: It is always a good idea to speak the language and understand the culture of the country that you are invading!" He pats the Sergeant's hand several times, smiles enigmatically, and departs with an air of prevailing conquest.

After the Mullah and his men are some distance away, the interpreter laughs hysterically. The Sergeant asks what he thinks is so funny. He gathers his composure and says, "Well, the

Mullah, as you call him, did a fine job negotiating… that is true. First, you gave the men three times what any Afghan would pay in this situation. As a rule, Afghans generally negotiate with a win-lose mentality. The goal is always to get the best for oneself at all cost." He then laughs even more uproariously. The Sergeant, already in a foul mood, barks, "What now, Ali?"

"But, the *really interesting* thing is that Mullah Akhtar Mansur, whom you allowed to settle your problem, is a high-level Muslim lawyer and scholar, but also very high-ranking in the Taliban."

The Sergeant's face turned bright red with anger. Kong jumps in. "Hey, Tiger, I bet I can blow that fucker up from here if you give me the word!"

"No, Kong, look at the lines of civilian traffic. The last thing we need is to not follow the ROE after all the negative press we have been getting lately. We will visit the Mullah on another day!"

"Excuse me for asking, but isn't this a fucking war?" Kong says, spitting dip juice.

"Yes, Kong, but we are not going to risk killing innocent people on my watch. All right, men, let's get this shit cleaned up, and get out of here."

Dope stands beside the old goat herder, now smiling ear to ear. "Man, this old dude is a M.F. PIMP." Dope says, laughing at his own humor. "Shit, this brother is looking fly!"

Reece is clearly agitated at our unprofessionalism. He orders us to shut up, get the melon mess cleaned up, and for us to be ready to pop smoke in five mikes.

We follow Dope's lead, and start humming the song "P.I.M.P." We pick up the remaining melons and hand them to the local children as gifts. I am certain they would prefer cash, cigarettes, or Kong's porn.

# Naan to Nothin'

THE PREVIOUSLY QUIET little square in the village of Patkheyl
is now bustling with people selling food, clothing, and small
household items. Next to Ahmad Khan's home is a stand where
I see Shahzada enthusiastically offering her naan bread, and I'm
reminded how hungry I am after this morning's fiasco on the
highway. I get permission from the Sergeant, and eagerly stand
in her line to buy some fresh, hot naan bread. The other guys
go back to the trucks to eat their MREs (meals ready to eat),
get some water, and sit in the shade to cool off.

Shahzada looks different today, clad in a somber long black
dress, and a white scarf covering her hair, in lieu of her festive
party clothes. Her sparkling eyes and big smile continue to light
up her surroundings. She offers niceties to each customer, and
has the uncanny ability to make everyone feel at ease, and to
make them laugh. Standing in her line, I notice the older man
from the highway fiasco. I don't see the other man, the Mullah
who spoke such good English.

A strange energy permeates the village, but I can't put my
finger on it. I don't really understand this culture—or this
war—well enough to trust my instincts. I remember Shahzada's
brother, Bahman, and the way he shot the man in black at the
well. Remember the plastic packages on the shelves in the grain
storage. Why would they have drugs and kill a drug lord's man,
who is actually our informant? Something doesn't add up.

Shahzada flashes me a huge smile. When it's my turn to be served, she scampers around to the front of her stall and gives me a big hug. *"Salaam Alaikum,* Mr. Books! I do hope that you are well today. It's lovely to see you so soon. I do hope you enjoyed our family celebration, in spite of the horrible interruption!"

"Salem Alukem to you!" I say with my Texas accent, causing Shahzada to burst into laughter.

"Oh, your Pashtun is lovely!"

"Why thank you, Ma'am, I have been working on it since eleven hundred hours!"

She crinkles her nose and I can see her lips repeating *eleven hundred.*

"Oh, sorry, since eleven AM this morning!"

"Ah, you are tricky, Mr. Books! I bet you are hungry for some of my irresistible naan bread. I noticed that you ate seven pieces at our home!"

"Yes! I would be honored and love some of your naan bread, if you please."

"I'll be right back. I'll make you fresh bread, hot from our tandoor oven."

As Shahzada skips to the compound door and opens it, I have a momentary glimpse of her father in the courtyard, standing with the wise old man and his son, the Mullah from the roadside accident. I feel a pang of alarm. At first I dismiss it as coincidence and tell myself not to get any wild ideas. But then I can remember Ali, our Terp, laughing and pointing out that the Mullah was a high-ranking Taliban. Why is a Taliban leader visiting Ahmad Khan? Just as I was considering running over and talking to the Sergeant, the side door opens and Ahmad Khan walks over to me with a big smile and friendly handshake. "Hello, hello, my friend!"

I was a bit confused, as the other evening Ahmad Khan didn't speak English the entire time we were in his home.

"How are you today?" he asks.

"I am very well, sir, thank you."

"Shahzada tells me you love her naan bread."

"Oh, yes sir, very much."

"Wonderful! She will be back soon. Please excuse me, I must attend to my guests, my cousin is visiting from Kandahar, Mullah Akhtar Mansur and Mawlawi Abdul Jan, Governor of Zabul Province. We have many pressing matters to discuss regarding our weak agricultural market and improving our infrastructure for irrigation for our crops. *Inshallah!* Nice to see you, my friend, please come again soon!"

As quickly as he appeared, he slips back into the compound and shuts the door.

On the highway, the Mullah introduced the other man as his father, but they have different names. This alarms me further. Soon after, Shahzada returns with a big smile. "I have brought you my finest hot naan bread, and, just for you, fresh butter and honey."

"Wow! That is incredible, thank you, thank you! How much do I owe you?"

"Oh, this is my gift for you."

"Oh, I couldn't do that."

"Please don't insult me!" she says boldly.

I thank her three more times. Just before I say goodbye, I ask her, "So, Shahzada, the men your father is talking to, are they father and son?"

"Yes!"

"Why do they have different last names?"

"I don't understand 'last names,'" she says with her sweet smile.

"Family name!"

"Oh, we don't use them in Afghanistan..."

"Well, it is great to see you, and I hope school is going well."

"Yes, I am presently reading Sir Lord Byron. Have you read any Afghan authors, Mr. Books?"

"No, but I would love to."

"Please wait one moment. I have something I would like to give you."

With that, she dashes hurriedly back into the compound and I try to make sense of what just happened with her father. I'm so hungry that I decide not to worry about it. How can he or his guests be anything but good people with a daughter like Shahzada? I can't contain myself and I tear some of the naan bread off and stuff it into my mouth. It is delicious. The guys at the truck see me and yell for me to hurry up. Shortly, Shahzada is back and puts a book in my hands. "This is very important and I hope it will help you understand our struggle more clearly."

I thank her and assure her that I will bring her one of my favorite American books, *Catcher In The Rye*. She seems very excited and says for me to hurry back to see her.

Again, I am unfathomably touched by her quick wit, charm, and depth of maturity for such a young girl. Then, I realize that her entire young life has been surrounded by war of some kind or another; she has no choice but to go from child to adult in an unimaginably short amount of time. The book she hands me, written by an young Afghan girl, illustrates this fact more than I could know: *A Woman Among Warlords*, by Malalai Joya.

When I get to the truck, the guys hassle me, saying stupid things about my little "Haji girlfriend." Kong says, "Man, you too will make the cutest Haji babies and you can be a gentleman farmer!" It takes everything in me not to slug him in the face.

"Kong, you are a *very, very sick man*. She's a child and she reminds me of my little sister, Gabby! Here, eat some bread!"

As I reach over to give him the bread, a huge, dirty gold-and-white dog rushes toward my hand and snatches the bread out of it, scaring the hell out of me! I hear the sound of a little boy cackle with laughter behind me.

"Mister, mister Kuchi Dog—very hungry!"

I look behind me, and a small boy with bare feet and a dirty face laughs joyously, pointing at the enormous Afghan mountain hound dog.

"You-bread-Kuchi-dog." He points his little fingers at the dog.

I give the dog more bread and he again starts laughing hysterically. Then I realize that these people are so poor that the idea of feeding fresh, hot food to a dog is actually comical, and in fact unbelievable.

I ask the boy if Kuchi Dog is his dog, but he doesn't understand my question. He pounds his two fists together and makes angry growling sounds and says, "Kuchi dog." Dope says, "The kid is trying to tell you the dog is a fighter." The dog may be a fighter, but when he looks at me with his big sad eyes, I just see a love puppy. I point to the dog, and then toward the boy. "Your Kuchi dog?" The boy just laughs and runs away.

As we watch the boy dart across the street, Corporal Ramirez says, "You guys see that young Haji on the motorcycle over by the well? He has been staring at us for the last fifteen miles. Something ain't right, fellows!" As we eye the guy on the motorcycle, I can just make out the multi-colored scarf of Ahmad Khan's visitor in his grain storage—the precise spot where his son, Bahman shot the man in black. I still can't bring myself to say anything to the Sarge, because I know these guys would kick the doors down on the compound and get to the bottom of it.

I can still see Shahzada at her stand laughing and helping new customers. Then Reece says, "OK, fellows, let's pop smoke, we have a long drive home ahead of us, and who knows what jingle truck might need our assistance on the way home."

Kong blurts out, "So, basically we got nothin!"

Mikey laughs. "No, we have a new mascot for the Deuce Four—Kuchi Dog!"

The Sergeant looks at me, then the dog, and shrugs. "Tacos, I'm riding with you. Mikey, ride with Books."

# Rolling in the Deep

BACK AT FOB HAMILTON, Kuchi Dog is a big hit with the guys and is immediately adopted as our new mascot. However, he doesn't really seem to warm up to anyone but me. He refuses to run, catch a ball, play fetch, or sit and shake. The one thing he loves is eating MREs, and he seems to especially love the chicken potpie. I'm not sure he has ever seen a chicken, but he loves to eat them!

Before I can clean up, the Lieutenant calls everyone together in the courtyard to give us one of his famous "Shit You Need To Know" speeches. He announces that President Karzai's half-brother, Ahmed Wali Karzai, a member of the Kandahar Provincial Council, was murdered today in Kandahar by one of his own men. The Taliban is claiming responsibility.

The men begin to cheer and say things like, "Shit, they beat me to it," "One less Haji fucker to kill," or, "Karzai was a fucking drug dealer and a thug."

The Lieutenant went on. "If you have forgotten, President Karzai helped us, back in 2001, to navigate the complex tribal hierarchies, and to identify who were the bad guys. In 2004, we put him in office as the President. Many of the Afghans say he used that appointment to eliminate his own enemies. After ten years, his fucktard half-brother has used the relationship with our CIA, and his brother's presidency, to garner tremendous power in Southern Afghanistan. It is said that he virtually controls the opium production. And of course, we are his biggest customer."

It is at this precise moment that I have my first epiphany brought on by war. This man, Ahmed Wali Karzai, spent his entire life praying five times per day to connect with the almighty and powerful love of God, as he manipulates other men for his own power and gain. I realize the full expression of his divide—the desire to be innocent and loved in the eyes of God, trapped in a material world that smells of greed and human sacrifice. The foul stench associated with manufacturing personal, social, and political illusions. The layers of lies that construct this implosive and fragile human society, and just how tenuous it all is.

My mind flashes to the grain tower at Ahmad Khan's compound, and the drugs I saw stacked up, but chose to ignore. I am reminded of Ahmad Khan's son, Bahman, suggesting that the bad guys were the ones attacking us, and sent by the drug lord, Mansur Khan. A perplexing visit from a high-ranking Taliban Mullah and the Governor to Ahmad Khan's home.

Something was happening. I could feel it in my bones and smell it in the air, but I couldn't put my finger on exactly what was happening. To quote the Lieutenant, "Gentlemen, you can expect a shit storm!"

Apparently the fighting in Kandahar is intensifying. Kandahar is the spiritual center of the Taliban, and it is only a two-and-a-half hour drive southwest from our base. Our British allies have been fighting block-by-block with high casualties to retake a Taliban stronghold on the so-called Pharmacy Road. If things don't improve, our squad will be sent to assist them. At this point, it becomes my life, or theirs, and no one gives a fuck if you voted Republican or Democrat, or if you think Mohammed Omar is the coolest fucker since Mick Jagger—you fight, you protect your brothers on the team, and you don't quit until the job is done.

The Sergeant gives our team some free time before our night-watch duty in the tower. Afgan National Army soldiers are taking early watch, but at night those guys smoke way too much pot and opium to be trusted to stay frosty with all the increasing Taliban activity.

My first order of business is to find the showers. Even Kuchi Dog smells better than I do. After two days of full gear and intense heat, I am ripe. When I ask Mikey where to find the showers, he laughs hysterically and says, "Oh they are in the spa area, next to the steam bath, in the main house on the third floor. I recommend the piñon-scented soap." Then, he throws me a big plastic container of hand wipes. "Try not to waste water!" I go to my bunk area and try to discreetly undress and clean up when Kong walks in. I turn the other direction and hear, "Holy shit, look at that ass... damn boy, I could hit that!"

Then the Sergeant walks in with the corporeal and Kong spits out, "Oh, hey Sarge!"

I didn't know what to do, so I flip around, buck naked, and stand at attention and salute. Tacos starts laughing. "Dude, nice tattoo! What the fuck is that?"

Everyone laughs, and I try to find a towel in my gear. After I cover myself, I respond, "Well, sir, that is a griffin; the body of a lion and the head of a dragon, and it is on our family crest."

"Family crest? Oh, excuse me, *Lord Books*. I didn't realize we were in the royal tent!"

Mikey jumps in, "Yeah, all those Southern white boys have crests. You may see it as a badge of family honor, but I prefer to see it for what it really is — my-castle-is-bigger-than-your-castle shit. The knights took them into battle to show their alliance to the king. Even back in the Middle Ages, it was about whose army is stronger and supports *the will of the king*."

Kong jumps in Mikey's face. "I am so tired of hearing your communist Indian bullshit!"

"I am not in favor of state-controlled ownership, so please refrain from calling me a communist! And, I've told you ten thousand times, I'm not from India, and therefore should not be called an Indian." Mikey's amused calm exhibits complete control.

The Sergeant says, "Gentlemen, seems you could all use some rest. I want Books and Mikey on the North Tower at zero hundred hours. Kong and Dope are free to sleep. Where is Dope?"

"He's throwing rocks with some ANA dudes!" Kong says.

"Throwing rocks? They are having a rock fight?" the Sergeant asks in disbelief.

"No, sir. It's some kind of game they play to gamble."

"Right, enjoy your rest!"

"I'm gonna go show those ex-Haji fuckers who's king of the rocks!" Kong says, exiting the tent.

Mikey picks up his Katsina and starts carving, then he looks at me, shaking his head. "Some guys are just made for killing."

After I finish cleaning myself up as well as I can with the hand wipes, a young soldier with round glasses and an affable face enters with a big carton of mail. He places a pile of letters, a small package, and a big box on Dope's bunk and says, "Merry Christmas, gentlemen, may all of your wishes come true!" and exits.

Mikey doesn't even budge from his carving, so I ask, "What's up, Mikey? Aren't you excited to get a letter from home?"

"No!"

"What's up, man?"

"It will be from my wife, Mary, and she'll tell me about her difficulties, and everyone else's, in our clan. She'll tell me about my mother's illness, and about my daughter, Ruby. About everything I'm missing and how big she's getting. Then, she'll tell me about her cousin's family being forced to move because of an energy company ravaging our sacred lands, and the hardship it has brought our clan. She will remind me to pray, and then I will be fucking depressed and, on, and on. It's a shame we can't buy whiskey on this fucking FOB."

He waved a dismissive hand. "So what about you? Anyone back home writing you?"

"Yeah, my brother probably wrote me. He'll tell me about what a sick fuck my stepfather is and how he wishes that Malcolm was fighting the terrorists instead of me, and wouldn't it be cool if he got shot in the dick? He'll tell me about his junior college back in Austin, and how lame it is, and how much it sucks that we aren't rich so he could go to a good private liberal arts school to study art. He probably sent me a book that he thought about for a couple weeks before buying it. I love that kid! So gifted and special and he grew up with a river of shit running straight through our house, but he tries to act as if it was merely an inconvenience brought on by circumstance beyond his control. Stoic little fucker!"

Talking to Mikey about my brother makes me homesick for the first time. I walk over to Dope's bunk and search through the mail. The smallest package is from Daniel, my brother. And as I imagined, he sent me a book by Rory Stewart entitled *The Places In Between*, about an Englishman walking across Afghanistan in 2002. He didn't write a letter, just a quickly jotted note: *Hey Bro, this might give you some insight to the people you are trying to kill!* Of course, he was being facetious, but even for me, an anti-violence sort of guy, I find the comment slightly irksome.

"What did ya get?" Mikey asks.

"As I thought, my brother sent me a book, not a letter."

Dope and Kong walk in quickly and Dope looks beside himself. "I can't believe I let that Haji Tom Cat hustle me out of all my fucking money!"

Mikey and I both laugh. "What happened, Dope?"

"That ANA dude with the scar over his eye and the beady eyes challenged me to play a game of Rocks. You know the game these guys play, drawing a line in the dirt and standing back to toss the rocks, and the one that gets closest to the line wins. This dude tells me, 'My friend, I have not played this game, but it looks interesting!' So, I say that I will challenge him to put up twenty dollars and play me. He takes the challenge and says, 'My friend, I could never put up so much money, I am a very poor man, but If I lose, I will introduce you to my very beautiful sister. She is very lonely after her husband died in the war!' He shows me a picture of the most beautiful woman you have seen in your life. She ain't wearing no blue pump tent over her body, she is fucking Haji Marilyn Monroe fine. We're talking Middle Eastern movie star wearing a tight red sweater with pointy titties and big, *beautiful* dark sultry eyes."

"So what happened?" I ask like an excited four-year-old.

"I say OK, but if I spot you the cash, and you lose, you have to introduce me *tonight* to your sister. And he says, 'OK, this is no problem. I will introduce you immediately after the game.'

"So, we start playing. This Haji shark allows me to win the first three games. I am thinking how nice it's gonna be to push up against that red sweater—am I right? Then, the shark man suddenly becomes a fucking rock-tossing, Michael-fucking-Jordan, NBA champion. That dude was ringing every toss, and smoked my ass but good!

"After he won my twenty dollars, I asked him, well, I know you won, but can I still meet your sister? He smiled and said, 'Sure my friend, here she is' and handed me the photo. What does that mean, I ask? 'She has been dead for three years... thanks to the United States' he says, starting to laugh, and then says, 'I told you I would introduce you to her... Did I not tell you her name? Did I not show you her picture? *Is this not an introduction?* Maybe my English is no good.' I wanted to knock that fool out!"

We all roll on the ground laughing. Kong continues boasting about what he would do to that guy.

"I'd like to see that dude play me in Monopoly! I'd fuck his world. I'd put a Boardwalk and Park Avenue, with hotels, *squeeze* on that bitch—no Get Out of Jail Free card, Do Not Pass Go, and do not collect my mother-fuckin twenty dollars..." Dope rants on, which makes us laugh even harder.

"Look on the bright side," Kong says, "if you had met his sister and held that red sweater in your arms, you would be married before you knew what happened. You'd be living in this shithole for the rest of your life with baby Hajis running around, while you work the fields as a gentlemen opium farmer."

"Man, all that red-sweater talk is making me horny. I'm going to the Jack Shack for my early evening *session.*" Kong adds, as if anyone cared about his smut schedule.

"Man, fuck that dude and my twenty dollars. I'm going to the gym!" Dope says, and leaves.

Mikey and I fall into a rare and very needed calm and quiet. Mikey continues carving on his Kachina and I relax on my bunk and begin the book Shahzada gave me. From the first sentence, the author speaks of her country, Afghanistan, in terms of tragedy. She illuminates the last thirty years of bloodshed and chaos: Russian invasion, civil war, and Taliban rule. She describes Afghans forced to become refugees in Pakistan, and hardships for women.

Reading her words while being at war in Afghanistan feels like I am a woman who is in an abusive marriage and reading a novel about domestic violence in the living room while my husband screams, "Hey bitch, come make my dinner" from the kitchen.

The author is a courageous young woman, chosen to represent her region in the first democratic national tribal gathering, the *Loya Jirga,* tasked with adopting a new constitution after thirty years of continuous war. She faces rival tribal chieftains, drug lords, warlords, mullahs, career politicians, and village elders. She confronts the warlords at the meeting, as she knows they can't possibly establish a fair democracy in her country. She receives death threats, is shunned and harassed by men and women alike.

She persists, knowing that it could bring danger or even death to her and her family. Her dear friend dies in the struggle, and she continues to stand up as a true voice of hope in the darkness. She describes women lighting themselves on fire to escape from the misery and shame of rape, or the exhaustion of being repeatedly beaten, or being treated as possessions by an abusive husband, often a cousin or a man many decades older.

The author's courageous words about democracy, empowerment and human justice begin to feel sewn into my flesh, like a fragrant rose tattoo over my heart. It makes the social complexities of the country have a pulse, a heartbeat, a context, and personal meaning. The more I read, the more I realize the insanity of my—our—presence in Afghanistan.

Afghanistan's social complexities are expressed in Shahzada's family. It all makes sense to me now, and the more clarity I receive, the more painful it feels being here. I feel divided. I tell myself to suck it up and get the job done. In one year I will be home, and back in school. I try to imagine what my future will be, and I can't even see a single image of what that might look like.

I get anxious, unable to concentrate on what I am reading. I decide to go to the pool. When I invite Mikey to join me, he just smirks. "Do you really want to swim in that water? Aren't you afraid of the surface glue floating on top?" I feel sick to my stomach and return to my bunk. He starts laughing and says, "Oh man, I'm joking, you can drink that water! You don't think The Ripper would allow men's body fluids to infiltrate *his pool.*"

When I get to the pool, several Rangers in Special Forces are horsing around on a big alligator float. It is funny to see these big, tough guys acting like they are in third grade at the public pool, holding one another under the water, splashing. One even suggests that they play "Mullah Omar" instead of Marco Polo. There is something different about these guys. Even the way they play around, they feel like an unbreakable steel chain of invisible links. I laugh to myself because they all sport thick beards, making them look like aquatic lumberjack warriors.

From the raft, this lean, intense-looking Ranger the guys call "The Heckler" looks at me sitting on the side of the baby pool. "Hey, bro, evening, where did you get that wicked griffin tattoo?" I laugh and respond, "Well, would it mean anything to you if I say I got it in the Hill Country of the Lone Star State?"

"No shit, son, that pretty much makes you a two-stepping, Shiner Bock-drinking, Willie Nelson-loving boy like me now, don't it?"

"Well, yes sir! I believe it does, all the way from Austin, Texas."

"So how did a homeboy like you get stuck hanging out with camel spiders in Zabul?"

"Well sir, it is a long, and sad tale. I ran out of money for school and heard joining the Army is a great way to finance my education. After Basic, I spent the next four years in the States learning about Army mechanics and fell in love with a lovely girl from Intelligence."

One of the guys quips, "Ain't that an oxymoron?" Laughter follows.

I answer, "Which part, the mechanics or the intelligence?" Then continue: "Well anyway, they sent her off to Iraq, and in my amorous confused state of mind I thought if they deploy me to Afghanistan, we would both get out in a year, and live happily ever after. When she arrived to Saddam's sandbox, she sent me a letter explaining how she had — *accidentally* — hooked up with her commanding officer!"

All the guys laugh hysterically, and the biggest guy says, "Yeah, I *accidentally* shot a Taliban suicide bomber in the face yesterday!"

A guy with a huge scar across his entire stomach, says, "Happens every time when these average looking girls get to the hot and dusty FOB with a ton of horny, jacked-up guys and they meteorically rise to Desert Queen status. They fuck everything that walks, including the other chicks on base! My buddies at FOB Washington say they even have a tent called Lesbos Island specifically designated for girl-on-girl orgies."

The other big guy in the pool says, "Turner, that is utter *bullshit* and you know it! You are a sick broke-dick Ranger who needs to go home and fuck his wife..."

Heckler looks at me for a long while. "Well, brother, if this shithole country doesn't make you proud to be an American, me and mine can drop you into some places that we've been that will make you a fucking bonafide patriot in about two seconds! Why, I seem to remember our squad in a certain situation in Somalia that would make the average American fall to their knees, soil their pants, and thank the Baby Jesus for being born in a country with stars and stripes on their flag. Is that the truth, gentlemen?"

The other guys both say, "You bet!"

One of the men adds, "Afghanistan is fucking grape duty!"

"What brings you men to FOB Hamilton?" I ask, sheepishly.

"We can't really talk about the details, friend. We just need to defrag from our last mission north, on the Pakistan border, and tonight we visit some bad guys around Qalat."

My stomach begins to tighten. *What bad guys? Are they going to raid Shahzada's family?* Something feels bad and I can't put my finger on it. I feel the need to get back to Patkheyl, and see Shahzada and her family.

Sergeant Reece walks over to the pool, and says, "Books, I need you and Mikey to get to North Tower in thirty mikes for night watch."

I don't know what is wrong with me. I am just so far emotionally removed from "playing Army" that I answer dispassionately with "You bet!" The Heckler gives me a Whiskey Tango Foxtrot glare, and I snap-to and crisply say, "Roger, Sarge!" The Special Forces guys give me a disapproving look and Heckler says, "Son, don't lose respect for who and where you are. Remember, Sergeant Reece is looking out for you, 'cause if he doesn't stay frosty, it might just cost you and your buddies their lives!"

I feel embarrassed. Then he adds, "You and me didn't cause this shit, and nobody made us join the Army, buddy. We volunteered because we are protecting our homeland: our family, our friends, and our loved ones. It is important for you to remember that we are responsible for defending a nation of people from groups of organized men who would happily rape your wife and children in front of you, and kill you after they make you watch it, just to have the satisfaction of knowing they took everything important you had in your life away. They hate everything about you, and they believe that their God has given them permission to kill you — and any other infidel — and they will be rewarded in heaven."

I humbly say, "Thank you, sir, I hope to see you back in the Lone Star State, I'll buy you a shot of tequila!"

Heckler gives me a salute. "Well, man, that would be my pleasure. Remember, brother, *we don't give up.*"

The other guys give a very quick and resolute *"Hooah!"*

I give him a crisp salute, and walk toward my tent with Reece. Sensing I was feeling uncomfortable after my misstep, he put his hand on my shoulder. "It's all good... those guys are a special breed. They are some of the toughest guys on the planet, and they don't allow outside concerns, fears, or influences to muddy their objectives, and they don't quit—*period!*"

"Wow, they didn't really instill that in my Army mechanic school back home. By the way, I want to tell you how much I appreciate you sharing what you did on the way to Qalat. We never really got to finish our conversation, but I'd like to do that sometime."

Reece gives me a warm smile. "Cool, maybe I can take you up on a tequila shot someday in Austin. I'll just surprise you! But, tonight, you better get dressed and head to the North Tower, or the Lieutenant will hang you over the wire as coyote bait, and me too, if I don't get you there!" I made a coyote howling sound and slipped into the tent.

●　●　●

Later, Mikey is sitting in the North Tower on night watch, with a 240B/.50-caliber machine gun, and me with my night-vision goggles and my new book about Afghanistan. All is quiet on the radio, and nothing is moving outside the wire. Mikey says he thinks something is off, that normally there should be some activity at this hour: bored ANA guys walking around, or the Haji Mart trucks coming and going. The Haji Mart guys are local vendors that bring us porn, cigarettes, Iranian candy, and men's underwear from Pakistan that looks like go-go-dancer jockstraps. They can also supply marijuana, hash, and opium for a "special price."

After two hours of listening to Mikey tell me stories about the beauty of the Grand Canyon and other sacred Hopi shit, I am lulled into a state of peace. It seems surreal for me to be eight thousand miles from home and learning about a beautiful culture, for which I am assisting to militarily occupy, that I knew nothing about. My stomach growls and I decide to head for the porta-potty. I haven't used the bathroom in forty-eight hours, and my stomach is not feeling good. Everything is so dark and quiet. I enter the potty and struggle to get comfortable. My night vision goggles are making this entire maneuver all the more uncomfortable. I finally sit—and feel a slimy wet pillow of mess, accompanied by a squish sound. I jump up and realize that one of the ANA guys had squatted above the toilet and missed. I try not to panic, and then try not to vomit. I frantically flail for the Handi-Wipes in my pack.

As I desperately try to clean myself, I hear a loud *pop-pop-pop* sound from the tower. Before I can pull my pants up, a loud blast from an incoming RPG rocks my porta-potty and slams me against the wall. I'm more worried about my little plastic fortress falling on its side and its filthy contents washing over me than I am about being blown up. I hear more *pop-pop-pop* sounds, and the Lieutenant screaming orders across the courtyard.

When I make it out, I stumble over a hole in the ground from the mortar blast. It is very close. I run toward the North Tower. When I arrive, Mikey is screaming obscenities and shooting across the valley. "Come on, you motherfuckers!" When I get to the top of the platform my eyes haven't adjusted yet to the pitch black, and I can't see anything. He yells at me, "Shoot the fucking guy in the orchard." I can't see anyone. I wait as Mikey continues to shoot at a cluster of Taliban fighters on the other side of a wall. Finally, I see the muzzle fire of the guy in the orchard. My stomach is cramping and I'm sweating. I aim and shoot several rounds into the trees. I wait, and don't hear anything. I am anxious. *Did I kill the guy?* I feel so many things I'm unable to reason well. Moments later, more shots ring out from the orchard. *Thank God I didn't kill the guy, but I want the fucker to stop shooting at us.*

Mikey, frustrated by my lackluster performance, moves his fire across to the orchard and I hear *pop-pop-pop*, then — silence in the orchard. I feel sick. Mikey yells, "Go get me some water! This shit makes me thirsty!" He smiles and gives me a nod.

Our mortar team is firing at the Taliban fighters in the distance. Our guys are cheering and screaming things like "Fuck yeah!" and "Try to mess with us, bitches!" and "Four Deuces, muthafuckers!" The courtyard feels electrified, the men certain of victory. I grab two water bottles and run back to the North Tower, and as I climb up the ladder I hear a *crack* sound and then a bullet ricochet above my head. Mikey stands to see the barrel fire, and as I arrive standing behind him I hear another *crack*. Mikey falls back against my chest and quickly slaps his hand to his neck.

He groans loudly and blood gushes through his fingers and flows in all directions. I scream at the top of my lungs for a medic. I grab his face. My eyes are filling with tears. "God damn it, Mikey, you can't leave yet. Hold on." Someone knocks me aside and starts barking orders at another guy. There are more cracking sounds, mortar blasts, and orders being yelled across the courtyard. The medic reaches into Mikey's throat and pinches his artery and screams, "Someone call a fucking Medvac — now." The medic orders me to take over holding his artery. He observes to ensure that I am getting it clamped. Mikey starts to choke and can't breathe. I panic and the medic calmly tells me how to adjust my fingers. The blood stops gushing and Mikey smiles at me with his eyes. I am trying to keep it together. The medic tells me he'll be OK, as if commenting on a leaking hose in a car engine, but I don't believe him. It feels like hours elapse, yet within two minutes the chopper lands and Mikey is flown out of the compound.

Thoughts rush through my mind. *Is it my fault that Mikey is hit? If I were in the tower, he wouldn't have stood up to see where the enemy fire was coming from? Will he make it? Would I see him again? What would I tell his wife and daughter?* I am so fucking angry. I start to feel something unexpected. I want to hunt down the guy that shot Mikey. I want to kill the motherfucker. I feel conflicted and divided: my love for humanity, and my rage and desire to kill the guy who shot Mikey.

Someone taps me on the shoulder. I turn and Sergeant Reece is in front of me. His face is calm and his eyes are trying to assess if I am OK. He puts his arm around my shoulder and I begin to cry. I am not embarrassed. I don't feel weak or afraid. I just feel. "This the hard part," he says, trying to comfort me. He lets me cry and I know that no one will think me less of a man for doing so. When I pull it together he says, "Mikey is going to be OK, Dylan. They will take excellent care of him. They will stabilize him in Kabul and then send him to Ramstein Air Base, and on to LRMC in Germany for surgery. I bet he will be back home with his family in Arizona within two weeks."

The Sergeant tells me to go rack out and walks me back to my tent. When I get there, Kong and Dope are sitting and staring at Mikey's empty bunk. In the middle of his bed is the cottonwood-root Kachina, representing our team. He has finished carving it, but it isn't painted. The unfinished work makes me feel hollow. Mikey's energy fills the tent, and I can feel what must be the Kachina spirit. The guys can see how shaken up I am. They greet me warmly. I don't really feel like talking and they understand. No words are necessary. As we say on days like this, "It was a *bad day.*"

I curl my body into a fetal position, pull my blanket over my head, Kuchi Dog jumps on the end of my bunk, and puts his head on my legs, and I fall asleep and have a vivid dream.

*I am riding on my motorcycle. I'm on an empty highway in Arizona. The road is flat, black, and heads toward the Hopi villages. I can just barely make out the gray silhouette of the mesas rising in the distance ahead of me. On either side are golden rolling hills. An eagle soars high above in large graceful circles. I ask the eagle if he is Mikey? The eagle doesn't speak. A large cloud forms in my view and I ask the cloud why the eagle will not speak. The cloud says, "You are the eagle, Dylan. I am the cloud."*

*"What do you mean?" I ask Mikey, confused that he has turned into a cloud.*

*"Remember, my friend, you are the eagle… you carry the prayers to the Great Spirit. I have left my body, and now I am a cloud, and I will give rain to my people for their corn; to feed and nourish them."*

*"But, I don't want you to leave!"*

*"Don't worry, friend. I am here. I wait for you at Oraibi."*

# The Divide

IN THE MORNING just before sunrise, Kuchi Dog begins to whimper and push his head into my arm. I think he wants me to take him out to pee, until I realize our tent is being swept by gusts of wind and sand so intense that it uproots the guy ropes and tent stakes. I hear Dope scream that he needs all of us to help secure the tent *on the double*. The hot sand stings my neck and is so strong it pushes me off balance. The guy ropes and stakes blow around like pissed-off snakes.

After we finally secure the tent and are back inside eating breakfast, Kong refers to it as the "Wind of One Hundred and Twenty Days," and I think, *If this shit goes on for one hundred and twenty days, I'm walking back to Texas!* The Sarge drops in to check on us and informs us that the Lieutenant wants a word with our squad at 0800 hours.

Kong makes an eerie sound and says, "The Ripper is hungry!" Kuchi Dog barks at him. We crack up until Kuchi Dog grabs the Kachina on Mikey's bed and starts using it as his chew toy. At first, we are all horrified. Then Dope says, "Man, Mikey, you got a great sense of humor. You know what he's saying: 'Oh, I forgot to carve Kuchi Dog, best start a new one!'" Suddenly, the reality of Mikey's injury came back into focus and I feel a heaviness hanging on me. My mind splices in images of me holding his artery, blood everywhere, and the stupid smile on his face when he knows I have stopped the bleeding.

Kuchi Dog pushes his nose into my side, which is Pashto dog-speak to say, *I sure would enjoy another Chicken MRE, Dad!* I feed Kuchi Dog and find such pleasure in watching him devour the entire package in a few slurps. Knowing that he has had a tough life, and I am able to give him a moment of peace makes me happy. The wind is less strong now, but still blowing at about thirty mph and is agitating everyone. I actually look forward to our brief with The Ripper, just for something to do and to get out of this tent. I can't concentrate well enough to read and Kong is blaring porn on his laptop and doing what he does best while talking to the laptop, and it is driving me insane. Even Kuchi Dog is annoyed and starts barking ferociously at Kong. Within moments Kong accepts defeat, and heads toward the Jack Shack for privacy.

At 0800 hours, we arrive to see the Lieutenant. Standing at the podium tapping his long, narrow fingers, with his usual air of superiority, the Lieutenant seems to be in his typical foul mood. We stand at attention and salute. He gives some kind of limp gesture in lieu of a respectful salute.

"As you know, conditions are not ideal for travel, gentlemen, but I'm going to have to send you out on a mission. It seems that some *idiot* in Kabul volunteered our MRAP to help some Afghan folks stuck in the mountains outside Band-e Amir. Also, some *fucktard* in Bagram, at a prison library, burned some old copies of the *Quran,* these folks most sacred religious book, thinking he was getting rid of 'just some old books.' Some local janitors found the charred remains of their holiest book and it has caused riots all over the country. President Karzai has called the guys who did this 'inhuman' and said they should face public trial.

"Needless to say, we need to do a better job with 'hearts and minds,' gentlemen. Kabul has asked us to do damage control and go on a PR mission, and wants you guys to head to Band-e

Amir to help some folks stuck in a mudslide in the mountains outside the city. Books, this shit is your chance to shine!"

I stand up promptly. "Well, sir, when it slides, I glide. Not a problem, sir!"

"Good man, let's get this done. You men will leave FOB Hamilton by oh-nine-hundred hours. You will spend the night at Camp Bulldog at Bagram Airfield. You will arrive there about five or six PM and spend the night, then head to Band-e Amir tomorrow, about five hours west. You will probably have to set up camp there. I expect you to be on best behavior and stay frosty."

"Sir, yes sir!"

"Dismissed!"

●  ●  ●

As our convoy leaves the compound, I struggle to see the truck in front of me. The sand and wind are still strong. Although I have visibility, I am nervous behind the wheel. Kuchi Dog is in the backseat and seems nervous in the truck, and occasionally sticks his big head around and licks my face. The Sarge is beside me, staring at Blue Force Tracker, GPS system, and seems more uptight than usual. I ask him if he is afraid of sandstorms and he assures me that is not the case, but doesn't understand why the Lieutenant is sending us to Camp Bulldog, and then on to Band-e Amir, when it is faster to go from Patkheyl, and then north. We could reach the assistance site today. Isn't that better PR?

I had a deep reaction to hearing the town of Patkheyl and begin to see Shahzada laughing and joking with her customers. I can smell the hot naan and the sweetness of the honey and hear her cute British accent asking, "Does it please you?"

My daydream is broken by the sound of the Sarge calling the lead truck, "Hooker-One, this is Hooker-Three, do you copy?"

"Hooker-Three, this is Hooker-One, I copy Lima Charlie. Over."

"Hooker-One, I am on the map and am changing the route. Proceed to Patkheyl. Over."

"Roger, Roger that Hooker-Three. Are we going dog shopping? Over."

"Negative Hooker-One. Just saving precious time, with a little grace. Over."

"Sounds like the Sarge is about to sing a gospel song. Over."

"Negative Hooker-One. Stay frosty. Over."

"Roger that!"

By the time we reach Qalat, I'm wide awake and the sand storm has subsided. The heat is sweltering and the sun is burning my arms. A street vendor is selling *shemagh* cotton scarves. I flag him over, point to the green one, and say *"Da somra di?"* I can't understand what he tells me, so I hand him a fifty-Afghani note and he shakes his head. I hand him a hundred-Afghani note, expecting change and he says *"Manana"* and walks away. The Sarge laughs. "You just got fucked, my friend!"

"Yeah, well if Uncle Sam would invest in actually preparing us to be able to communicate, we might be more effective shoppers! The GTA Culture Cards that they gave me didn't really teach me to speak the eleven *languages* spoken in Afghanistan. My favorite culture card is the one with the headline, WHAT ARE SOCIAL NORMS AND MORES (MOR-RAYS)? They try to offer a definition and then they actually write, *Norms are 'social lubricants' that help people interact smoothly.* Are we fighting the Taliban in the gay bars?"

I laugh, and the Sarge gives me a disapproving glare. I ignore it, and try to catch up with the other trucks. After a few minutes he says, "Why would you associate fighting the Taliban with a gay bar?" I can tell by the way he asks that he is not happy about it and launches into a curt retort.

"Next month it's expected that 'Don't ask, don't tell' will be repealed... probably a good idea to start being aware of what you say now!" It dawns on me that what Dope and Kong said might be true, so I just jokingly blurt out, "I will work on it, and does that mean you will be able to be openly gay?" A long pause elapses, and then he turns his head and gives me an ironic look that conveys, *What is he going to do, shoot me?* And says, "Yep!" I didn't know what to say, so I just said, "Cool." Sarge seems pretty stirred up and continues talking.

"Why does the United States government give a shit if some-one is gay? Alexander the Great, Julius Ceasar, Lawrence of Arabia, King Edward II of England, and King Richard the Lion-heart are all known to have slept with men. There have always been, and always will be gay men who are soldiers and warriors.

"Gay people are pushed off buildings in the Middle East, yet their so-called fierce macho warlords have young boys as sexual toys. Men don't fight because they are gay or straight... As you probably could deduce from what I shared with you before, I joined the Army for many reasons, some good, some bad. I was trying to get away from my father, small-town America, and from the bad memories. Not to date men! I believed that the terrorists responsible for September 11, 2001, had to be stopped and wanted to protect my country from the threat of terrorism invading our shores."

"Me too!" I say and launch into a passionate diatribe.

"Now, I see what a fucking farce this place is. We shouldn't be here. The Taliban is fucked up and I don't like their brand of rule, but they don't want to attack the United States on our own soil. The original 'bad guys,' Osama bin Laden and his gang, were just passing through. Meanwhile, back home all the terrorists seem to be young, psychotic white males with an interest in shooting innocent school children.

"When I think about that, it really pisses me off. I just keep seeing Mikey's face, his smile, and it breaks my heart that we are in this shit storm." I stop because I can feel the tears pushing behind my eyes.

The Sarge continues.

"What does that say about our 'social norms and mores?' It is now the 'norm' for our own people to use violence against one another, pass legislation that does not help or forward and protect our own citizen's lives, but ensures the protection of oil companies, insurance companies, banks, car manufacturers and multi-national interests and profits."

"I'm not sure that any of the old governmental systems are in place. We sure as hell are not a true democracy. Who has the balls to find the new system, for the benefit of the majority of humanity?" I offer, realizing how futile that sounds. The Sergeant continues to talk.

"For these miserable bastards, after the Russians invaded, they were socially torn apart. Regional warlords ruled, abducted small children, took lands, and perpetuated social chaos. The country was illiterate and in turmoil. The Taliban seemed like the good guys who wanted to restore order and unify the country. They did so by torture and intimidation. Soon people realized that all of their freedoms had been taken. Women were forced to stay home and not be educated. The men couldn't play cards, watch videos, or have any pleasures. Then, we invade and bring the promise of a democracy, by putting a Pashtun warlord in power, and as you know, his brother is now dead. This will certainly stir up all kinds of shit in the region..."

I am kind of overwhelmed by the intensity of our political discussion and say, "I seem to have struck a nerve!"

He smiles. "Yep! Why can't humanity get their peanut brains around the idea of basic dignity and respect for all human life? We are all in this fucking sandbox together!"

"Agreed, but our people can't even seem to figure out drive fast on the left, slow on the right!" I say, and take a deep breath to try and find some emotional calm.

As we reach the outskirts of Patkheyl, I can see a motorcycle with two young men in the mirror racing from behind. Soon, they pass our truck. The man on the back is wearing all black, with aviator sunglasses and a headscarf that covers his mouth, and the guy has an AK-47 machine gun slung over his shoulder in plain view.

"The last time we took out two guys on a motorcycle, they were on our side. Sarge, what should we do?"

He jumps on the radio, "Hooker-One, this is Hooker-Three. Over."

"Hooker-Three, I read you. Over."

"Be advised, two possible unfriendlies, armed, coming your way quickly on a motorcycle. Over."

"Roger that, Hooker-Three. Do you want us to act? Over."

"Negative. Charlie Mike. Stay frosty. Over."

"Roger, roger that!"

The atmosphere is poisoned in an instant. I can see the Patkheyl village in the distance. I think about Shahzada, Ahmad Khan, and his family. Sarge gets on the radio with FOB Hamilton, and the Lieutenant is furious that we have rerouted our trip without his approval. After blasting the Sarge and some bantering back and forth, the Sarge seems to have convinced the Lieutenant that his plan is the better route.

"Hooker-Three, Hooker-Three, this is Hooker-One. Over."

"Go ahead Hooker-One. Over."

"Our boys on the bike are stopped up ahead. Break. We made eye contact and they have jumped back on the road. Break. I smell an ambush. Over."

"Yep. They are teasing us, boys. Break. Get ready for a firefight. Over."

I hear him say the words and I feel really anxious.

"Hooker-Three, this is Hooker-Two. Over."

"Go ahead, Hooker-Two. Over."

"I spot Hajis in the orchard ahead, something's strange. Break. Need OK to take out boys on bike. Over."

"Negative, Hooker-Two. Hold fire. Break. Let's move ahead and see what we have. Over."

Before we can reach the courtyard, an RPG is fired from behind a mud wall, and explodes between the lead truck and Hooker-Two.

"Hooker-Three. We are taking enemy fire. Over."

"Roger that Hooker-One and Hooker-Two. Return fire. I repeat, return fire!"

Corporal Ramirez is in the MATV with a MK-19 mounted on top, and I can see him shooting, but can't see what is going on with Dope's truck. I hear multiple blasts and then all the trucks stop.

"Hooker-Three. This is Hooker-One. We are taking too much heat. We need to get out of the trucks *now*. Over."

"Roger that, Hooker-One."

"Hooker-Two. This is Hooker-Three. Over."

"Hooker-Two. This is Hooker-Three. Over."

The Terp in Hooker-Two is terrified, and not able to respond on the radio, and Tacos is up top, unable to stop fighting long enough to talk.

The Sarge orders me to get out of the truck and stay behind him, and take cover. We need to move up and join the squad. Kuchi Dog is freaking out, barking, and desperately trying to get out of the truck. I am in such a hurry that I leave the door open. When we start toward Hooker-Two, I hear Tacos yell, "Goddamn it, take this you motherfuckers!" He continues to fire and then his body jerks spastically, and slumps over the side of the Humvee. Blood spills everywhere. The Sarge screams, "Ramirez, can you hear me? Ramirez, hang on buddy." He screams into the radio, "Man down," and then puts his fingers on Tacos's neck to check his pulse. He shakes his head with pain in his eyes. Sarge says, "Come on brother…" with so much care, as he leans him back inside the truck. Mortars are blasting around us and finally, he says, "I'm sorry, brother, to leave you…" He points ahead of us, and screams for me to *move-move-move*. We have to leave Tacos and run at full speed to join Dope and Kong.

Kong is screaming, "Really, you want some of this?" We move forward in a shallow stream of water with a thick three-foot mud wall between us, and enemy fire. We know that there are men in the orchard to our northwest. Kong has already taken out the guys on the motorcycle. Shots whiz past us from the open field behind us, and soon from the mountains to our northeast. We are stuck in a triangulated ambush fire. The Sarge gets on the radio and screams, *"Troops in contact,"* and calls for an airstrike, giving the grid coordinates for the mountain and the orchard. I suggest that we push forward to Ahmad Khan's compound for a tactical advantage. The Sarge agrees, but orders Kong to take out the sniper in the field behind us. Kong quickly suppresses the fire with an AT-4.

We all move swiftly along the wall heading toward the compound, and within a few minutes we see our guys arrive in an AH-64 Apache attack helicopter. They shoot a series of Hellfire missiles and obliterate the mountain target. The chopper circles back and releases another missile directly into the orchard. The noise is deafening. The Sarge screams, *"Push on, get to the compound, and take out anyone holding a weapon regardless of age, or gender."*

We run as fast a possible with all of our heavy gear and arrive, breathless, to Ahmad Khan's compound. I bang on the door, hoping to see Shahzada's sweet face. No response. The Sarge orders us to clear the area and throws a grenade, landing just in front of the door, instantly blasting and shattering the opening.

We storm into the compound. Kong and Dope rush to the right, and the Sarge and myself to the left. My heart is pounding heavily, and I find it hard to breathe. Kong and Dope run toward the main house, and Sarge and I head to the grain storage tower. The Sarge is in the lead, and kicks the door open. He pushes on to clear the tower, looking at all possible points of enemy fire, and instructs me to keep eyes below.

On the second level, where I saw the opium stored before, there are now only sacks of almonds stacked in piles. When we reach the third floor, we look out beyond the courtyard, the well in the square, and we can see the bombsite in the orchard. The Taliban guards are littered and bloody on the ground. Large sacks hang from several tree limbs. I imagine, it must be sacks of nuts hanging, with firewood below the bags to keep animals from eating them, or perhaps to dry the almonds.

We see Kong and Dope re-enter the courtyard, still on high alert. The Sarge screams, "Clear?" They respond, "Roger that, Sarge!" He tells them to stay put, and we rush down the stairs. I am relieved that the family is gone. That must mean that they are safe, and I assume that Shahzada is in the neighboring village at school with her British tutor. When we rejoin the guys, we carefully make our way to the orchard to make sure the enemy isn't still in the village.

In the orchard, I am immediately sickened by the gore and carnage. Kuchi Dog runs around the horror scene, with blood splatter everywhere, barking frantically at each dead soldier. He makes his way to the sacks hanging in the trees and begins to bite at one of the bags with his strong jaws, growling, and viciously tearing the sack. I think, *Wow, how can you be hungry?* He finally succeeds in tearing the sack, and from the bottom falls the lifeless body of a small girl. Her sweet face jerks toward me, and her eyes are expressionless.

Seeing Shahzada's body lay splayed, bloody, and cold over the jagged firewood causes me to fall to my knees crying and vomiting.

I hear the Sarge scream something and a second attack by enemy gunshots rings out. Dope screams, "Get up, man, we gotta pop smoke."

My legs are frozen. Dope grabs me and yanks me up. I hear *pop-pop-pop* and feel a burning sensation in my leg. I think that I've pulled a muscle when I fell to the ground, but we have to move fast. We make our way back to the trucks. Dope gently picks up Tacos and lays him on the ground gently. He climbs back up on the truck and shoots the M-19 toward where he can see muzzle fire and smoke on the far side of the orchard. Kong joins him shooting the .50-cal. The Sarge runs over to me. "Oh, fuck, man, you are hit. I'll call a Nine Line."

I look down and see the blood gushing out of my leg, and I pass out.

When I regain consciousness, I am in a Medevac chopper and the medic smiles at me and says, "You are one lucky son of a bitch. The bullet missed your femoral artery and bone. Congratulations, dude, you are going home!"

# Part Two

• • •

"What if I'm not the hero...
What if I'm the bad guy?"

— GRIM REAPER TATTOO

# Miasmal Mist

ONCE AT SSG Heather N. Craig Hospital in Bagram, after five years, nine months, and three days of being in the Army, my war on the battlefield ends. I'm in pain, but conscious. On the way in, I notice, stenciled on the wall above: I WILL NEVER FALTER, AND I WILL NEVER FAIL.

I am in the company of young guys with their heads wrapped in gauze, their arms in bandages, and many missing their feet or legs. A dull, degenerative and deafening silence is followed by the medical team's hushed whispers, medical-device beeps, and bold orders from the surgeons that ricochet down the hall with urgency. We are all united in the same concern, the same question: "Will we live, or will we die?"

We all feel it, the uncertainty, vulnerability, and the desire to leave — some to get back to their teams, and others home. Many are frozen in fear. Others are glib and chatting up the nurses, still others too damaged to communicate. One of the Special Forces guys tells the doctor, "Fuck this shit, I have to get back to my men. Just set my fucking shoulder back in place, put a fucking bandage on my arm, and let me go!" The doctor, obviously exhausted from his twenty hours of continuous ER trauma patients, curtly responds, "You will be of little use to *your men* if you get an infection in that arm and lose it!"

My physician, Dr. Matthison, reiterates how lucky I am. I have no damage to the bone or arteries — which he declares as a fucking miracle — but the tissue trauma is serious and I need to keep the in-and-out wound clean and dry to prevent infection that could cause me to lose my leg. Compared to the guys around me, I feel like I have the common cold.

In the evening I am assigned to a Critical Care Air Transport Team and hoisted on board a C-17 cargo plane that was converted, in a miraculous ninety minutes, into a flying medical center. When I am inside the plane, I wipe a thin layer of fine sand off my forehead and notice that my fellow passengers seem a great deal more injured than I am. We are stacked three racks tall and I am placed in the middle, which I find comforting.

A nurse comes over and introduces herself as Trudy. She's on my transport care-team for the next thirteen hours until we reach Ramstein Air Base in Germany. Trudy is as sweet as they come, and she checks my security belts: "I bet it's nice to be out of your *battle rattle!*" I smile, point to the bunks, and say, "Well, a patient sandwich isn't my idea of fun!" She gives me a sweet smile for trying to be upbeat, and is off to help the next guy. Within minutes we are departing down a dark runway with no lights, and lift off with a swift, and steep, vertical climb to avoid Taliban attack.

This is the part you don't see in the movies: the focused care team on the plane, the medical staff, and the overall approach to helping our wounded in the Middle East. It's like precision poetry. Every action is with such genuine concern to give the soldiers state-of-the-art care, and to get them home alive. Of course, we don't all make it. I hear the guy next to me telling Trudy, "Please tell my wife, and little girl, how much I love them… her name is Katy and she is four. She has blonde hair like her mom." He dies within the first hour of the flight.

Watching them zip that body bag brings me tremendous pain and I think about losing Mikey, Tacos, and Shazhada. I am so stoned from the pain medications. I say a prayer — something

I haven't done in many years—with the hope that I will find a nanosecond of peace. I pass out.

Somewhere over the Black Sea I wake up, startled by an Afghan man standing over me and smiling. My first impulse was to reach for my gun, but it wasn't beside me, which really upsets me. He gently offers an introduction, in perfect English: "Hi, Dylan, I'm Dr. Najib. I'm sorry, I didn't mean to startle you... I am the physician in charge of your care. I was just checking on you, and was surprised to hear you speaking in Pashto."

"What did I say?"

"You kept saying '*Shahadah,*' and I was surprised that an American soldier knew about this custom!"

"I wasn't saying that word. I must have been saying Shah-za-da! The name of a girl I knew in Zabul."

"Oh, I see. You knew a princess! Do you know what shah-*a*-dah is in our culture?"

"No."

"At birth, the *Shahadah,* profession of faith, is whispered in the baby's right ear.

Sugar, or a date, is placed in the baby's mouth so the first taste of life is sweet. At death, *Shahadah* is whispered in the deceased person's right ear. The dead are then washed, rubbed with perfumes and spices, wrapped in a white cloth, and buried without a casket, facing Mecca."

Again, I hold the customs of an ancient culture in my heart, reminded of what all humans, perhaps since the beginning of time, want for their children: to thrive and to become fine human beings, and for them to be spared from the pain and suffering that this life can bring. Images of my sweet Shahzada visit me, and I mourn that no one was there to whisper loving words into her right ear.

When I wake up, the cabin lights are fully illuminated in preparation for our landing in Germany. In the hospital the physician has a look at my wound, and says I am good for transport in twenty-four hours, as long as the wound is not bleeding, and there are no unexpected complications. The reality of my situation is fully clear for the first time: I am returning to the United States of America, still *officially on active duty,* wounded, and depressed.

When my Army transport plane arrives at Fort Bliss, Texas, a strong wind is blowing, and the plane is rocking from side to side, and several of the guys let out a loud cowboy *yeeeeee-ha* as we touch down. The atmosphere is lively and everyone seems very eager to see his or her families. We are escorted to the gymnasium, where I can hear the younger women squeal at the sight of their husbands, and the sound of children screaming with excitement, "Daddy!" The room is a cacophony of yelling names, tears, and laughter. I want so badly to be hugged, and welcomed home, but there is no one waiting for me.

I walk slowly through the crowd, trying to adjust to my cane. My leg is sore and hurts with every step. I have to locate a taxi to get me to the El Paso airport, and on to Austin. On the way out, the cutest little blonde girl points at me and says, "Mommy, Mommy, that man got shot like Daddy!" Then, in a horrible moment, I remember the man on the CCATT plane back in Germany that didn't make it. Before he died, he said to the nurse, "Please tell my wife, and little girl, how much I love them. Her name is Katy and she is four. She has blonde hair like her mom." How would they tell this sweet child she wouldn't see her daddy again? I feel so angry. I walk outside and the 115-degree heat envelops me, and the dry semi-desert terrain surrounding me makes me think, *Fuck, I'm back to Afghanistan; this has all been just a bad dream.*

• • •

On the way to the El Paso airport I think about how I'm trained to harness deep inner rage to become a warrior and to stay frosty for combat, and to assess every situation for danger and possible threat, expect the unexpected. In Basic, they told me, "Son, there is the right way to do something, the wrong way to do something, and the military way!" As much as I love the world, and thirst for knowledge and involvement, I am utterly confused about how to function in a new civilian life.

For almost six years I knew exactly what I was suppose to do and when to do it. I had every decision made for me. Everybody had the same mission: personal safety, your buddy's safety, and kill the enemy. Entering the American social jet stream brought on a profound sense of uncertainty: What will I do—*what can I do*—when I get to Austin?

I have some money saved, but not enough to finish school. I suppose there's not a huge demand for MRAP mechanics, or a Recovery and Power Generation Specialist. Army advertising slogans are rolling through my thoughts: "Be all you can be!" Be "Army Strong!" I don't feel like applying for my military benefits to go to school now, which was the whole fucking reason I joined. Somehow it feels dirty, like I'd be using blood money, Shahzada's blood, Taco's blood, and Mikey's blood, to pay for my college degree.

My brain is a cluster fuck of mismatched and hazy thoughts with a deep, rich inky miasma of fear and pain. I am overwhelmed by the infinite amount of choices at every step. Personal choices feel like I've been sick in bed for five years, now walking for the first time. My brain is screaming: *Walk, goddamn it, walk!*

At the airport, I'm overwhelmed by the air conditioning, the bright colors of plastic, the bombardment of advertising messages, the lack of strong earthy smells, the absence of farm animals, and children and old people. Women are everywhere, animated and talking so quickly and voluminously. They don't wear big mysterious blue tents, so you can see their smiles, body shapes, skin, hair color, their fingernails painted sky blue, teal green, red, and black. In some cases, their breasts are exposed, their navels, their asses hanging out of their short-shorts. It is strange and exotic. I almost feel awkward and embarrassed.

I'm back in a land of urban *individuals*. Instead of trying to please God five times per day like the Afghan people, they are pleasing themselves all day with specialized coffee drinks, personalized playlists of pop music, self-help gurus, teeth whitening, gluten-free organically grown, farm-to-table fast food, luxury cars that park themselves, and porn. Instead of an M-4 machine gun glued to their hands, it is a cell phone. In lieu of using it for an IED, they are used as an ESM (explosive social media) device.

In spite of feeling like a new-born kitten on a Ferris wheel, I am *so happy to be home,* or at least the idea of home: a place where one is safe and loved. I just need to find some love and human touch. I make my way to the airport saloon and sit at the bar and try to catch my breath for a moment before my flight to Austin. I take in the hideous compilation of garish colors, and adjust to the golden light from the neon beer signs overhead. The spicy nuts make me thirsty.

A buxom brunette with thick red lips greets me with a nonchalant "Hi, darling, whatcha havin?" I take a deep breath and ask if she has any Tuica. She laughs and says, "Is that a tequila, honey?"

"No, ma'am, that is the most celebrated twice distilled plum liquor in all of Romania!"

"Is that a fact?"

"Why, yes it is!"

"Well, we don't serve a single vampire beverage. How about a good old-fashioned Mexican tequila shot?"

"Now, *that* is a great idea! May I have a double shot of your best añejo tequila with a Dos Equis chaser, please?"

"You bet, darling, coming right up!"

"Sorry, Ma'am… make that a triple shot, please!"

•  •  •

I wake up and my leg hurts like shit and my head is thumping like a bass drum. I'm naked. I remember nothing. The room has white walls and high ceilings — really high — and thick concrete columns. The windows are tall with heavy, industrial metal frames and thick expensive curtains. The sheets are soft and white. The pillows are fluffy down pillows and there are six lying around in various forms of being smashed and folded. A large black armoire is hiding a flat-screen television. I hear a faint voice singing in French softly, and it echoes from around the corner, followed by the sound of a bathroom shower. My mind perks up. *Where the hell am I, and who is that?*

I manage to pull myself out of bed and tear back the curtain. The sun is bright and causes me to squint. I feel nauseous. On the writing desk is an empty bottle of champagne and the ice is not fully melted. I see a woman's handbag hanging on the back of the chair, and based on the quality of the design and leather, it appears to be very expensive. An image of an older blonde French woman flashes into my mind, sitting at a long, impressive bar. I remember her laugh, heavy red lipstick smile, and continuously telling me how "cute" I was, but I don't remember her name. She wore a wedding band.

I look at the stationery neatly tucked to one side of the desk and notice a gold and white logo that looks like a cattle rancher's brand, and can't make out the letters. Below the insignia, in bold type, I see the words HOTEL EMMA. Looking further, to the bottom of the smoothly textured white cotton paper is the hotel address: SAN ANTONIO, TEXAS.

After recovering from the shock of my unexpected port of call, and not clear about why I didn't make it to Austin, I realize that I am starving. I look at the In Dining Menu resting on the desk and decide that thirty-two dollars for eggs is beyond my budget. As I am searching the mini-fridge for possible fruit, I hear my suite host say from the bathroom, "Good morning! I hope I didn't disturb you. You seemed to need the rest!"

"Good morning!" I try to say in an upbeat manner. "I do hope that I was pleasant enough company last night. I'm afraid, I've been living a really *rustic* lifestyle lately!"

"Yes, you told me all about it last night. You don't remember your passionate discussion on the plane, and then here at the bar, the guy next to us interjecting his thoughts about the Afghanistan involvement? I thought you would throw him through the window when he said, 'What kind of idiot would join the Army?'

"Do you remember that you just looked at him, smirked, pointed at yourself, and said, 'This kind!' and bought the guy a drink, stood on a barstool, and delivered an impassioned speech, something like, 'My friends, fellow countrymen, since World War II, the United States of America has been in a fog of illusionary democracy... Remember the foreboding and clairvoyant warning given to us by our very own President Eisenhower in his 1961 farewell address to the nation, 'In the councils of government, we must guard against *the acquisition of unwarranted influence,* whether sought or unsought, by the military-industrial complex. The potential for the disastrous rise of misplaced power exists, and will persist.'

"Everyone applauded and sent us several more rounds. *You are so cute!"*

She walks in the room and I am taken by her lovely manner. Last night she wore her hair up and was clad in serious business professional attire. But now she's in tight jeans, a silk tank top, and high heels, and her silky blonde hair is down. She wears a Cartier tank watch with several gold bangles. She seems relaxed and happy as she grabs her purse, jacket, and computer bag.

"I have to catch a plane, but I thought we could have a bite in the restaurant before I leave. Does that sound good?" I nod. "Great. I have to do some work emails and catch up on calls. Why don't you meet me in the restaurant downstairs after you take a shower."

After she leaves the room, I call the front desk and say, "I'm sorry to disturb you, this is Alex Baldwin. My wife is in the spa and I wanted to check out soon. Can you tell me what name she put the room in? Did she put the room in my name, or hers?"

"Mr. Baldwin, we have the room registered in your wife's name, Sara de Rosier, but we will be happy to take your payment information when you are ready to depart, or we will conclude the room charge with your wife."

"Great, thank you so much."

Sara. Lovely Sara. I need to take a quick shower to join her, but I realize that I don't have anything to protect my wound. Then, it occurs to me that I can use one of the guest plastic shower caps to protect it. I poke a hole in the cap and slip my leg in and happily find that it works like a charm! I take a good, long look at myself in the mirror. I still sport a "farmer's tan" from being in Afghanistan. My face, neck, and arms are tan; everyplace else is white. I need a haircut. My blue eyes are bloodshot. I've had to shave every day for five years and I'm sick of it. I decide not to shave. I rummage through my pack and find the nicest t-shirt and jeans I own, but my military boots look less stylish and polished than I would like, given how nice the hotel is and I'm guessing the restaurant. Finally, after examining my wardrobe,

I think, *fuck it. What are they going to do? Throw me out for a fashion violation?*

I find Sara on the porch outside, surrounded by fresh-cut flowers, pastries, fresh-squeezed orange juice, and coffee. When I sit, she smiles. "You clean up nicely! I ordered an omelet for you, and millionaire bacon! No place like Texas!"

"I knew I felt lucky this morning," I say with a laugh and take a bite of the bacon. It is thick and crisp, laced with a drizzle of maple syrup. Shortly, a lovely waitperson in a long bistro apron arrives, carrying two plates of food. She serves Sara two poached eggs with wilted spinach over wheat toast, grilled asparagus and organic purple heirloom tomatoes, and places in front of me a gorgeous golden omelet with potatoes, green chile chorizo on cornbread, and says, "Your Mozart egg omelet, sir!" I am perplexed and ask, "Did the chef add sheet music to the mix as an ingredient?"

The server earnestly explains, "Our chef has a relationship with a local farmer, who has located a hatchery that will deliver her newborn chicks that have never been fed a meal. She gives them their first meal of pure flaxseeds, loaded with the richest whole food source of the omega-three fat, and only plays Mozart music. Their diet of flaxseed and Mozart continues everyday for their entire lives. I think you will find a noticeable difference in taste, texture, and their rich golden color. Bon Apétit!"

Sara seems amused by my appreciation and enthusiasm for everything we are experiencing. Without saying so, quality is something that has obviously always been a part of her life. In fact, she takes it for granted. I know she is a seasoned traveler by the way she communicates with the staff and how efficiently she navigates her every move. It occurs to me as she is talking that I don't have the slightest idea how we met yesterday.

"Forgive me, but I don't really remember how we met last night. Are you in San Antonio on business?"

"Yes, I am a public-policy consultant for Kazon Corporation."

"The defense contractor?" I ask, slightly caught off-guard.

"Yes sir!" she says with a big smile.

"How did you get involved with those guys?"

"Well, I'm a Princeton University political-science graduate, with a master's degree in public policy from the Kennedy School at Harvard, and a PhD from Brandeis University. I graduated with a pile of student loans and was living in Washington D.C. without a job. Kazon was looking for fresh talent to help with public relations, with their growing demand for a lobbying presence on the Hill, and developing deeper relationships with our emerging cyber-security programs. I'm in San Antonio because we are initiating a five-year collaborative partnership with the University of Texas at San Antonio's College of Business to conduct research, and that brings me to our meeting at the El Paso airport bar, after my meetings at Fort Bliss. *You were so cute!*"

"Is that a good business to be in?"

"Well, last year the United States federal government spent seven hundred and eighty-one billion of taxpayer money on defense. Kazon is in the top five of contractors and we grossed about $23 billion last year. If we can get Congress to stop capping the spending, we will be doing very well over the next decade. You might want to consider using your military expertise, good looks, and winning personality to land a good defense job."

I sit quietly, sipping my orange juice, enjoying the pulp tickling my tongue, and then I say, "I think I've had enough war. I do have a question for you, if I may? Have you actually been to the Middle East and experienced how your products affect those in war?"

Sara stopped smiling and slowly leaned into the table. "Let me guess. You went to war, to get money for college, on your own free will, to be a warrior, and now that you have been shot, you don't want anyone to play war? Is that it?"

Shahzada suddenly appears across the table from me and begins to laugh.

"Something like that. I'm not trying to be rude or self-righteous, I just find it hard to understand how we are spending hundreds of billions of dollars on war, with over a trillion-dollar deficit on a country that we say is a terrorist threat to our country—and it is not! I have been there. How can a country with a GDP of about twenty billion, a seventy percent illiteracy rate, and a ninety percent agrarian society, with internal fighting and no strong central government, be a true threat to the United States of America and Western Europe? How can we rationalize trillions of dollars in spending since 2003? Is that a good ROI for our nation? Seems to be to be a fine example of *Koyaanisqatsi*..."

"*You are so cute* when you get riled up. What the hell does that mean?"

"In the Hopi language *Koyaanisqatsi* means 'Life out of balance'."

Sara looks at me with a big smile and takes a deep breath. She obviously likes me and enjoyed our tangle in the sheets, but she really doesn't want to talk about this stuff, much less her personal life, and the fact that she represents the kind of company that profits by the politics of aggression in the name of defense. Sara seems to exchange her emotional connection with a real community of people for *buying power,* the projection of social acceptability, and sexual conquest.

She's not looking at the fact that she's married and picked up a stranger in an airport bar, that she ships her kids off to boarding schools because she is too busy to deal with them, and I'm fairly certain that she is not looking at how her relationship with politics in Washington D.C. are affecting the people of the Middle East.

"How do you know so much about the Hopi?" she asks, trying to turn the conversation to a less gritty direction.

"Well, I had a friend back on the FOB Hamilton that is Hopi and he loved to tell us *for hours* all about his culture and how in balance they are and just how out-of-balance we are."

"Well, darling, 'balance' is a big word in today's world…" Sara says, as if speaking to her overly idealistic son in boarding school, who doesn't have a clue about how the *real world* works.

A very tall man in a dark suit walks over to the table. "Excuse me, Mrs. De Rosier, your car is waiting for you in front of the hotel when you are ready."

She thanks the man and turns to me. She clasps her hand on my hand, as if we are shaking for the first time. "I really enjoyed spending time with you—*you are so cute!* Good luck in Austin and maybe I will see you there sometime. I have to make trips to visit with the governor from time to time. My email is sara@kazon.com. You take care of yourself!"

"By the way, what does your husband do for a living?"

"Robert is the CEO of Kazon Corporation." She kisses me on my cheek and briskly heads toward the front desk.

As I watch her navigate confidently through the café, I realize how badly my leg hurts. And how utterly sad and alone I feel.

# Barn Swallow

WHEN MY BROTHER DANIEL picks me up in San Antonio, I can't believe how much weight and muscle he's gained. In Marble Falls, he was a quiet, skinny little kid. The kind of guy that you notice, but don't talk to because they're so shy that you feel like it would be cruel to scare them out of their shell. It's been almost two years. He's cultivated an air of intelligence and strength, without affectation. It's great to see him.

On the way to Austin, Daniel talks about school, his rental house in the suburbs, the crazy roommates, and finally about Mom and Malcolm, and the kids. How they struggle financially to keep their head above water, and as usual the conversation always funnels into an upsetting discussion that leads to Malcolm. Daniel says he's been too busy with work and school to go home for a visit. He tells me that Gabby has a new boyfriend. He thinks he's a drug dealer. I think about our little sister, Gabby, and Malcolm's drunken late-night visits to her room, and it makes me want to kill that abusive bastard. I understand her need to get out of the house, but she is hooking up with the wrong guy. I've had Malcolm's boot on my face for almost my entire life, but I'm not that scared, little kid any longer.

I stop talking to Daniel. We listen to music. My mind is skipping. I can't concentrate. I'm still back in Afghanistan, with Shahzada, her family, and my teammates back on FOB Hamilton. I'm so fucking wound up. I feel so violent. I can't stop thinking about ridiculously serious subjects. Politics and philosophy are wrapped around my neck like a python squeezing me to death.

I worry about Mikey and I mourn the loss of Tacos. He was so excited about being a new dad and having a "Little Tacos" running around the house. As strange as it seems, I want to go back and help my squad get those fuckers responsible for his death. I feel heavy with guilt that I'm at home, and my squad is dead, wounded, or still back in Jaldak dealing with this crazy shit.

In my lifetime, I've been deceived by my mother and father, two presidents, church leaders, and employers. Every unifying philosophical structure that I was taught as the "truth" has been derailed at some point. I don't think it is just my experience. As I see it, we, as a nation, are in a state of confusion, polarization, and impudent sarcasm.

Being home, back in the United States, makes me hyper-anxious about the condition of our society and how we relate to the world—and to one another—yet there is an internal scream due to feeling completely ineffectual. It's too fucking overwhelming.

I close my eyes for the rest of our trip back to Austin, but I'm too wound up to sleep.

By the time we get to Daniel's house, my leg is burning and I am exhausted. The intensity of the last week has caught up with me. Daniel leads me upstairs to a small back bedroom with a single mattress on the floor and no furniture. For me, the accommodations are pure luxury: the first time in almost six years to have my own personal space, and complete silence.

Daniel's roommates are at work, or school, and I'm finally able to lie down and exhale. I take a couple of painkillers the doc in Germany gave me, and as the quiet envelops me, I notice my surroundings. The popcorn ceiling is dull and lifeless. The closet sliding doors have mirrors that allow me to see the big dark bags under my eyes, and the branches of a live oak tree outside the window. The carpet is beige with stains, but I am grateful it isn't sand.

I listen to my breathing and feel the weight of my body sink deeply into the mattress. I'm so ready for rest, for deep uninterrupted sleep. As I retreat into myself, soon I am dreaming that I'm back in Patkheyl and seated at Ahmad Khan's table. Ahmad Khan smiles and laughs while playing the *rubab*. He says, "You see, I play just like the Jimi Hendrix—no?" I am eating with one hand and feeling so happy to be alive, and to be with his family. I respond, "No, you are more intoxicating than Jimi!" He stops playing and stands abruptly, no longer kind, or smiling. He points his finger at me, and screams, "Why did you kill her? Why did you kill my baby girl? This is your fault. *You are no hero. It is you who is bad...*" Shahzada opens the door, in her best clothing, covered in blood, and she says, "Don't worry, Books... I will read *Catcher and the Rye* someday, and we will discuss it over tea and hot *naan* bread with honey. *You can count on it!*"

As I begin to wake up, I hear a voice within, "Dylan, you are going to die..." I hear these words and panic, no place to run, and there is no comfort. I have the sensation of being a black hole and all of my life's energy is imploding within myself and I am terrified. I am panic-stricken.

I wake up sweating, shaken to my core. My mind starts negotiating myself off the proverbial ledge. *It's OK, there is life and death, light and darkness... one is not more entitled than the other... death is as beautiful as life... you just can't see it.* I feel horrible and my leg hurts. I try to get up, but I feel dizzy and fall back. I hold the pillow, as if it will comfort me. I hear some noises downstairs and panic. I reach for my gun—it's not there—*more panic.*

Then, I remember that I'm in Austin, Texas. I'm safe. I'm in Daniel's home. *Fuck, am I going insane?*

I decide to go downstairs. I need to be around someone, so I can get out of my head. Putting on shorts isn't easy with my wound. When I walk into the kitchen, some guy wearing all black, with a topknot, samurai-hair style, is rummaging through the fridge, and finally pulls a Lone Star tallboy beer from the far back. When he turns around, he smiles. "Dude, these house vultures swoop down on my beer supply! You must be Daniel's brother, the war hero! Hey man, I might have another beer, do you want one?"

I manage, "Sure," and he continues talking. "Dude, the counter was crazy today! My arms are tired from pump-pump-pumping all that mocha madness for those snooty high school girls."

"Where do you work?"

"Danny Boy didn't tell you? We all work at Starbucks down the street."

"Wow, how did you guys all meet?"

"Well, I met Daniel at an outdoor concert when I was hanging with Natalie, and he was vibing with her friend Kyra, and so he invited us all over to his crib to smoke and hang out. I had the job at Starbucks, and we needed someone at work, so I hooked Daniel up with the job, and then Natalie got a job, but she and I broke up. We are just chill roommates, but occasionally she gets fucked up and we, you know, it's complicated! I'm from El Paso, and my brother Tito just moved in, but you'll never see him, unless he and his girlfriend fight, or if he needs some stash, or to swoop one of my beers!"

"Sorry, I didn't catch your name."

"Wow, my bad. I'm Charlie... well, actually I am Carlos Nuñez, but everyone calls me Charlie! *Here*. Back home they called me Nunchucks."

"Cool, nice to meet you, Charlie!"

"Likewise. So did you just get back, like today?"

"I got back yesterday, but had a layover in San Antonio..."

"Whoa, did you meet a River Walk señorita?"

"Something like that! More like a señora..."

"Nice. When you are in a strange city, it's always better to roll with experience! So, did you kill a bunch of bad guys before they got your leg?"

My brain explodes with sounds followed by images: *pop-pop-pop-tat-tat-tat*. Mikey's neck hemorrhaging blood, Captain Ramirez slumped over the side of the Humvee, and all the Taliban fighters dismembered in the orchard. I see Shahzada next to Charlie in the kitchen, laughing, and she says, "He *really* doesn't understand, Mr. Books!"

I take another long, slow sip of my beer and then I smile and say, "You know, man, it's all kinda foggy!"

"No doubt! Dude, you should totally get a tattoo of a mandala and make the center, where the bullet entered your leg. Get rid of the entrance Karma..."

"Do you know a good tattoo artist in Austin?"

Charlie pulls his t-shirt off and smiles. "You tell me, dude!"

His small, muscular torso is a kaleidoscope of elaborate Japanese-inspired fantasy with two enormous *koi* sensually interacting from his chest to his stomach.

"Wow, you got that in Austin?"

"No, I got the first one, this small cross in the center of my chest in El Paso when I was a freshman in high school. My mom almost had a heart attack and thought I was joining a gang, and selling drugs, or some shit. The whole tattoo thing is lost on her."

The front door opens swiftly, and a thin, beautiful girl with long silky brownish-red hair walks in and says, "What's up, Charlie Checkers? Who's your G.I. Joe boy buddy?"

"Whoa, Natalie, boy buddy? We just met! Give me some time to get to know him before the bromance commences."

"What a minute... bandage on the leg and Army-man shorts. Dude, you are Danny's brother! Nice to finally meet you and welcome back to civilization! Do they have a Starbucks in Kubutz?"

"Thank you! Nice to meet you too... and, no, no Starbucks in *Kabul*—yet!"

"Charlie, do you have any more beers?"

"No! You vultures cleaned me out last night. And *who was* that dude barking like a dog last night in your bedroom?"

"Oh my God, that little adorable, freaky frat boy with the amazing body I found at the Yellow Jacket Social Club... he was so *wasted,* he went canine on me!"

"Apparently. I almost called Animal Control! Girl, you are addicted..."

"So G.I. Joe, what are your plans now that you are back?"

"Well, I am still in the United States Army, until my contract ends in October. I have to report to Camp Mabry, Thirty-Sixth Infantry Division—*eventually*—but for the next three months, the docs tell me that I have to heal my wound, and given my profound state of disrepair, I think that will involve copious amounts of booze, women, and song!"

Charlie raises his beer. "Damn, I knew I liked this dude. Welcome to crib Barn Swallow! Tomorrow, in honor of your return, I'm taking you to my favorite tattoo artist in town at Electric 13, to get a commemorative tattoo for your return."

"That would be awesome. Why do you call this place Barn Swallow?"

"That's the name of our street. I always think, barns can't swallow, but then I remember that we live with Natalie, and it all comes back to me why the name is perfect!"

"Dude, you are sick and soon to die if you don't improve your discourse. Besides, no beer, no boys, no smoke, and no food... this place is like a suburban crack house! Ya'll wanna go to a food truck and get some grub?"

"Totally! I am craving Pig Out, specifically, The Persecuted Pig: with jerk pork, mortadella, Swiss, love mustard, and pickles on a toasted hoagie."

Charlie looks at me. "That is the shit that blew Kennedy's head off, son! As you can see, Natalie gets excited about food! It's part of her amazing multitude of skills. Besides studying math—the girl can swallow!" He gives us a Cheshire-cat grin.

"Yeah and Charlie has skills, always a crowd-pleaser, the only hot little daddy in Austin to have girls buy him drinks all night, do blow, have a sleepover, and make it in to work for opening shift at four-thirty AM, and keep a smile on his face all day long! So, G.I. Joe doll, I assume you want to come with?"

"I do, but I can't move very fast, or go far, with this leg and a cane."

"No worries, you don't need to be bipedal to play, just have an earnest desire to eat and drink! Besides, should you fall, we will carry you! Isn't that what you Army boys say?"

"Something like that!" I think of Mikey, and feel crushed with sadness.

"¡Vamanos! To *Pig Out,* dudes!"

# Koyaanisqatsi

THE NEXT THREE MONTHS feel like a blur of alcohol, cocaine, weed, and everything other. I have developed a routine of trying to sleep all day, reading, or surfing the Internet for news, especially about the Middle East, tons of porn, and for deals on motorcycles to restore and resell.

Today in the news, some young white guy walks into a movie theater and kills twelve people and injures seventy others. It makes big headline news and then is forgotten in two weeks. I don't forget. I think about it a lot. I went to Afghanistan to protect our country, fighting with guys his age to make America safe, and our own people are killing one another. What the fuck has gone wrong?

As I observe folks around me, they appear totally self-absorbed, taking pictures of themselves constantly for their social media representation. It's like personal "Brand Special": Aren't I cute, sexy, and leading a wonderful life? But when you talk to him or her, and pull back the onionskin, you may discover that he or she is fucking miserable: hates the job, wants to travel the world, and has no relationship, or hates the one they are in. But, online, he or she is thriving and living large. The entire country is politically polarized, and therefore ineffectual and pessimistic.

At night, I try to avoid being alone, and sleeping. Sometimes I drink espresso at Starbucks and read while I wait for the Barn Swallow gang to get off work, and we go over to the East Side

and party all night in cool spots. One night Daniel introduced
me to Bob and Janie, the couple who owns our house. They are
really nice. Bob made a fortune in high-tech, developing Internet
security solutions for big companies that were bought by bigger
companies. They live in Seven Oaks, a fancy neighborhood a
few miles away.

They are totally down to earth and ask me about my deployment in Afghanistan, about how I am doing, and about our
family in Marble Falls. I guess I feel safe around smart, caring,
older people, and I tell them every dirty little detail of my
family's lives. They aren't judgmental and make me feel very
safe to talk about my feelings honestly. They invite Daniel and
me to come over and have dinners with them. We seem to be
getting very close. I think Janie kinda is attracted to me, but I
could be confusing motherly concern for Mama's interest in a
new toy. She seems to drink *a great deal,* but then so do I and
everyone else we are around.

When Daniel gets off work, we have dinner downtown and
head to his favorite bars. Daniel is always inviting people to
the house to chill and enjoy some pot, booze, or cocaine. On
payday, we call "The Weatherman." That is what we call our
coke dealer, who is happy to deliver "snow" to our house. For
hallucinogens, we mail order from the "dark web."

Charlie introduces me to his tattoo artist, and the first thing I
get is a tattoo on my back in script letters in Latin: WHAT IF I'M
NOT THE HERO... WHAT IF I'M THE BAD GUY? On my chest
I get a huge Egyptian Eye of Horus, the symbol of protection
and good. Then, I get work on both arms: full sleeves of images,
Asian-inspired mythology, personal significance, and beauty. My
hair begins to grow out, and I let my beard and mustache grow
full, thick, and natural. I have no fucking intention of going
back to the Army, shaving, or wearing a uniform. I'm done. I
just haven't told them yet.

By September, with my leg fully healed, the God Pathos (the God of sexual longing, yearning, and desire) unleashes on my world by introducing a new digital application that allows one-stop shopping for consenting adult sexual frivolity. With a simple swipe of my finger—*presto*—I am in the arms of a pre-selected and eager companion who just wants to "hook up" for sex. The entire household is enthralled with the ease and convenience of the brave new tool. But like everything in life, if it looks *too good to be true,* it probably is.

I think my younger house companions feel both intrigued and mystified by the sheer volume of digi-date hook-ups flowing through our house, and love to make lewd comments after my new friends leave. "Oh wow, Dylan, she seems really wholesome—NOT!" and "Gee whiz, D, didn't know a girl could snort passionately using pig noises, nor did our *entire* neighborhood!" or "Dylan, did you find her in a Halloween pageant? I have never seen someone with pink and purple hair and that many tattoos and piercings in my life!" and "Shit, were those girls twins?"

I began to question my hook ups after meeting Letter W, turned sideways: a gender-fluid, non-binary woman who became flustered when I used the term 'her' in reference to her. She did give one hell of a back rub!

It got even stranger with Tessa. She presented herself as postmodern, feminist, independent and fiercely political. All of that got communicated in bed. She loved to be on top and in control, and to get off before me. The way she pleasured me felt more like a demonstration in technique and attack than someone trying to connect with me. After sex, she would disappear downstairs for an eternity. She would then triumphantly re-enter my bedroom as some kind of Martha Stewart domestic diva with hot chicken pot pie made from scratch, and feed me like I was a sick four-year-old.

Tessa never really communicates in a traditional manner, and out of nowhere she shows up at the house with homemade apple strudel, a chocolate pecan pie, and some kind of Italian fish soup. My housemate Natalie jabs me: "Oh, Tessa is showing you what a wonderful little wifey she will make you someday." I have to explain to Tessa that while I think she is amazing in the kitchen, I really only signed up for the bedroom skills. It wasn't *her;* I just wasn't ready for a serious relationship. She throws hot, delicious fudge cookies at me, and screams, "You suck in bed anyway" and storms out of the house.

I decide to stop digi-dating for sex and start to get really anxious, and feel something new and horrifying after-wards — *invisible.* Everyone around me is in school, taking some classes and working, trying to develop their career, or at least do some kind of crazy artistic passion. When I'm introduced, it goes something like, "Oh, hey, this is Dylan, he's in the Army and just got back from Afghanistan." I guess they think it is the most interesting thing to offer-up about me. Whatever the reason, it makes me out to be one of *those people* — a vet — someone who has probably killed another human being, and therefore they feel awkward, as if we will have nothing in common, better to simply ignore and move on.

Any person you are meeting socially, normally has a reference to war based on every movie they've seen, or their alcoholic uncle who served in Vietnam, or their grandfather who was a bomber in World War II. There is a new tendency in this war to label anyone who serves as a "hero." This is a kickback from the American response to those who served in Vietnam, and were discarded. There is absolutely *nothing* heroic about me. I did see others exhibit extraordinary courage and bravery, and act heroically, but it wasn't me. Of course, there are also the folks who know that there were no weapons of mass destruc-tion, and that neither Afghanistan nor Iraq is or ever will be a real threat to our national security. They are so disgusted with the politics, and I am therefore guilty by association—a foolish political pawn.

Because I went to war, I always feel as if I am treated as someone *other*, like someone who served time in prison. Even though I attended college for three years, read voraciously, and have skills in mechanics and technology, I always feel like I am just moments away from being the guy on the street holding the cardboard sign: VET. HUNGRY. ANYTHING WILL HELP. GOD BLESS. How does a nation allow the men and women who fought for their freedom stand on street corners, or commit suicide? This reality keeps me in constant anxiety, and really interested in remaining drunk and stoned.

I'm starting to get official notices from the Army that I am supposed to report to Camp Mabry to finish out my contract. My new CO, Staff Sergeant Manning, and I speak on the phone and I try to explain that I'm still not feeling well, but he is adamant that I report for duty. I try to invite him for a beer, to meet me at Deep Eddy Cabaret, but he just barks that the United States Army is not a social fraternity, and I need to get my ass to Camp Mabry on Monday. I just can't drag myself to that base. I can't even think about putting on my uniform without having a panic attack. I'm sure as fuck not going to shave, or cut my hair. My emotional anxiety is getting worse and I'm having horrible nightmares. I'm seeing Shahzada babble on, about every bizarre subject in the far reaches of my brain.

The more I watch the news to try to stay informed, the crazier I feel. It starts with Benghazi, Libya. Our ambassador is attacked and killed. A huge mess ensues, with the conservative right reporting that it was Hillary Clinton's fault. The presidential debates are in full swing and the conservatives are accusing Obama of being a socialist. Obama wins the election.

I read everything I can get my hands on about our involvement in Afghanistan. The words are painful for me to read. It conjures images of men making deals in backrooms that destroy other people's lives to improve their own career interests, with no consideration or knowledge about the very people they fight. As I read an article in the *New York Times*, certain words jump off the page like IED blasts in my eyes:

> *...A plan for changing the way Afghanistan is wired. We ended up thinking about how to do as little wiring as possible.*

> *..."Light footprint" strategy*

> *...Why Americans were dying to prop up a leader, President Hamid Karzai of Afghanistan, who was volatile, unreliable and willing to manipulate the ballot box.*

> *...By what the war's cost would be if the generals' counterinsurgency plan were left on autopilot — $1 trillion over 10 years.*

> *...We had been at war for eight years, and no one could explain the strategy."*

> *...Ultimately, Mr. Obama agreed to double the size of the American force while training the Afghan armed forces, but famously insisted that, whether America was winning or losing, the drawdown would begin in just 18 months.*

> *...He understood why we needed to try, to knock back the Taliban. But the military was 'all in,' as they say, and Obama wasn't.*

> *...Mr. Obama concluded that the Pentagon had not internalized that the goal was not to defeat the Taliban.*

*...After a short internal debate, Mr. Gates and Mrs. Clinton
came up with a different option: end the surge by September
2012 — after the summer fighting season.*

●  ●  ●

I start seriously feeling pinned down. I'm growing weary of
"hanging out" with the gang, getting drunk and stoned every
night, but they're my family. Without them, I'm alone with
my misery, nightmares, and Shahzada babbling at me. My skin
doesn't look healthy and I have bags under my eyes.

I don't own transportation and have to depend on friends, the
bus, or ridesharing drivers to go anywhere. But then a miracle
occurs. A check comes from the United States government to
compensate my injured leg, a check for $15,000. I feel like I have
won the Texas Lottery! I've been seriously lusting after this
sweet BMW K1300R motorcycle, a sexy black crotch rocket. It's
built around a water-cooled, four-stroke, in-line four-cylinder
engine with two overhead camshafts and four valves per cylin-
der. I have to buy it. After insurance, tax, and license, I walk
away with $1,242.43. I call The Weatherman and plan a celebra-
tion party.

The following week, I am sitting at Deep Eddy Cabaret, my
favorite dive bar, and I am having several pitchers of beer and
smoking a joint with the bartender, and doing the last couple
of lines of coke in the bathroom. My commanding officer pays
me a surprise visit. Sergeant Manning says something short
and sweet like, "Son, do you want to spend the rest of your life
in prison — drink yourself to death, or stick a *fucking gun in your
mouth?* Don't you want to have a *good life,* and find yourself an
American Dream?"

I am so drunk I give him a bear hug, start sobbing, and singing
the pop song "Call Me Maybe." I tell him I love him, ask him to
marry me, and then puke all over his uniform.

He escorts me back to Camp Mabry, issues "convalescent leave," and orders me to see "The Wizard."

My entire life I was told I was a piece of shit and all that I had to do was put my faith in Jesus Christ, and ask him to be my personal savior, and God would take care of the rest. I wasn't experienced in talking about my feelings, especially when it came from a commanding officer's order.

I sit on a couch staring blankly at Dr. Trimble. She asks me so many fucking questions. I give her obtuse, dry, measured responses. She tries to comfort me by saying things such as, "I understand what you're going through... this must be very painful for you." Her eyes are deeply loving and her face is tan: I attribute this to daily jogs and weekend campouts with her family. She's obviously happy. How could she understand what I'm going through—what I feel?

It is hard for me to concentrate. I stop listening to her probing questions and begin to daydream. I imagine her walking over to me, pulling her panties down, kissing me *very slowly,* and sweetly whispering in my ear, "I got you, baby. You are going to be OK."

I feel as if I am falling into a room filled with fluffy white feather pillows. This moment of tenderness is shattered by loud mortar blasts and rapid-machine-gun fire ripping through me. Blood spatter hits the white walls and the scene changes. I see the pedestrian chaos outside our main base in Mazar-i-Sharif. There are lifeless, bloody bodies of men in turbans and waistcoats being stacked hastily in the street. A pack of dusty boys, with funny hats, are making jokes, pointing, and laughing. They are unaware of the macabre poetry before them.

The scenes continue. The horrors and memories my mind uses to taunt me always end on the most painful image. *Shahzada.* My throat constricts. Tears involuntarily erupt.

Dr. Trimble seems frustrated by my "absence" in our sessions and my lack of progress in sharing my feelings. She suggests that

I write down my experiences as a child. She wants me to try and see my "inner child" from my adult perspective. To revisit all the feelings of when people hurt the little boy, Little Dylan. She also wants me to write about what I experienced in Afghanistan. But there are certain things I can't—or will not—share. I don't really want to talk about "it," I'm not even sure what "it" is. I just want it to end. And it doesn't.

Dr. Trimble offers me acronyms to describe my condition: PTSD and Adult ADD. With anxiety, attachment, and abandonment issues. I just call it FLS, or *feeling like shit*.

She prescribes gobs of medications. I won't take that poison, but I am going to take her up on the idea of writing. I didn't watch my friends die in some remote FOB to become invisible, to become the great American janitor, sweeping the bloody sand over and over, expecting to clean it all up so we can open counter-service restaurants in Kabul. Fuck that!

I know that I have to deal with my situation. I can't keep living with so much anxiety. I'm going to try and have a look at my "inner child," wherever the fuck that little guy is, and maybe if I go home to Marble Falls, it will help me get in touch with that shit again. I think I will go with Daniel for Thanksgiving.

●　●　●

When I call mom to tell her that Daniel and I are coming for Thanksgiving, Gabby answers the phone and when she hears that it's me, she says, "Oh my God, Dylan, it's been a long time, bro!"

My first thought was that she is high, and I am not happy. "Is everything cool?"

"Yeah, more or less. Mom and Malcolm are driving me fucking crazy."

In the background, I hear Mom yelling at the youngest and Malcolm barks bluntly, "Who's on the phone?" He repeats his question and Gabby ignores him. He yanks the phone from her hand and says, "Who is this?"

"Howdy, Malcolm, this is Dylan Griffith, I'd like to speak to my mother, please."

"She's busy. What do you need?"

"Oh, I just wanted to let her know that Daniel and I are coming for Thanksgiving on Thursday."

"OK, I'll tell her. You boys be here at three, my game starts at three thirty—don't ya'll be late!"

"Got it! Can you put Gabby back on the phone, please?"

"She left with her boyfriend."

"Boyfriend?"

"I have to go."

After Malcolm abruptly ends the call, that familiar acidic burning sensation churns in my stomach and I am infuriated—I am going to go kick his ass.

•  •  •

My new motorcycle feels amazing on the road.

It's a cool, sunny day in the Texas Hill Country and being Thanksgiving Day, very little traffic on the road. There is a golden hue over the grassy pastures. We don't really get the New England transcendentalist-poetry seasonal thing in Texas. Ralph Waldo Emerson would walk through the Texas hill country in the fall and say, "What the fuck! How am I supposed to find inspiration in this shit?" But for me, the evergreen live oaks and cedar trees make up a part of my DNA. It seems to serve as a gentle reminder that I do, in fact, belong somewhere.

A Marble Falls highway sign appears after about forty-five minutes, and my stomach starts feeling tight. I can't believe my eyes: a new Starbucks coffee shop with a drive-thru. We cross the Colorado River and soon I can see the old iconic Blue Bonnet Café, where I had my first grits, Texas toast, and pecan pie as a boy. I remember feeling embarrassed by the way Malcolm talked rudely to the waitress, "Hey lady, I ordered my pie about an hour ago…" Everyone in the restaurant stopped talking and stared at our table. Then he told Daniel and me that he would "kick our ass when we got home if we didn't clean our plates."

When we arrive, Mom's beat-up car is in front of the house, with a SHIT HAPPENS bumper sticker, but Malcolm's old red pickup truck is gone. I am relieved. Maybe he went to see his family in San Angelo. Daniel and I bang on the door really hard to give the kids a scare, and scream, "Open up—police!"

We can hear the kids squealing excitedly, "Mom, the police are here!" Mom opens the door with a cigarette hanging from her lips and a beer in her hand, and an exasperated look on her face, and says. "Oh, it's my baby boys!" The kids all run over, jumping on us and hugging me. As horrible as it is to return to this house, it is wonderful to feel the kids' hugs and excitement.

Mom is trying to cook Thanksgiving dinner for the family, but she burned the turkey, and Malcolm is headed to Kentucky Fried Chicken to buy a couple of buckets of crispy chicken and some mashed potatoes. Mom did manage to cook corn on the cob without burning down the kitchen.

Mom goes straight back to sit on the couch, where she always sits next to Malcolm's chair, and has a huge ashtray filled with cigarette butts and an assortment of beer cans. She is wearing a Pepto-Bismol pink tracksuit, with pink plastic clogs, and her hair is worn in pigtails. I notice how thin she appears, and she is just beginning to look older. The little kids could barely talk when I left for the Army and now they are seven, eight, twelve, and fourteen.

Gabby must be around seventeen or eighteen, but isn't home.

"Mom, where is Gabby? Did she ride with Malcolm to pick up the chicken?"

"No. Gabby left the house a couple of weeks ago."

"What? Where is she?"

"I *don't* know."

"Surely, you know *something*."

"Well, I fussed at her about cleaning up the back bedroom before she went to meet her boyfriend. She told me that I couldn't tell her what to do, that she would be an adult, eighteen, on her birthday next week. I told her that if she was such an adult, she could just pack up her shit, and find her own apartment and pay her own goddamn bills. She cursed me out and left. I haven't seen her, or heard from her since."

Daniel adds, "She's with that dude they call Raven. He lives over near Uncle Buddy's house, on the lake."

"I went to high school with that idiot. Gabby is seeing someone my age?" I ask, and that reality pisses me off even more. Before I have time to think about it further, the front door opens abruptly, and Malcolm walks in with two huge plastic bags in one hand and a case of beer in the other. He ignores Daniel and me, and goes straight to the kitchen where he screams, "Goddamn it, Sara, aren't you going to clean all this burnt shit up?"

"Now, Malcolm! Your boys are home, aren't you going to say hello!"

"They ain't *my* boys!"

I feel my gut tighten and I hold my breath. My first instinct is to scream back, "Well, you sure as fuck aren't our father!" Instead, I look at the kids playing on the floor in front of the television. The two youngest seem to be oblivious to how horrifying the adult interaction is, but the two oldest have the same sullen stare that Daniel and I had, unsure what might happen next and wondering if it is safe to stay in the room.

"Malcolm honey, will you please bring me one of my pills from the pantry?"

"Which one?"

"The Oxy. The little white one!"

"Shit, there are twenty bottles with little white ones... get *your* ass up and get it!"

"Come on, darling!"

"Is it the one with U24 on it?" Malcolm asks, as if it is his last attempt to find her pills.

"Bingo, baby!" my mom says, extending her arm like a spastic cheerleader.

Daniel looks at me with a smirk, and whispers, "Mom is an Oxy—*moron!*"

"Malcolm, I set the dining table. We are going to eat together at the table today, honey, OK?"

"Y'all can sit at the table, you can have a fucking picnic in the backyard, but I'm watching my game, in my chair. The Cowboys are going to whoop New England's ass today!"

"Honey, we need you to say grace."

Mom sticks another cigarette in her lips, and tells the little ones to get ready and wash their hands for "Thanksgiving supper." When Malcolm walks in, he puffs his chest out and says, "You can let our *war hero* here say grace!" My mood turns acidic and my arms tighten.

He yells at the youngest boy, Pooh, to get out of his chair and he sweetly responds, "OK Mao-cum." He sits down with a beer, hands my mom her little white pill, another can of beer, and reaches over to grab a soft pack of cigarettes. After he pinches one out, he looks at my mother and says, "Shit, Sara, I just opened this pack and they're almost gone!" Then he screams at Johnathon, who they call Eeyore, to get his little ass up and get him and Mama a new pack of cigarettes.

"We got a new carton in the pantry, darlin," she says as if to convey an air of being on top of her household responsibilities. They both stare at the television, but my mind is spinning out of control in this unbearable, toxic shit.

They live like this every day of their miserable fucking lives. Mom asks if we are hungry. Daniel and I say we are, to be polite. Malcolm says, "You two little faggots better eat before my game starts, 'cause I don't want to be listening to all that noise once it starts!"

I hear the words "little faggots," and without thinking, I jump to my feet. My instinct is to rip Malcolm from his chair and end this fucker's life, but as I stand, I realize in a split-second that he was saying to Pooh and Eeyore the same shit he said to Daniel and me our entire lives. His abuse continues with the next set of boys. I stood there frozen in anxiety and looked at the oldest girl, Mara, wondering if he abuses her like he did Gabby.

Everyone else stares mindlessly at the television: a show about home makeovers is blaring, and Mom keeps saying how much she would love to do a makeover on their house. I never really noticed how ugly our houses were growing up. Mom never really made interior design a priority. Our family priorities were cigarettes, beer, drugs, and Malcolm's chair. Intellectual life was nonexistent.

The only social interaction is Sunday mornings at the local evangelist Baptist church. My mother has no awareness that exchanging ideas, reading, travel, or trying new things could enhance one's life. They are content maintaining their addictions, attending their small-town evangelical church, and leading a devil-may-care lifestyle.

As the cigarette smoke in the room engulfs me, I realize how tense I am, and remember Dr. Trimble's words: "Dylan, in order to begin healing, you are going to have to first accept where you are in the moment. In other words, breathe into what you are feeling. Notice the feelings. Don't react, or judge them, just listen. I want you to think about what Little Dylan is feeling at that moment. Notice what comes up…"

What is coming up is how dysfunctional and depressed I feel in this house. My mother is popping OxyContin like they're SweeTarts. They are made from the very opium we were supposed to "disrupt" in Afghanistan. Malcolm has only one speed. He is a self-serving, petulant, spastic excuse for a man and I am struggling to find any compassion. I'm not sure Mom would appreciate me killing him on Thanksgiving.

Mom announces that it is suppertime and tries to get the kids in the dining room: a table with a bunch of mismatched chairs with ancient stains, tears, and rips. I sit at the head of the table and look at everyone gathered around me. In the center is a large bucket of fried chicken, several containers of mashed potatoes in Styrofoam containers, corn-on-the-cob on a plate, a tub of margarine, and a stack of KFC napkins. The kids all have orange drinks in various plastic cups, and Daniel is drinking beer from a can. My mind wanders to Ahmad Khan's home and the amazing meal we shared. I remember the beauty of the food and dress of the guests, the laughter, and celebration: the warmth and generosity of the family. I imagine how nice it would be if Mikey and the guys were sitting around the table with us today, eating, laughing and joking.

Everyone at the table is staring at me as if to say, *Come on man, we are starving!* It occurs to me that they want me to say the grace. It's been so long, I don't remember the words, and I feel nervous. "Lord, we thank you for the food which we are about to eat, and ask that you bless this family, and those who are unable to be with us today." I think about Gabby, and then Shahzada, Mikey, and Tacos. I want God to bring them back. The family doesn't notice that I didn't finish and say, "Amen!" The younger boys already have drumsticks in their mouths.

I look up. Across the wall, in thick red marker, is one of Malcolm's famous biblical quotes: *"For God has not given us a spirit of fear, but of power and of love and of a sound mind."* (*2 Timothy 1:7*)

Strangely, I am comforted by the words. They are no longer a symbol of Malcolm, but instead serve as an assurance that I'm not afraid, that I am empowered, and that I do know the essential importance of love. As I try to let that into my heart, Malcolm screams, "Sara, I need some more mashed potatoes... Well, looky there, the Redskins starting quarterback is named Griffith. Things are looking up for my Cowboys if this Griffith dude is as much of a faggot as *these* Griffith boys!"

Mom starts to get up to get Malcolm what he wants. I stand up slowly and say, "I got it, Mom." I grab a container of mashed potatoes off the table, dripping with hot brown gravy, and head toward Malcolm's chair.

Malcolm is eating a chicken drumstick and growling, *"Come on..."* at the TV. I fall into a dream state. It is so real, I feel like it is happening. I walk in front his chair, which is fully extended, and kick it as hard as I can, causing Malcolm to slam backward on the ground, upside down, and he begins choking on the chicken bone. I pull him out of the chair and grab the bone and rip it from his mouth, and wrap my hand around his throat, and squeeze his fat neck, and whisper closely into his ear, "I'll show you *faggot*. I'll stick this chicken bone up your ass and snap your fucking neck. Watch yourself, you fucking rapist. *You touch anyone in this family again,* or say one disrespectful word to me or Daniel, or my mother, and I will fucking end you."

I take the container of mashed potatoes and slowly smash it into his face and leave him whimpering on the floor... and I think, *what a waste of perfectly good mashed potatoes.*

And then, I hear Malcolm say, "Are you going to hand me that?"

I just stand there. I don't move, or say a word. I look deeply into his eyes. Dylan the warrior is ready to end this problem, once and forever. I slowly hand him the mashed potatoes.

"Thank you, Dylan!" Malcolm says, politely.

It was the first time in my life this bombastic bag of noise has ever called me by my name. In that moment, I realize I don't have to rip his fucking throat out, because he already knows I will. I've already done it a thousand times. I have taken back my power.

"No problem," I say with a smile of victory.

I yell to Daniel, "Come on, buddy, we're going back to Austin!"

Daniel isn't very happy with me for wanting to leave our family gathering so early. I feel bad for leaving in the middle of our Thanksgiving, but even though Malcolm and I had some kind of detente, I don't want to be around him. Besides, I have some business to take care of with Gabby's boyfriend.

• • •

By the time we get to Raven's house, it is getting colder. Daniel doesn't know exactly where the house is on the block. I go to a random house, and a large woman wearing a bright-green kitchen apron emblazoned with a cheerful multi-colored felt turkey, dressed as a Pilgrim, answers the door. She kindly directs us to the correct house. My heart begins to race as I walk up the small, uneven driveway. I am negotiating if I am going to kick his ass, or just take Gabby. It occurs to me that we were on a motorcycle, and if I bring her back to mom's house, she has to deal with Malcolm's shit. I can't drive forty-five minutes to Austin on the highway with my brother and sister on the bike. So I decide to leave this guy a strong message.

When I bang on the front door of his dilapidated house, I hear a huge dog barking. I knock again and another dog begins to bark.

There isn't an answer and after five minutes, Daniel says, "Come on man, we'll take care of this later, it's Thanks-fucking-giving."

# Phoenix in Flames

ON THE WAY HOME Daniel insists that we stop by Bob and Janie's house. I feel *really* uncomfortable going to their house so wound up. The thought of being in a home with warmth and love overflowing somehow makes me nervous. I'm not really in the mood to pose for a Norman Rockwell holiday portrait. I want to go home, and get fucked up, but I feel like I owe it to Daniel.

Bob and Janie's house is pretty amazing. It's on a hillside, with a sweeping view of the hills to the west. It is a completely walled compound. When we enter, even though I have been here several times, I am taken by the beautiful balance and scale of the architecture. My mood is transformed from morose to calm.

Bob and Janie warmly receive us and give us both hugs. They apologize for their dog's enthusiastic welcome, big wet kisses on the face, and for the fact that their son, Martin, would not join us tonight due to skiing with friends in Vail. Bob says that "Marty" loves skiing more than any living being.

Bob offers us an amazing glass of French Sancerre, which I had never heard of, and we walk around the property admiring the landscape, enjoying the cooler temperatures as the sunset brings lavender, orangey-gray, red, and golden hues into view. Daniel obviously needs to get his frustration out about our visit to Marble Falls and begins to explain, in horrifying and long detail, our family visit: giving characterizations that make me feel embarrassed, until I turn my head and notice Bob.

At first his eyes appear glassy and then he turns his head to look away, and before I have time to add to Daniel's story, Bob begins to cry. I don't know why, but my first instinct was to just grab the guy and hug him, and not let go — so I did!

Bob flinches and I can feel his discomfort, uncertain if all this emotional display is too much. I want to cry with him, but I won't allow myself. I feel the need to take care of Bob. I open my eyes and I see that Janie and Daniel are emotional. *What just happened? This is so fucking weird.* They must know something about Bob that I don't. After a moment, Bob pats my back and says, "Whoa, didn't expect that!" He moves over to Janie and gives her a hug, and she gently caresses the back of his head and shoulders. Then he gives Daniel a big hug and says, "Dude!" Daniel smiles his patented jocular grin. I wonder if the Pilgrims were this emotional."

Bob doesn't talk about what makes him feel so much. He simply excuses himself in the name of preparing dinner and selecting the right red wine for tonight's celebration. It seems pretty clear to me that Janie is the adventurous one in their household and loves to nurture men. Janie nonchalantly invites us inside to chat and to have more wine. The more she drinks, the more she touches my arms and hands as she talks. I take a break from the conversation and walk around to look at some of their art.

The split-level living room is phenomenal, filled with art objects, built-in shelves with old Native American pottery, and small bronze statues by the likes of Joan Miró and Pablo Picasso. They have extraordinary hand-knotted tribal Persian and Afghan prayer rugs.

It strikes me as strange to admire the Afghan rugs on the floor of Bob and Janie's home as art objects, instead of their intended use as prayer rugs. When my eyes see one rug in particular, I have a vision of being in Shahzada's home, and she appears seated on the floor beside me. She's laughing and says, *Hello, Dylan! Do you miss me? It's a shame we can't spend more time together.* My disturbing hallucination ends when Janie tips the bottle of wine toward my glass, and sensually asks, "Are you OK?"

"Yes, just remembering the beautiful rugs I saw in Afghanistan."

"I can only imagine. You guys must be starving!"

Bob comes back in with a couple of bottles of wine. "Well, I have decided to open two of my best wines for us to celebrate our Thanksgiving meal. As we aren't having turkey, I've opted for dry-aged beef tenderloin, and therefore will open two bottles of my 1982 vintage, Chateau Margaux, Bordeaux!"

Janie says, "How wonderful, Bob!" I don't really have anything to add. I like wine, but I don't really understand what is special about this one.

Bob busily buzzes around the open chef's kitchen and Janie tells us stories about the various art objects: where they found them, about the artists, and the cool travel they've been able to do since Bob sold his company. She explains that they have a particularly important collection of Hopi pottery, including pre-Nampeyo-era work. I remember the dream about Mikey, as a cloud, "I'll wait for you in Oraibi." I miss him and his stories. As Janie talks about the Hopi, I have to fight back my tears, and I have an overwhelming need to know if he made it back home.

When we finally are seated at the table, I start to feel guilty that I'm here, in the presence of such beauty, and I think about my buddies back in Afghanistan.

Bob carefully pours the wine into each of our glasses, and after he sits at the head of the table he says, "I would like to say a kind of *gratitude prayer,* if I may. I'm really not a very religious man, in the traditional sense, but I'd like to share some words with you briefly. Please, let's all hold hands for a moment. I'm so grateful that we are all gathered in love and friendship, for the excellent food, and wine, we are about to enjoy, and for our wonderful friends, and new members of our family, Daniel and Dylan!"

After enjoying the food and wine for a while, Bob asks me what I think I might like to do with my life. Normally, when this question is asked of me, or someone else, I have instantaneous emotional recoil, and my first inclination is to run as fast as I can from the question, or say something surly like, "I'm going to Paris to be a hand model!" I don't know if it is the magic of the moment, brought on by some kind of Bordeaux induced aurora borealis affect, but words begin to magically leave my mouth.

"I would really like to help other people. Ideally, I would like to help them realize the futility of war, the essential need for true democracy, and a system that is designed to foster exceptional, *extraordinary* problem-solvers, and to eradicate companies who exploit humanity and create an imbalance on the planet... and to ensure that natural resources are distributed fairly."

Bob smiles lovingly. He takes a deep breath, and I can tell he is gathering his thoughts.

"That is wonderful, Dylan," he says sincerely. "To serve mankind is the highest calling and a bitter pill to swallow when you actually are in the arena, and you realize that the major-ity of people may not even understand, or value, what you are trying to do for them. It's important to have an idealistic goal, or *intent*. The cause-and-effect is powerful.

"An easy-to-get-to example: What if the United States didn't aspire to have safe highways and streets, had no traffic lights, driving-age requirements, standards for vehicle safety, insur-ance, and everyone was permitted to do just what they feel and drive as they pleased? Even with all that in place, in this country they often think those rules don't apply to them."

"Yes, I've experienced that very scenario while I was driving in Afghanistan!" I say, laughing.

"Did you know that even with our stringent efforts, laws, and safety standards, one-point-three million Americans die every year in traffic related deaths? That is 3,287 deaths, per day. All of our citizens are instructed on the importance of safety, yet every day people drive drunk, stoned, fast, ignore lights and signs, and take chances that risk other people's lives. Which is why you guys are sleeping here tonight!"

I offer, "Well, if we can't even get our own people to drive fast, in the fast lane, and slow, in the slow lane, how can we expect other cultures to accept our democratic process, as we superimpose our will on other nations and cultures?"

Daniel blurts out, "Whoa!"

Bob again smiles lovingly at me, and stares deeply into my eyes.

"Dylan, when I was a kid, the world was so exciting. I was a sweet, loving little guy who wanted to talk to everyone. That is why I got emotional outside listening to your brother talk about your Thanksgiving gathering with your family, and Malcolm's abuses to those small children really hit a nerve.

"My father, now deceased, was a horribly abusive man: to me, and to my siblings. When I was a kid, it wasn't acceptable for me to laugh, make jokes, or act silly. He never once asked me how I was feeling, or what I was thinking about, or was interested in what I was doing. For him, it was a constant demonstration of showing how tough he was, trying to 'toughen me up' and somehow this made him, and me, more of a 'man.' He didn't understand how to invite me into his feelings, or have fun with me. He just told me what to do, and who I should be in the world. Make a lot of money was his mantra."

Daniel says, "As Andrew Carnegie said, "There is no class so pitiably wretched as that which possesses money and nothing else."

"Very true, Daniel. His world was very small. I made a choice that I would find a way to make my world very large, and that is why I became a computer-science engineer. At that time, it felt as if my world of possibility was infinite, but I always felt impoverished by the lack of love and connection with my father. When I was young, that caused me to do crazy things to try and get other people's affection. I was literally starved for his attention. The only place I seemed to be able to draw attention to myself was in a science class. I was *really unhappy*... that is, until I met Janie!"

"Whoa, dude, tell us the love mystery!" Daniel says.

"Not tonight, we will save that for another evening, I'm telling you this because Janie and I have something we want to share with you both, and I need to make sure that you truly understand the spirit of our Thanksgiving."

Janie smiles at Daniel and me in such a way that it scares me. I think they are going to go into some kind of long, intense diatribe about how "Jesus will save us" and offer to pray with us, or try and involve us in some kind of multi-level marketing business, or some kind of kinky shit. I'm not prepared for what comes out of Bob's mouth. Bob smiles and says, "I hope I can get through this without crying..."

"Don't worry, we both know how to swim," Daniel says with a laugh.

"OK, as you guys know, we've grown really close, and fond, of you, Daniel, over the last couple of years, and then when we met you, Dylan, we were both instantly taken by you. The fact is we love you both, as if you were our own kids. It seems too late at this time in your lives to adopt you legally, but we would both very much like the honor of adopting you — spiritually, as members of our little family.

"What that means to us, is that we happily and willingly include you in our hearts to ensure that you are loved and cared for in a healthy, unconditional, and supportive way. We want to create an opportunity for you both to thrive, because we believe that you are both very special and have much to offer the world.

We've been very blessed financially, and we want to share our prosperity."

"Daniel, we think you are so creative and smart, and we want to ensure that you have the education that you deserve. So we'd like to offer you a full financial scholarship, including living expenses, to any liberal arts, or art school, in the country."

Daniel begins to cry, which causes Janie to cry.

"Dylan, I know it feels like we've just met, but somehow I'm so deeply connected to you. I sense that you have some personal things to heal and work through, that I can't help you with, and that no amount of money will 'fix.' It's your journey of healing. With that said, we would like to help facilitate that in our own small way.

"We've happily decided to gift you the Barn Swallow house. We'd like to provide you a safe place to continue your healing without worrying about things like rent and where to wash your clothes. We'll also give you a monthly allowance for a period of two years, which will cover all your living expenses, and give you enough support to have some freedom to figure out what you'd like to do with your life. You don't have to answer to me about how you spend it, or what you want to do. If you want to go to Mexico City or Biloxi, Mississippi, it's your business."

I am completely overwhelmed. I feel deeply grateful for Bob and Janie's kindness, and to be a part of their loving family. I'm most happy for Daniel. It is so great to see his impish little face light up with exhilaration and joy. I've never seen that expression of joy on anyone's face in my family.

●  ●  ●

For the next couple of weeks, my head is swimming and I feel schizophrenic. On the one hand, I've just been given an amazing gift, and a chance at establishing myself, maybe even find some happiness, by Bob and Janie's generosity, but on the other, my feelings of guilt, nightmares, and panic attacks are not getting any better. I've slowed down on the cocaine use, but I am still drinking *way too much.*

Shahzada is whispering random shit into my ear as I move through time and space: *Look at that idiot driving… he knows that there is a detour ahead, yet he flies ahead of everyone trying to merge, and acts like Oops, I must merge, let me in…* Or, she's screaming while I am trying to read the news: *Wake up, people… the Electoral College is just a safety device to trick you when the power elite need to trump a candidate! Is this democracy or is this is political manipulation? And you call us the bad guys?*

I'm actually looking forward to my appointment with Dr. Trimble on Tuesday. Her office is cheery and she offers good coffee while you wait, but she is *always* late. I don't mind because I love reading the books in her waiting room. She doesn't put crappy lifestyle magazines out for her clients; instead she has interesting old picture books, vintage *Life* and *Look* magazines, short-story compilations, history books, and poetry collections. I have grown to appreciate being able to tell her what is really going on with me, and she seems to give a shit. When she finally comes out, she senses that I'm having a difficult day, more than usual, and she adjusts her energy for me.

I tell Dr. Trimble about my experience in Marble Falls with Malcolm. As I describe my behavior, I'm somewhat alarmed by the sheer violence of what I want to do to him. I am ensnarled in a contradictive divide. I crave anything, and everything, other than violence. I want to feel peaceful and loving, yet I struggle with constant anger. Anytime I'm in the company of a person or situation that is blatantly unjust, or unfair, I just snap and want to fuck snap their fucking head off. I'm not sure I can explain it. It's like, the crazier the shit happens in the world around me, the more I seem to focus in on what feels like the greater *philosophical derailment of our country,* and this causes me to overreact and to respond to situations in a way that is normally considered "inappropriate." It keeps me wound up. As we say in Texas, "Tighter than Dick's hat band!"

Like when I go to the gym. I love letting off some steam at my neighborhood gym. It feels good to sweat out my anxiety and booze. When I go to the locker room and negotiate moving through a door, or to my locker, I will say, "Excuse me" politely, and some douche bag with a new set of muscles will give me a *fuck you* look. After being in war with guys who know how to use basic manners, his rudeness makes me want to slam his face into the lockers and say, "Your fucking mother didn't teach you how to say, please, you're welcome, excuse me, or thank you, but I will!" It is stressful to know that I can snap his fucking neck in an instant, but I choose to remain polite.

Mrs. Trimble sweetly says, "So, you're feeling some anger!"

"Yeah."

"Do you want to talk about it?"

"What's there to talk about? Our country is manufacturing unnecessary war, polluting our people with floods of information, most of which is bullshit. You heard it from me. During the Cold War, the communists said religion was the opiate of the masses, well, now it is news and information! Even a smart person, concentrating, and trying to find real and useful information, has to dig and study. Is the non-vetted 'my opinion panel,' news-entertainment crap providing people what they need to be informed and make good choices? So everyone is just walking around fucking dazed and confused about what is really going on! What's really going on is that we are drinking the Kool-Aid and chanting we are a great country, we live in a democracy, we are Christians, and the truth is, we are a very diluted facsimile of the before-mentioned—"

Dr. Trimble gently but firmly cuts me off.

"Dylan, don't you think that all people throughout history have had to contend with abuses of power, manipulation, misinformation, war, famine, disease, injustice, and natural disasters? I think the difference is that it is all instantaneously delivered to us through the media and internet, by the good, the bad, and the stupid. My friend Lori calls CNN *Constant Negative News*. Maybe it is time to stop accepting the bait. The only person on this planet that you can truly control is yourself and how you relate, or respond to the external world.

"Is it OK for Dylan to be happy, in the presence of all the ugly things you know about the world? Is it OK for Dylan to experience peace? Is it OK for someone to love Dylan? I understand what you are saying, Dylan, and I agree, there are many, many horrible things on our planet... but, there are also many, many amazing and lovely things and people as well. We get to choose where we put our attention, what we fight for, and where we hold our consciousness. We get to choose if we let go of the events of the past that hurt us. We don't have to hold on to that pain. It doesn't have to define us. In your case, you no longer are under the thumb of his reckless parenting. You are free to parent yourself. To bring things into your life that make you feel good. It is OK for you to be happy.

"It's important for you to realize that you have to let go of what you can't control. Let go of the pain, and don't attach to the madness of the world. I think it is time to go within and find love for that angry and hurt little boy, Dylan... and let him know he is safe now."

"Wow, Dr. Trimble... you make it all sound so easy! *Abra-fucking-kadabra.*"

"I'm not saying it won't be hard, or that you can just wake up one morning and—presto—everything is lovely. But, I am saying you can consciously choose your actions and where you place your thoughts. You can begin to integrate positive thoughts, people, and experiences into your life to give you a greater sense of balance, inner peace and self-esteem."

"I just find it hard to think about 'peace' in Austin: crazy roommates, clubs, drugs, girls, traffic, et cetera."

"I don't believe in 'geographical cures,' but maybe you should take a trip somewhere that you've always wanted to go. Spend some time writing about how you're feeling. Re-set your life compass."

"Yeah, maybe!"

"Well, it'll give you something to think about until we meet next! I'm afraid our time is up for today."

•  •  •

When I wake up on Thursday morning, I hear Charlie and Natalie downstairs making noise. At first, I think they are fighting, which is a fairly routine occurrence lately. The first words I can identify are from Natalie screaming, *"Oh My God!"* Followed by Charlie, "What kind of sick fuck would do this?" The television is blaring. I can hear a news anchor say, *"At this time we are uncertain of the exact number of children that may be injured or dead. Numerous gunshots have been heard inside, and the state police are arriving on the scene. The local police have confirmed that a 911 call was made by the school secretary and reported a shooter. We are not clear at this time if there are multiple gunmen, or if it is a lone shooter."*

My mind replays the words *children* and *dead*.

I hear Charlie scream, "What's wrong with these young, rich, white dudes? They are fucking crazy!"

Natalie says, "Dude, you don't know if it is a rich white dude! It could be terrorists."

I see Shahzada in the corner; smiling. She just stares at me. After a moment, she says, *You see, Dylan, you have survived, and now it is time to teach others… Shhhhhhh, be very quiet. You're not listening, Dylan.*

This freaks me out. I'm certain that I've now officially gone insane.

This is not the way I want to begin my day. I am getting really freaked out and decide to go downstairs and find out what crazy shit is happening.

Charlie and Natalie are both on the couch glued to one another, and the television. The moment Natalie sees me she says, "Landlord, this shit is horrible. Some guy is shooting little kids at some elementary school!"

"Where?" I ask.

"Some place in Connecticut, called Sandy Hook."

They know the name of the shooter—just twenty years old—and it is confirmed that twenty children and six teachers have been killed. In just five minutes. I feel nauseous. My mind starts skipping. Natalie notices my strange breathing and the uncontrollable bouncing of my leg. She asks if I am all right, and I say that I am fine, but I'm not. I go back upstairs. The sky is gray and looks cold. I am really anxious. I want to call someone and realize that I have no one to call. Daniel is at work and I can't talk to Charlie and Natalie about this, or at least I don't feel like I can. I collect myself, brush my teeth, wash my face, and go back downstairs.

Charlie and Natalie watch the television like its "News of the Weird." They're more fascinated by the horror than impacted by the loss of twenty six- and seven-year-old children. We have no way to process it. It's too horrible.

Back in Afghanistan, if we lost one soldier it was a *big fucking deal*. We felt it down to our bones, and it hurt. Watching another report on a "mass shooting" turns the reality of the horror into a palatable term; it gives distance, and space, for the listener to be off the hook of having to really process—feel the feelings—of pain and horror of the event. Just as we do by using words like "collateral damage" to nullify the horror of innocent people slaughtered in a war.

Now we, as a nation, don't have to own that the 20-year-old kid grew up in *our system*. That he grew up in an idyllic community that prides itself on beauty and safety. He was given access to guns, taught to shoot, as if he was expressing some kind of sacred constitutional privilege. He played violent video games, came from a divorced family, was depressed and bullied. Violence, fear, and anxiety are so commonplace for him that it erodes his young mind: burns away the possibility of safety, spiritual development, and happiness. Instead, he fosters emotional isolation, anger, and violence—and chooses to kill children.

How can we accept this violence as our reality? I remember Mikey telling me that his grandfather said before you make a decision, think about *how it will affect the next seven generations*. I don't think our legislators think about the next seven minutes with gun-control legislation.

I want my mind to stop all this scrambled, frenetic digging about the problems of our country. I try to remember what Dr. Trimble told me about the world, that it will always have pain and problems, but what can I do to create peace for myself? This seems to calm me down and I allow myself to breathe. I lie down, close my eyes, and hold a pillow on top of my chest and try to stay in this place of calm. It feels good to breathe.

Just as I surrender to the peace, Natalie opens the door and whispers, "Dylan, are you asleep?"

I don't say anything at first, because I hope she'll just leave and let me rest. Then I feel her crawl up my mattress like a cat. She lies next to me and gently places her arm around my chest and the pillow, and buries her head in my neck. It feels nice to have her next to me. Within moments, I'm fast asleep.

An hour or so later, Charlie opens the bedroom door briskly. "Whoa, *isn't this* a cozy love nest..." Natalie says, *"Shut up,*

Charlie" into my neck, which gives me a startle. Charlie laughs
and says, "Hey, Landlord, some dude, with big biceps is downstairs to see you. Says he served with you in Afghanistan!" At
first, I think it must be Kong, and then I realize it has to be
Sergeant Reece. My heart leaps, and I'm so excited. I don't know
why, just am. I run into the bathroom and throw water on my
face and push my hair around, and run downstairs.

When Reece sees me, he smiles warmly. "Well, I was in the
neighborhood and thought I would let you buy me that shot of
tequila you mentioned back on FOB Hamilton!" I walked over
and gave him a huge hug. I was so glad to see him my eyes
involuntarily began to get glassy. I say, "Wow, dude, I am so
happy to see you. Are you out of the Army?"

"I'm a free man! *Officially retired* from the United States Army."

"Man, I have so many questions for you and so much to talk
about. How long are you in Austin?"

"Just tonight. I came to check it out for my new business. I
don't know if I told you back in Afghanistan, but I am starting
my specialty travel agency, touring the country, and I needed to
check out Austin on my way to Dallas."

"Wow, that is great!"

Charlie and Natalie come down and Charlie, being Charlie,
starts teasing Reece immediately.

"Whoa, dude, what's happening? I'm Charlie, and this is
Dylan's other *rent slave*, Natalie. You must spend a minute or
two at the gym. So, you and Landlord were in the desert together
playing battle games with the nefarious dark forces?"

Reece smiles at Charlie, because Charlie is impossible not to
find cute, harmless and funny.

Charlie continues, "Dude, I was reading online about these
crazy army guys who take home videos of dead guys, and share
with other soldiers. They pose them like they are jerking off,
Sharpie their faces, and crazy shit like that."

Reece looks equally amused and horrified.

"Well, Charlie, my men didn't do either of those things. But, sometimes the stresses of war, and losing your best buddies, brings out a strange sense of humor in some men."

Natalie couldn't stand having a handsome young guy in the house and not try to spray her feminine mystique on him. She blurts out, "You are so cute! You can *totally* crash in my room tonight if you need a place to stay." She sounds like an intoxicated groupie talking to a rock star.

"That's nice, Natalie, thank you."

I try to save him. "OK, Tiger, I'm taking you out for that tequila shot and for some Tex-Mex food, and then for some more tequila shots, and then we can meet up with these crazed rent slaves. We'll show you the town!"

•  ●  •

It is so strange having Reece on my bike, behind me, in Austin, Texas. The last time I saw him, I was behind him and we were dodging mortar fire and trying to get the bad guys. Having him with me brings up emotional memories of my experience in Afghanistan, as if I'm there in the moment: the ancient architecture, the vast valleys, orchards, mountain ranges, poppy fields, the crowds of men, the veiled women, and the curious, lovely children trapped in a lifetime of senseless war. I hear *pop pop pop* and I'm holding Mikey in my arms, bleeding and fighting for his life. It's a bittersweet symphony.

As I'm trying to navigate the road, the emotional intensity sets me on fire. The feelings are so complex. I don't know how to process them. Using words feels cheap. We get to Congress Avenue and I look for a parking place. It's cool weather and there are tons of people everywhere. I feel uneasy. I don't like crowds. There's some kind of art thing going on, and people are

outside the door of the restaurant at the South Congress Hotel,
so I make a sudden U-turn and head toward the east side. Reece
screams, "That was a fast tour!"

We find a cool, small restaurant on East Sixth, in an old house,
and I feel calmer. When we get off the bike, Reece laughs. "What
happened, buddy?"

"Man, I saw all those people and kind of freaked out."

"You OK?"

"Yeah, just need a minute to breathe, and a tequila shot!"

Reece smiles warmly, the same smile he offered me in Afghanistan. The one that says, *It's OK, buddy. Doesn't feel like it, but it
is. I got your back!*

The small cantina isn't crowded and the people are nice. We
sit outside on the patio, next to a fire pit. The waitress is cute
and tiny with long wavy hair and big hoop earrings. She tells
us that she is an art student at the community college and just
moved to Austin six months ago. Her name is Chula.

I look into the fire. It occurs to me that the last meal we
shared was outside Shahzada's family home. My mind flashes
to her brother shooting the man in black, and her family dropping his limp body into the well.

"Are you guys ready to order?"

The sound of Chula's voice causes me to jump. "I'm so sorry.
I didn't mean to startle you!"

"No, it's all good. Just a little jumpy today."

"I understand. That happens to me when I stay up studying
or painting."

Reece gives me a compassionate look, and says to Chula,
"This guy and I have just come back from a very big adventure
in Afghanistan."

"Oh Wow! That's so cool. I bet it was amazing."

"Yes, it was *amazing*."

"Are you guys archeologists, or were you making a movie?"

"No, we were stationed there in the Army."

"No way, you guys don't *even* seem like that type of guy."

"What do you mean 'like that'?"

"Well, you know… all, Army-man, kill-people sort of guy."

I wasn't able to speak. As usual, Reece steps up. "Well, we aren't anymore. Tonight, we are just two old friends who are excited to eat your delicious food and have a drink."

"Awesome! Do you know what you would enjoy?"

"Well, I'm from New Orleans and don't know much about this kind of food, and I'm probably not pronouncing it correctly, but that Cochinita Pibil, achiote braised pork, sounds amazing."

"It is awesome. Oh, I'm sorry… I forgot to tell you about our special item on the menu. The chef made Barbacoa de Chivo tacos, braised goat, and that is served with guacamole, black beans, queso fresco, and a stack of fresh handmade corn tortillas. They are to die for!"

Reece and Chula both look at me, interested in what I will order, and see that I am crying. I am both embarrassed and relieved to let the emotion out. Chula sweetly asks if I am OK. After a moment I say, "I'm so sorry. I didn't expect that. It's just that you have goat tacos tonight, my buddy and I are enjoying our evening, and we lost a friend of ours in Afghanistan who loved goat tacos. Just a little sensitive today…"

"I'm so, so sorry." Chula is obviously taken off guard by the unexpected emotion she feels that she has caused.

"No, I'm sorry. I promise to get it together. I do think I will have a *strong* margarita on the rocks with salt, with a mezcal floater, please."

"Make that two!" Reece says.

"Coming up!"

When Chula is gone, Reece reaches across the table and rests his hand on my forearm. He gives me his usual kind gaze "Man, it's tough to forget. I don't think we are supposed to. The important thing, as I see it, is how we remember." He pauses.

"We can't be responsible for our enemy. We can't be responsible for the bad decisions by our government, or the politics — they are naturally flawed. We can't hold the sadness of all the deaths, and human loss. The only thing we can control is our own reaction to it, and *what we give to the world* now. If you try and be responsible for all of this shit, it's like taking the sum of human insanity, giving it weight, tying it to your ankles, and casting yourself into the ocean. You will surely plunge and drown in misery, and sorrow."

"I know, Tiger. What I don't know is how to live and thrive in a society that is so fucking self-absorbed. Everywhere I look, I'm frustrated. They told me I was going to war to preserve our freedoms and democracy. Yet, all I see is greed, corporate fascism, racism, discrimination, poverty, homeless people on corners, mass murders, on and on. Why can't we sort that shit out?"

"Man, do you think this is new? Nothing is new, my friend, it just changes forms. Remember in physics, learning about energy? You can't create, nor destroy energy — it just changes forms! That's why I'm not afraid of death."

"Wow, I find it really tough to let go. It makes me feel like a fucking chicken broiler, going down the conveyor belt for slaughter."

"My friend, you need to go on a vacation and have some laughs, see some new landscapes, and enjoy new cuisine, people, and romance. Do you have a girlfriend?"

"No, I haven't really been up for romance. It's kinda hard to explain to your girlfriend that you are experiencing delusional visions of a young girl you met in Afghanistan in the corner of the room talking incessantly during PTSD moments. But you are right, I do need to get away, and you are *perfect* for your new tour business. Maybe I'll go somewhere on my bike. I've been really feeling strongly about visiting Mikey in Arizona. I can't stop thinking about him."

Reece looks uncharacteristically sad. I can tell that he wants to tell me something but he doesn't want to upset me or ruin our brief time together.

"What is it, Tiger?"

"I'm so very sorry to tell you this. We lost Mikey in Bagram. Our team did everything they could, but they couldn't save him."

I close my eyes and try to breathe deeply. Waves of pain and emotion move through me. Images of him laughing, I see him talking, sharing his culture, I hear his voice telling me to come visit him at Oraibi, as if it is another planet, a sacred place, that only he can show me. *How can you know someone so little time, yet be so impacted by them, love them so deeply, like a brother?* I didn't have the energy, or the emotional strength to talk about this now. I know I'll have to suck it up, and move on with our evening. It would be too much to process, and Tiger didn't come all this way to watch me fall apart. I know I must go to Arizona. I'll have to speak to his family, pay my respects, and find closure.

"Have you heard any news about Dope and Kong?" I ask.

"Yes. Kong, for his heroic performance the day you were shot, is now in Ranger School and from what I gather, happy as an Alabama clam. Dope is still in Afghanistan, and I haven't heard any news. I think his contract should be over soon."

Before we could go further, Chula brings our food, and more drinks. She says this round of drinks is on the house for "serving our country." Tiger and I raise our glasses and say, "To Chula, and the Four Deuces!"

After several more tequila shots, we leave to meet Charlie and Natalie at the Yellow Jacket Social Club. Natalie is holding court on the patio with a group of adoring fraternity boys. She is wearing a super-tight short black dress and high heels, a flowing multi-colored silk scarf, and has her hair in a ponytail sticking straight up. She has on deep red lipstick that accentuates her full lips, and dramatic eye makeup that makes her big brown eyes appear huge. She is wearing a bunch of mix-match bracelets that cling and clang on her excited arms as she talks. She sees us walk in and screams, "Oh my God... Landlord and G.I. Gorgeous!" She hugs me and jumps into the arms of Reece and plants a big kiss on his lips that seems to linger for several seconds too long. He turns red.

I make my way to the bar and order a couple of tequila shots and beer chasers. Charlie is talking to a table of three University of Texas sorority girls. Charlie seems to always be fascinated with those types of girls, and they with him. They are unlike the girls he grew up with in El Paso, the sturdy Latina desert flowers.

We listen to Natalie pontificate about the silly men in her life who just use her for sex, because they are reckless little boys who want to hurt her, because they are too stupid to actually commit to anything other than their own dicks. Reece starts laughing and Natalie looks at him, aggressively asking, "Are you gay?"

Reece laughs even louder and says, "Yes! Why do you ask?"

"Well, I didn't know, I mean... I wouldn't think so, but you seem so tuned into what I'm saying, as if you totally get it!"

"Yes, I do totally get it!"

"Dude, I am totally *depressed*. All this time, I thought we had a real connection."

"We do have a real connection!"

"Really?" Natalie blurts out.

"Yep, we do!"

"*Really?*" I ask.

"Yep!"

It feels good to laugh and to just let go.

Tiger says, "I feel like dancing!"

Natalie says, "Oh, my God, me too!"

I say, "I'm not dancing."

"Come on, you're dancing!" they insist.

Reece suggests that we all go to a gay bar, and dance. Natalie gets all excited because she's never been to one. I'd never thought about a gay bar. I don't know why, it just never entered my mind. Besides, they don't have "gay bars" in Marble Falls, Texas — we just have highway rest stops for those kinds of hook-ups.

We try to get Charlie to come with us, unsuccessfully, as he is invisibly chained to his new sorority girl. There's a club close by, so we walk.

Basically, the rest of the night is a blurred memory of more tequila, cocaine on the patio, hysterical laughing, dancing, hugging and kissing, somehow getting home, and waking up with all three of us naked in my queen-sized mattress on the dirty, stained beige carpet in my bedroom.

●　●　●

"*Dylan... Dylan,* are you awake?" Natalie whispers really loudly.

"*Dylan,* do you smell that?" she says.

"No."

"Oh my God, the house is on fire."

Natalie jumps up and runs out, and I hear a shrill, "Shit! Get up, everyone. *Now! Fire!*"

Charlie is screaming, "Shit, I'm so sorry dude. I didn't mean to — *fuck* — where is the extinguisher?"

I throw on shorts and run downstairs. The kitchen is full of smoke and a grease fire blazes on the stove. The fire alarm is shrill and screaming. Charlie is throwing glasses of water at the fire, but it isn't going out. I grab the extinguisher and finally smother the flames.

The house smells like poor judgment, wet smoke, and grease. My head is pounding. Natalie and I open doors and windows. I rip the battery out of the smoke detector. Reece comes around the corner. "Well, I was going to cook eggs for everyone, but I guess we'll have to go out!" Charlie *will not* shut up about how sorry he is, and how it was an accident. We all hear a pathetic whimper of a call — "Chawee" — and out of Charlie's bedroom emerges a young blonde girl in a Pi Phi T-shirt, wearing Charlie's Pac-Man boxer shorts, and that makes us howl with laughter.

This is way too much excitement for my hangover and mood. I go back upstairs to lie down. Natalie goes to her room to take a hot bath. Reece comes upstairs and lies down next to me and put his arm over my chest. I feel *really* uncomfortable, and he can tell, and asks, "Are you OK?"

"Yes, I'm just a little wigged out from last night, the amount of alcohol and drugs we did, and the fire!"

"Yeah, a bit too much fun. But, seriously, are you OK?"

"Yes. I don't remember much about whatever happened. I've never been sexual with another guy. The thing is... something about you I really love. You are so kind and warm. I've never had that from a man. It is confusing to me, and at the same time I desire it. It's just something I can't really process right now."

"I understand. It's all good. You're my friend, and I'm happy about that. If you need me, please know that I am here for you in a real way. You don't have to explain anything, or "be" anything around me. You don't have to 'fit'."

"I appreciate that, man."

"I'm going to have to pop smoke! I have to head to Dallas, and check it out."

"Yeah, last night I decided to go to Arizona to pay respect to Mikey's family."

"I left my business card," Reece says. "If you are in New Orleans, call me! Call me any way, and let me know how you are doing."

"I will. You be safe, Mr. Tour Guide."

"Always! It's going to be all right, my friend."

Reece gently closes the door, and I close my eyes and let my mind float to a peaceful place. Soon I am asleep, and can hear Native American drums playing softly. The intensity slowly rises, and I can hear ceremonial chanting. I have the point of view of an eagle, and I'm soaring over the golden landscape heading toward Second Mesa. Suddenly, I'm hit, shot, and I'm falling toward the ground. I am in pain and I see Shahzada running frantically across the landscape to try and catch me as I fall. Crying and screaming, *No... no, you can't die.* I burst into flames, and when I crash into the ground, my eyes open.

I am relieved to discover that I'm alive, sleeping in my bed on Barn Swallow. My house smells like wet burnt smoke and bacon, and the television is blaring downstairs about the Sandy Hook shooting, but I'm alive.

# Part Three

• • •

"Take a breath of the new dawn, and make it a part of you."

— HOPI PROVERB

# Road Trip

I THROW TWO PAIR of jeans, four black t-shirts, wool sweater, underwear and socks into a backpack. I put on some comfortable, warm clothes to ride, grab my leather jacket. I am packed for my trip. I have no idea if Mikey's wife and daughter will appreciate me coming unannounced and uninvited. I don't know if his grandfather is still alive. Mikey spoke about him as if he is. A deep feeling of *importance* draws me there, yet I'm still so uncertain about what I'll discover—or more honestly, I'm a little afraid of what I'll find.

My first obsession is about what route to take, and I keep changing it every fifteen minutes. My second obsession is the weather. It shows rain in places, and heavy snow farther on in New Mexico. Maybe I should just go west on Interstate 10 to Phoenix, and then north to Winslow, and forget the smaller roads in New Mexico. I begin to second-guess my decisions, and start to have doubts about my trip. My third obsession is what if I get there and the Hopi say, "Sorry, we only allow Native Americans on our land"? Then, I realize I am being paranoid. Besides, even if I can't find Mikey's family, I need a vacation. Jesus, I haven't been on a vacation in about four years, and I hardly call my stay in Afghanistan fun vacation travel.

After a shower, I stand in front of the mirror naked. It has been a long time since I have really looked at myself with any kind of interest in how I look. I haven't really thought about that since I don't have a CO screaming about dress standards, and kicking everyone's ass. As if the Taliban gives a shit about how well shaved we are before they try to shoot us in the fucking face. My hair is long enough to put in a ponytail, I have a full beard, and both arms are covered with tattoos. My blue eyes are very clear. For the first time in my life, I wonder if other people will perceive me as dangerous, or some kind of hippie or badass. *Now you are thinking like a crazy man... people will respond to how you treat them, not what you look like. Time to go!*

Downstairs, Charlie and Natalie are still glued to the television set listening to new details about the shooting in Sandy Hook. I am feeling sick from the burnt bacon smell, the noise pollution, and the essence of *strange world* in the air. Natalie is perky and chatty, as usual, and seems absolutely unaffected by the fact that we had sex last night. I, on the other hand, feel *very odd* and don't really remember what was said, or the details of what happened. I feel like my body has been turned into a cardboard box, dry and lifeless. I assume that is attributable to lines of cocaine. Emotionally, I'm like helium, or more like a helium balloon with no string, and no one to hold it...

Natalie gives me a hug. "Bye, Landlord. You be careful on that moto-scooter!"

Charlie adds, "Yeah, no popping wheelies on the interstate, dude. Don't forget to say, 'thank you' and brush your teeth."

"Thanks, L'il Charlie. I'll be good." I'll miss my crazy little roommate family.

Natalie walks me out to the bike and gives me another hug. Even though we both knew that we'd never sleep together again, it felt nice to have her see me off on my big adventure. That's the language I need to give this trip meaning: my *big adventure*. It was nice to hear the purr of the bike when I started it, and when I sit on her it feels like I am in the right place. The vibration causes me to relax.

•   •   •

My first challenge is to get to Highway 71 without getting killed. The flow of traffic in Austin is much faster than the speed limit. If I go slower, I am essentially a target for some idiot in his BMW 7 Series late to a meeting. As I head west, the views open up to the Hill Country, with new neighborhoods and large homes dotting the hillsides. Soon, I reach Paleface Park on the Pedernales River, near Willie Nelson's recording studio. I've never been there, but somehow, growing up in Hill Country makes you feel like you are related to Willie.

I pass Opie's BBQ, and decide eating ribs and brisket at nine-thirty AM isn't what I need, so I push on west toward Llano, Texas. Minutes later, a green highway sign announces MARBLE FALLS 12 MILES. It triggers a wave of anxiety, and my mind replays my desire to kill Malcolm. Who is that person, with so much anger and violence? Is that who I've become? I always thought of myself as a compassionate, loving person, but lately I am experiencing myself as a violent man. I don't mean like the guy who opens fire on elementary schools, just a serious case of pissed off.

As I drive, my mind transports me to a scene in Marble Falls that I had long forgotten. It's in the middle of the night and my mom was drunk and high, wakes me up. She tells me, "Mama has to go out for a while. Be a big boy and watch the other kids." She leaves me and I am terrified. What if something happens? I don't know anyone in this town to call for help and besides, we don't have a phone. I'm so upset that I can't sleep. I imagine that someone is trying to break in and get us. I sneak into the kitchen and grab several large knives. I go back to the bedroom and lay them in a semi-circle around me for protection. What if there is more than one guy?

I remember that Malcolm has a .410 shotgun under their bed. I sneak into their room, thinking that he is asleep. He is gone. I grab his gun and return to the bedroom. I have the knives and gun. I play with the safety. Safe is black, fire is red. Or is it the other way? I switch the safety to red and feel exhilarated, and afraid. I switch it back to black and I am ready to protect my brother and little sister. I fall asleep holding the gun. I hear something in the den. *It must be the back doors rattling from wind. Is someone trying to get in?* I fumble with the safety switch, and I am too nervous to look. I run toward the den and trip in my socks. I hit the hallway floor with a thud, and a loud blast. I accidentally shoot the sheetrock into the bathroom wall. I don't know which I'm more afraid of at this point, the imagined intruder, or Malcolm's inevitable beating.

Soon, I am in the town of Llano. The locals refer to Llano as "Lan-o." It is a community of small-town folk who get their hair cut at the local salon, Cut or Dye, purchase doe urine during deer-hunting season at their local gas station, and eat home-style baked goods at Krissy's Bakery.

I decide to stop and get some coffee and a quick something to eat for breakfast at Krissy's Bakery, I notice that the tiny stucco building, with a historic marker in front, looks like a miniature Alamo. When I open the door, my nostrils are filled with the smell of warm dough, sugar, and I see a beautiful girl in a soft yellow sweater, overalls, and a long white apron. She has long, wavy, dirty-blonde hair pulled back into a ponytail under a red bandana. I imagine that she sings Joni Mitchell songs when no customers are around. She sees me standing at the small counter and gives me a sweet smile. "Be right there, darlin!" Even though I am viewing an ocean of sugar and carbohydrates, I feel as if I am in the healthiest place on earth.

I stare at the fresh pies, kolaches, donuts and glistening sticky buns, and help myself to coffee. "Good morning, sorry, my pecan pies needed to go into the oven. What can I get you?" She really looks at me for a minute and seems so open and kind. She has seafoam-green eyes, white creamy skin and full red lips. I want to hug her. She can sense my attraction, and it causes her to chatter about the bakery items. She explains about the many kolaches, and all of their various fillings: sausage, jam, and one with eggs and bacon.

"I'll have the eggs and bacon, please!"

"Good choice. One of my favorites."

"What do you do when you aren't baking?"

"Well, my husband and I like to take our daughter to the lake and fish... or, I like to build bird houses. The fun part is painting them!"

I smile. She wants me to know that she is not available, and I'm okay with that, but I just want to continue talking, because I find her beautiful. As she chatters on about her cute, sweet daughter, I think only about how nice it would be to kiss her. That is, until the local sheriff walks in, and gives me a dirty look. The sheriff is as solid as a fire hydrant, with thick black boots and a Smith & Wesson, M&P 9 mm pistol on his hip. He says, "Good morning, Krissy! How's little Katie?"

"Fine! Katie has discovered flying kites, and now that is all she wants to do."

I am transported back to Afghanistan and remember the young Afghan boys flying kites with such skill and excitement. As I look at the fresh baked bread, I can see Shazada in the corner laughing at me, "You want to kiss her! They don't have naan bread, Mr. Books!" My attention shifts when the sheriff asks me, "You awake enough to ride that bike, boy?"

I realize he's talking to me. "Sorry, I was remembering something about Afghanistan."

"Did you serve in Afghanistan, son?"

"Yes, sir."

The sheriff comes over and shakes my hand firmly, and looks me directly in my eyes and says, "I'm glad you made it back, son."

"Thank you, sir!"

"I was tromping around in the rice paddies and jungles back in Vietnam. It ain't easy to come home, is it, son?"

"No, sir."

He pats me on the back, and thanks Krissy for the bag of donut pretzels, and walks out.

"He's a character!" I say.

"Bill Henderson is one of the nicest men that God ever put on this earth."

"Seems like it!"

Krissy's mood has changed. I didn't say anything to her that could upset her, yet she seems really sad. I decide to take a chance and ask her if she's okay. She leans against the counter and places both of her hands over her eyes, and lets out a big sigh. When she moves her hands, I can see a tear, and she apologizes.

"I'm sorry, I didn't tell you the truth a minute ago. I have to be careful with so many folks just passing through town. I didn't expect to get all emotional."

"It's OK, you don't have to explain… it's cool." I say, feeling bad for her. She begins to cry harder, and I am beginning to feel slightly uncomfortable.

"You see, I lost my husband, Buck, a year and a half ago. Katie was only four years old. We'd just opened the bakery and I was so happy. Everything that I ever wanted in life… well, it wasn't always easy. Buck was a handful, even before he went to Iraq. When he came home, something was changed in him. Buck was the life of the party. He loved to tell jokes and laugh. He loved to drink and dance. He would talk to a fence post. When he got home for the last time, he started having problems sleeping. He drank whiskey every night. He stopped going hunting with his friends. We stopped touching, and he got really, really depressed. It scared me and I had no idea how to help him. We didn't have any psychological services for vets here."

Krissy is crying so hard that I'm afraid someone will enter the bakery and think I've done something horrible to upset her. I ask her if she would like to go somewhere and talk. Without hesitation, she walks over to the front door and flips the sign around to CLOSED. "Let's go to my house. It's just two blocks from here and Katie is in school for several more hours. Just leave your motorcycle where it is."

We walk to an old white German farmhouse with a tin roof and a wraparound porch. She apologizes for "the mess." Her house is immaculate, with some toys scattered around on the floor. I follow her into the kitchen. It has high ceilings and old floral-print wallpaper. We sit on built-in white benches next to a big bay window looking out onto her garden. Everything feels like her—warm, beautiful, and cared for. It occurs to me that I've never felt this peaceful in someone's home in my life.

Krissy puts the teapot on the stove and says she will be right back. She returns with a tin box that I assume is filled with delicious cookies, and places it beside her on the wooden bench. "It's really nice of you to listen to me carry on about my husband. I don't really talk to anyone around here about it, and my parents are both gone. I try to stay strong for Katie. I swear I don't know what I would've done if that sweet angel wasn't in my life. She lights up a room with her smile and adorable laugh."

"Does she remember her dad?"

"No, not really, but sometimes she will surprise me with comments like, 'I sure miss Buck, Mommy'... or, 'I wish Buck were here with us, Mommy!'"

Krissy looks out the window, and I can tell she is imagining her husband in the yard. She gets up and pours the hot water into two mugs with teabags. "I hope you like this. It's ginger hibiscus tea."

"Actually, that sounds wonderful, but I'm afraid it will put me to sleep on the road. I have to get to Ruidoso, New Mexico tonight, about another eight hours, and I had a couple of really late nights. Would it be too much of a bother to ask for a cup of coffee?"

"Oh, I'm so sorry. I don't know what I am thinking! Also, you never got to order something to eat back at the bakery before I went into my boo-hoo attack. I am going to make you breakfast!"

I can't believe my eyes, but in little time she makes me an omelet, with bacon and wheat toast. It's delicious and I begin to feel the life come back into my toes and fingertips. She chats about the old farmhouse, about living in Llano and the crazy cast of characters that visit the bakery. I love listening to her talk. She has the sweetest voice and laugh. Her warmth radiates goodness.

We talk about Austin, and all the traffic, and the fun restaurants to try, and how she loves the Blanton Museum. I learn that she studied art in college, but when she met Buck, they had big dreams to own their own business and start a family. They both knew how to cook and they thought a bakery would give them more free time, and less problems, than a restaurant.

After I finish breakfast, and drink another cup of coffee, she politely asks what brings me on a road trip through Llano? I explain how much I love riding on the open roads in the countryside and how much I enjoy meeting people like her, and sharing a moment together. How I love to drift, explore, and learn about people and how they live. I felt like it would be a bit much to talk about Mikey's death, given I brought up all the emotion about her husband, Buck.

It feels very easy to talk to her and I find myself wanting to know more about her — *a lot more*. After we reach a long pause, she looks at me pensively. "Maybe this isn't appropriate, 'cause

I know you need to get back on the road, but I feel the need to share something with you."

"I've never shared this with anyone and I really feel that I want to with you. Somehow, it feels like you will understand."

"Sure, anything!" I say.

"When Buck took his life, he wrote a letter to try and explain why. Would you mind if I read this to you?"

"Of course."

I'm terrified that I won't know how to react, or what to do, if she falls apart. Then, she takes a deep breath and begins reading slowly.

When she finishes, she drops the letter on the table, and closes her eyes, and breathes deeply.

I understand Buck's pain. I can feel every word, every one of his emotions burning into my heart, as if it were my own letter. And while my experience in war was different, and I had never committed the feelings to paper, it was always with me, the unwanted torment and pain, the uncertainty if what I did was wrong, or worth it... to watch my brothers die for a senseless war.

I gently put my hand over hers and she held it for the longest time in silence. I can feel her emotions as she explores the touch of my hand. Tears gently fall down my cheek. I close my eyes and feel a great sense of deepening. She gracefully moves, and sits beside me and places her face against mine. The light from the bay window brightens, giving her kiss the sense that it's ordained by a higher power. I lift her into my lap and hold her tightly. Our communion is rich and filled with life, connection, and abundance. I begin to kiss her passionately. "Wait," she whispers.

"I love this feeling. I like you. I want this but I just met you. Maybe on your way home you can stop by and we can have dinner and talk some more. I'd love for you to meet Katie. She will love you!"

Krissy can see my disappointment, and I know that she wants to make love, but she obviously is more emotionally mature and realizes we need to wait. *Maybe she is right. Maybe I am just caught up in the moment and it would just be sex and ruin this amazing connection we seem to have.*

Last night was crazy, I got basically no sleep, slept with two people, and now I am kissing a beautiful stranger in her kitchen. I don't know if I should call Dr. Trimble or get back on the road, if I'm ever going to get to Second Mesa, Arizona.

"You're right, Miss Krissy! I should come back and get to know you better. You sure know how to make a great first impression."

She smiles and gives me a sweet hug. "You're not so shabby yourself. Well, maybe that beard!"

Krissy walks me back to the bakery and gives me a bag full of kolaches. She insists that I not ride too far today, that it would be dangerous to ride another eight hours without a break. It always strikes me as amusing when people try to take care of me. I have just returned from war, where my job was to stay awake for sometimes thirty-six hours and function at top speed. All the same, it was sweet of her to worry, and I find it hard to say goodbye to her warm smile, touch, and those big green country-girl eyes. I had the overwhelming feeling that we would be together someday.

●    ●    ●

Leaving Llano took me deeper into the Texas Hill Country. Live Oak trees and sage-green fields with grazing cattle dominate the landscape, with small signs of early settlers: an old pioneer chimney still standing, or the remains of a small limestone frontier house. I recall the ancient remains of Qalat-e-Gilzay and can hear Mikey telling me about how Alexander the Great conquered

Afghanistan over two thousand years ago. This landscape feels so youthful and insignificant.

As I curve and lean into the road, I think about what fate might befall the United States of America. Will it all end someday: absorbed, conquered, destroyed, transformed, integrated, or removed by natural disaster? What cultural elements would remain? What would future people say of us? What would remain as our contribution to human history: a musical film, a jazz song, a Rothko painting, a comic book, or an Ansel Adams photograph? Would the hamburger stick around for the future? Would archeologists dig up a baseball and a Louisville Slugger bat and deliberate with amusement about how the Americans played a game they called "baseball," as we do with the Mayan people in Mexico and their game courts?

Whatever our fate, every human relationship, and every culture throughout human history has its season, and I seem to be in my winter of discontent.

After hours, I begin to imagine that I can shape-shift and fly off my bike, as an eagle, and soar over the fields to Arizona. Leave my tired arms, the pain in my leg, and the strange intensity of the last forty-eight hours. As much fatigue as I feel, I am happy to let my "self," my true spirit, escape words and relationships. I am alone and free. I am traveling fast. I'm aware that at any moment a farm truck can pull onto the highway slowly, and it might cause me to crash the bike and die. I go faster. Now the trees and the large round hay bales lose their distinct shapes. The cool air is charging me, and I feel exhilarated. I worry that a buck will jump the fence and cause my certain death, but I continue to fly.

Before I know it, I'm in the town of Brady. The town welcomes visitors with huge still-lifes of black metal cutouts: a large buck, ducks flying, and a wild turkey mounted on a limestone entrance marquis with two gold stars. I turn right on Highway 87 and pass the old granite stone courthouse, with a World War II monument, and I imagine the town's men returning from that war were met with a hero's parade, and respected for saving Europe, and the United States, from the threat of fascism. I imagine that the hardships and horrors that those men endured to protect the world from the tyranny of Hitler, Mussolini, and Stalin were slowly forgotten, as they worked their family's land and felt the warmth of the Texas sun on their backs. When they attended church, they would have felt a part of a community that, together, supported the men and their path to healing. Will I ever have a sense of community and truly heal from war?

As I slow my speed to enter the town of Eden, Texas, I notice that there isn't a heavenly *anything* in this Garden of Eden. The only sign of life is behind the razor wire that spirals into view from the adult "Detention Center." It's privately owned and managed. It reminds me of the multitude of companies making billions of dollars off "Operation Freedom" in the Middle East, selling the idea that the private sector always does it better, cheaper, and more efficiently—*right?*

I feel sick looking at this place. It reminds me of a bunch of broiler chickens being raised for slaughter. No one *really wants to know* what is behind the door of the hen house: the conditions, the steroids, and forced feeding. We just want to see "All natural" chicken. Just like we don't really want to see the lost, unsupported souls branded as "criminals." And for that matter, nobody wants to see the innocent dead women and children killed in the Middle East reported as "collateral damage." No, we Americans love to publicize ourselves as *something to be, and something to see.* Just don't ask how we got there, or what's behind it! Don't demand transparency when the illusion is so sexy! We love illusion, and we are the world's chief manufacturer of it twenty-four-seven. You just can't see the smoke stacks.

I feel restless until my surroundings begin to change outside of San Angelo. I'm leaving the Hill Country for the drier, flatter, landscape characteristic of West Texas. Soon, the oil-field pump jacks dot the landscape, as do vast stretches of cotton fields, and this allows me to really open up the bike and make up some time.

Back in Austin, I bought an old 35mm Pentax camera at a garage sale. I haven't really used it, so I thought this trip might be a good time to initiate my renewed interest in art photography. I tried it out in high school, and loved it until Malcolm got stoned and pissed off at me for some bullshit, and threw my camera into the wall, and then stomped on the case until it resembled a cheese blintze. He yelled, "You stupid dipshit, you can't take pictures worth a fuck, I don't want you taking pictures of me and your mother, and you sure as hell will never be any kind of artist. Only faggots are artists anyway!"

San Angelo is where my mother first took us when we moved to Texas. She met Malcolm here before we moved to Marble Falls. Apparently, San Angelo is named after a Mexican nun, though it was a notoriously dangerous frontier town. It's easy to imagine Malcolm's ancestors—coarse frontier rednecks—holing up until they hear about a mining strike, go off to kill Indians, or join a territorial conflict. I imagine their rough burnt faces, unshaven with sweat soaking their half-broken bodies after fighting in the Civil War. Illiterate, and ambitious men expanding, by any means necessary, the American influence westward, as our new self-appointed ambassadors of a fledgling democracy. Ironically, that sounds like the current condition of Afghanistan.

Next stop: Big Spring. The actual spring that inspired the town's namesake is long dry, but once served as the watering hole for the Jumano, Apache, and Comanche tribes in the area. It was discovered by an U.S. Army captain, who mapped it as a campsite on a trail to California. By the 1870s buffalo hunters resided in the town, mostly in "hide huts" and saloons. Then, ranchers worked homesteads. The railroad brought more folks in the 1880s, and in 1920 came the big oil boom in West Texas that lasted until the 1950s.

The town's interesting history seems presently eclipsed by fast-food restaurant chains and convenience store gas stations. The obvious eroding economy makes me sad. I am too tired to really think about it. I'm only halfway to Ruidoso, New Mexico, where I plan to spend the night. If I go the speed limit, it will be dark when I arrive, and I still have to find a place to stay. The road is flat, with no cars in view. If I maintain my speed of 100 to 110, I might be able to get there before dark. The espresso kicks in and I decide to go for it.

Mikey's stories about the Hopi are on my mind, and I hear him telling me about how his people are corn farmers in the desert with only twelve inches of annual rainfall. So many of the Hopi tribe's spiritual practices are, in some way, related to praying for rain. Our cultural approach is to outsmart Mother Nature, try to manipulate her, and create our own destiny. The Hopi prefer to live in harmony with nature, offering absolute respect, and reverence for the earth, on her own terms. It seems to permeate many areas of modern life. How many women do I hear tell me about how her partner tries to manipulate her to get what he wants, and doesn't respect her needs, her body, or her happiness?

We strive to remove burden and toil, investing heavily in technology. At first glance, it all appears miraculous, but there are possible snags in the magic show. Everyone runs around like his or her fucking hair is on fire. What have we left behind? What have we forfeited to gain speed? Would you say that removing man from the farm has given him a deeper sense of purpose, connection, and reason for living? Have our urban city centers given us a deeper sense of connection and community with our fellow man? Have we not been further divided by the very thing we hope will bring us closer?

At the New Mexico state line, I see the continuation of pump jacks, uneven flat landscape with no trees, no road signs, no retail stores, and the occasional sand dune. I imagine the Spanish explorers marching across this arid, hot hell on the back of a horse in search of gold. Will it be as elusive for me as it was for Coronado's seven golden cities of Cibola?

On the outskirts of Roswell, New Mexico, I see pecan orchards and no alien spacecraft. Farther on in town, there are tourist shops with oversized little green men on rooftops, with storefronts beckoning alien believers and tourists. The old cinema on the strip has been converted into a UFO museum. Even though commerce is visible, there is little evidence of the urban evolution that I experienced in Austin: no chef-driven restaurants, no new modern architecture, and no visible signs of alternative fashion. The city feels dependent economically *on the idea* that an event occurred in 1947, an alien crash, with enough evidence to give it meaning, life, and vitality. I wonder if it is metaphoric for our entire national identity. The idea of democracy: if enough people believe we are, it might be true.

Heading on to Ruidoso, the landscape changes to gentle curves and rolling hills with golden grass. A mountain range in the distance inspires a shift within myself from anxious to calm. I feel as if I am in a new place, one filled with spiritual possibility and peace. I feel Krissy with her arms around me. I feel our kiss. I have kissed many women, but I have never felt like I did in her arms.

I'm on a magical stretch of highway, with beautiful curvaceous hills enveloping me on either side. In forty-five minutes, I've climbed to 6,900 feet above sea level, and the temperature drops by twenty degrees. The cold mountain air tries to penetrate my jacket. The hillsides are filled with tall pine trees and snow

covers the highest elevations, with some hills barren from recent
fires. The excitement of ending my nine-hour ride for the day is
mounting. The sunlight is vanishing rapidly. As I reach town it
begins to snow. There are small inns and shops on both sides of
the road. One seems perfect: the Sitzmark Chalet Inn. The old
hotel has split timbers as siding and evergreen paint trim, giving
the quaint quarters a feeling of a snowy hillside in Switzerland.
A neon OPEN sign is slightly obscured by a huge wooden carving of a bearded mountain man, holding what appears to be a
pet raccoon. The place seems just the right amount of comfy.

I decide to first ride deeper into town to look around. There
are shops selling pottery, Native American jewelry, t-shirts,
pistachios, leather goods, dress shops, and green chile cheeseburgers. A bar entitled WIN, PLACE, AND SHOW catches my eye,
and it looks like a great place to have a drink. I can now see the
big snow-capped mountaintop the locals call the Sierra Blanca.

I'm charmed by how inviting the little town is, and I decide
to go back and settle into my hotel room, take a hot shower,
and have an early dinner. One thing the Army taught me is
to appreciate everything: good food, toilets, hot showers, and
especially a soft bed. This is the first time since I can remember
that I feel good, relaxed, and capable of sleeping the entire night
without nightmares, or my crazy roommates waking me up from
partying too loud. The mountain beckons me to be calm, and I
accept the embrace.

At a New Mexican-Mexican restaurant, Casa Blanca, I have
fried green chile strips and green chile enchiladas with a couple
of strong margaritas on the rocks. I have my second wind after
dinner and decide to check out a bar behind a gas station called
the Gas Lounge.

When I walk into the bar, there is only one old dude sitting
at the bar, half-slumped over, drinking whiskey. It looks kind
of like a mid-priced hotel bar. I sit against the wall in the back.

After a few minutes, I hear the bartender yell, "Francine, honey, you have a guest!" Then I hear a Texas twang: "Be right there, Angie."

Francine, an attractive woman in her early thirties with blonde hair, bright red lipstick, and freckles, nudges her way through the crowded floor of empty chairs and tables, and gives me a friendly, "Hey, honey, how are ya tonight?" I am alarmed by Francine's black eye, and it's obvious that she didn't get it from tripping in the storage room. After taking my motorcycle helmet off, I re-arranged my wild, wavy hair into a Japanese *samurai* topknot to get it out of my way.

"Well, Francine, I'm happy to be here, after riding nine hours on a motorcycle!"

"Lord have mercy, darling. Where d'ya ride from?"

"Austin, Texas!"

"I'll be damned, my sister lives in Austin. I'm from Abilene!"

"No shit?"

"No shit!"

"I went to Abilene Christian College for three years."

"Well, it is a small world. Honey, you're so snuggly, you kind of remind me of the mascot, Willie the Wildcat!"

"You have no idea!" I say, realizing that I might actually have some fun here.

"What can I bring you, honey—to drink?"

"I guess I'll have a strong margarita on the rocks with salt, you pick the tequila!"

"Coming up!"

Francine seems like a sweet woman that hasn't had anyone in her life be sweet to her. I feel like this is going to be a good experience and we'll have some fun chatting, I'll get home early, and finally get some very needed sleep. When she returns with my drink, she asks what brings me to Ruidoso. Since she has no other customers, I decide to tell her the real reason. After several minutes of emotional storytelling, she says, "Oh, honey, I'm so sorry about your friend." Before she can say anything else— unexpectedly—her eyes tear up, and she looks down. "I'm sorry, darling, I lost my husband in Iraq nine years ago. He was just nineteen years old, and my life has been pretty rough ever since."

"I understand. I'm sorry for your loss."

It's amazing to me how many husbands in small towns are affected by wars in our country, and how much pain and loss wives, girlfriends, lovers, and children have to endure. It's like cancer: no one thinks about it, or talks about it, until someone in their immediate family is dying of it! Before I can try to offer comfort, the front door of the bar swings open and I'm jarred by a screeching—*loud*—female voice, "Hey, howdy, Angie baby, it's Saturday night, it's snowing, and I'm ready to party!"

I hear Francine faintly say, "Oh shit, Kara is in one of her moods!"

Two huge cowboys, bookend lumberjack ranchers, flank the little brunette spitfire. The energy in the room changes from sleepy to uneasy. Francine says, "Excuse me, honey, I'll be back in a jiffy!"

Kara, the wildcat, en route to the ladies' room, loudly calls out orders for Angie the bartender to "Line um up, sweetie... Mama is *in the mood!*" One of the cowboys looks at me with a long hard stare, and it doesn't seem particularly friendly. I watch Francine pat him on the back, as if to reassure him that I was fine, and there's no problem. I hadn't really considered that I might appear odd to these folks. That my two arms, full of tattoos, my untrimmed beard, and my long hair in a topknot might not be the usual mountain-man fashion.

When Kara returns, she has a life-size Marlboro Man promotional cardboard cutout between her legs. She screams, "Come on, cowboy, ride!" Everyone in the bar is laughing, except me.

She makes a beeline toward my table. "That is one nice jacket you're wearing, honey cup. Can I try that on?"

"Sure!" I say, ready to enjoy the show.

I stand up and take off my black leather motorcycle jacket, which I love almost as much as my bike, and hand it to her. She puts the jacket on. "Thanks, *it's mine now!* If you want it, you'll have to come to Quarters later on and get it!" She turns to the giant twins and says, "Look boys, I have a new coat. Just like Dolly Parton. My very own coat of many colors!"

I assume she will return my coat after she has her fun, at my expense. But, watching her shoot about five tequila shots with her big-boy escorts, it is pretty clear that she actually thinks she truly will keep my expensive leather coat. Last thing I want is Mountain Princess puke on my coat, and I still have to ride hundreds of miles, with no place within one thousand miles to buy a new one.

After I finish another margarita, I ask Francine if she thinks Kara is serious about running off with my coat. She says, "Honey, she'd take your coat, hat, and wallet and leave you in the snow naked if she thought it would make her appear more *outrageous.*" Given the ugly stare from one of the guys earlier, I need to get my wits about me and get my coat, and get out of this place without a brawl. My road fatigue is finally hitting me after my fourth margarita.

I leave a hundred-dollar bill on the table and make my way to Kara to politely ask for my coat. Before I reach the table, the cowboy giving me the stink-eye kicks an empty chair at me and says, "Join us!" Kara adds, "Yeah, blue eyes, join us for a tequila shot!" The other guy smiles and doesn't say anything. Kara screams for Angie to get another round ready, and to bring one for her new friend. My gut is telling me that I need to go. Kara looks at me. "Miss Francine says you are going to visit Indians on some reservation, and you just got back from Afghanistan...

what the fuck do you want to visit those drunk bastards for? And, where, and why, were you in Afghanistan anyway?" She points her little fingers in my face.

The guy giving me the stink-eye blurts out, "To kill those fucking raghead terrorists that murdered three thousand Americans on 9/11... that's why!"

I know better than to open my drunken mouth, but I do.

"Man, that's not why we are in Afghanistan." There's a lot of energy behind my voice. "And just as you *don't know shit about the Native American culture,* you don't know *shit about the United States of America's policies on war,* or why we are spending trillions of dollars there, instead of educating village rednecks like you."

"Oh, really, Einstein? We're there because those Afghan guys love to protect terrorists like Osama bin Laden. Man, our own *nigger president* is related to that guy. You know that dude is a Muslim? Wasn't even born in this country? That's why he doesn't go over there and take care of this shit like he should!"

"You stupid fucking racist. That has nothing to do with our national policy, and furthermore, our president has more intelligence in his little toe than you do in the entire sum of your body."

"You think I'm going to take that from a fucking hippie-faggot communist?"

He stands and starts walking around the table. Before I could stand up all the way, he swings a left hook at my stomach, which I block. I jab-cross-left upper cut-cross and knock him back onto an empty table. I walk over to hit him again, but Kara jumps on my back and starts slapping me on the side of the head. Her little hands don't hurt, but her jewelry does, so I shake her off my back by throwing my shoulders forward quickly. She curses and screams as she falls forward onto the bar floor. Just as I turn around, the other guy hits me squarely on the jaw and knocks me to the ground.

I look up and Francine is slapping the shit out of Kara, and Angie the bartender is screaming from behind the bar at the cowboy who hit me. I stand and swing my helmet into the guy's stomach so hard that he doubles over and struggles to breathe. I pull Kara off Francine, and take my coat off her body. Angie comes around the bar with a twelve-gauge shotgun and pumps the shell into the chamber. "If you idiots want to throw any more punches, you best go outside, or you will be picking your bloody heads up off the floor. I want Kara, Billy and Ned to leave—*now!*

Kara is still screaming obscenities at Francine. She announces: "Bitch, this is not over." The cowboys give me hateful glares. The first guy that hit me says, "I bet you're one of those freaks that cut people's fingers off and makes a necklace out of um for a souvenir."

"No, I'm one of those soldiers that stood beside my brothers in my battle, held my best buddy as he was struggling for life, and lost him, because I thought I was protecting the freedom and lives of illiterate redneck assholes like you to make the world a better and safer place…"

"I don't need a *faggot like you* to protect me."

Again, I meet the divide. I realize at this moment, that I want to kill the guy. I truly want to hurt him. Underlying that is a profound sadness for the loss of Mikey, Tacos, and the other guys that didn't make it back, and sweet Shahzada. I suddenly see her standing on the bar. She says, *Dylan, there has been enough violence on this planet to last until the end of time… let it go, let it go!*

•   •   •

Francine follows me to my hotel in her truck. She says she's afraid that Kara and the boys might follow me, and it could be dangerous. She informs me that her brother is on the *Ruidoso*

*Police Department,* as if that fact will protect me. I'm so tired. My jaw feels like Muhammad Ali hit me in the face repeatedly for fifteen rounds. She follows me into the room and says she will stay over and protect me. We fool around a little, but I'm just not in the mood for sex, and I'm a bit freaked out that I keep thinking about Krissy, as I'm holding Francine. She says she is comfortable to just hold one another, and within a few minutes she is asleep in my arms, naked, and snoring like an Afghan mountain yak.

In spite of the fatigue settling my bones, sleep is impossible. My mind replays the bar brawl with the cowboys, over, and over. I indict myself for starting the fight. Why didn't I handle it better? Why didn't I just let that redneck blab on, and use the opportunity to educate him? Why did he *get to me?* After what feels like hours of restless turmoil, Shahzada appears next to me. She starts whispering softly in my ear, but this time it doesn't terrify me. I must be deeply asleep, but I think I'm awake. She says,

> *Dylan, you really must stop harming yourself — nothing good will come of it! You are just angry because that terrible man reminded you of Malcolm… and, you are feeling guilty for sleeping with a man, and finding him attractive… and the cowboy called you a faggot… just like Malcolm did when you were a boy. You are clearly not a bundle of sticks! You are a man in every way, in the truest sense. You don't really believe that killing other men and fornicating hordes of women makes you a man? Or, making lots of money and having expensive things contributes, or adds value to your character? Surely, you are not that misguided! Do you know how to find your true strength? Do you know how to live in real and lasting peace?*
>
> *For now — rest — my friend… the best part of your journey awaits you…*

Francine tries to wake me up quietly by caressing my arms and kissing me lightly on my chest and neck. I act as if I'm still asleep, because I don't want to wake up and have the sweetness stop. She slowly moves her hand over my stomach, up and down my thigh. I stir slightly, and she rests her hand on my cock and whispers, "Somebody is waking up!" I begin to laugh, realizing how childish I'm acting, pretending to be asleep. We both say "Good morning" to one another, smiling into one another's eyes, and she gently moves on top of me, and begins to kiss me beautifully. Our breathing deepens and I am surprised by how connected I feel to her.

In the morning light, I can see how beautiful her eyes sparkle. I slowly kiss her breasts and hold her close to me. I love the way she whispers into my ear. As she pushes against my thigh, I am getting lost in the moment. I roll her over onto her side, kissing her neck, moving my hips slowly against her, teasing her. We are both oblivious to the outside world, and I'm falling deeper into the dream, until the sound of a loud *bang* on the door, followed by an older women's husky voice: "Housekeeping!"

This was not meant to be for us this morning. So Francine takes me to a cool little place to eat breakfast. I love the excellent *huevos rancheros* and Francine seems to be enjoying her eggs, bacon, and homemade biscuits with grape jelly. I ask her about the Apache Indians. She shrugs. "Well, I really don't see um around town, except the guys who buy booze at the pharmacy, and then go around back and get stinking drunk. If you go to the Inn of the Mountain Gods casino or Ski Apache, you can see some… they own it, but they pretty much keep to themselves. Folks around here say they are rude."

I ask Francine about her husband. His story is familiar to me, like so many guys I served with in the Middle East. A young man, who wants to make a difference, get the bad guy, protect his loved ones, and defend democracy.

I begin to feel anxious, and I need to get on the road. She encourages me to stay a little longer and even sweetly whispers that we could enjoy finishing our interrupted pleasures from this morning at her place. It sounds great, but I have to ride about seven hours today to get to the Hopi Reservation before sunset. We exchange information and she encourages me to stop back on my way home. She gives me a sweet kiss farewell, and the grape jelly she ate on her biscuits lingers in my mouth.

As I climb toward the Sierra Blanca ski area, it occurs to me that I haven't seen a single Native American. I see stores filled with their cultural footprint, Native American jewelry, art, pottery, golf courses with names like "Kokopelli", but no sign of indigenous people. I see on the map that the Mescalero Apache have a huge reservation that borders the city of Ruidoso, some 463,000 acres. They own a really nice casino and ski resort, yet, outside of their interests, they are nowhere in sight. I find that sad and strange.

I make a ton of stops for coffee. I decide to try to make it to Winslow, Arizona, and spend the night. I'm even more exhausted. The landscape begins to change as I head north to Socorro, New Mexico: beautiful rolling hills with few trees in sight. I imagine the exhausted conquistadores in 1598, led by Juan de Oñate, having come through the desert south, Jornada del Muerto, reaching Socorro hungry and tired in search of riches. The local pueblo Indians, the Piro, offered them food and water. I'm sure they felt ordained by God and the royal crown, rationalizing their claims as bringing civilization to the lives of "Godless savages."

Even though the beauty around me is offering a calmer environment than I have ever experienced, I know that I can't continue to live at this level of anxiety. I hear Dr. Trimble's voice: *Dylan, it's a good idea to look at the events of your childhood and identify what hurt Little Dylan, but then you have to let that go. Accept that this is not who you are, that they are simply events that happened.*

Should I do the same with my experience in the Middle East? Should Americans do the same as a nation about 9|11? Slavery? Women's rights? Gay rights? Human rights? Do we all need to simply acknowledge the pain of the past and "let it go?" It always makes me feel like I'm naked, facing a wall, powerless, and without the ability to change what I so dearly wish I could. I breathe deeply and pay attention to the ride. In the middle of nowhere I want to let myself feel: present to the sun, hills, and the enormous blue sky.

As I pass another tiny town, I begin to climb to a higher elevation into the mountains. It's snowing and, while it is beautiful, I'm having a hard time feeling safe on the bike. I try to slow down. Somehow this is making me really anxious and frustrated about time. I want to go faster. As I reach the elevation, the roads are completely covered with snow and I am rolling through several inches of powder.

When I reach an unexpected sharp curve, an enormous bull elk is standing in the middle of the road. I don't see him at first, and by the time I make eye contact, I have to turn sharply to avoid hitting this magnificent beast. I hit a patch of frozen ice, slide in slow motion into an embankment of snow, and fly off the bike. After I land, realize I am alive and that it's a miracle.

As I lay crumpled in the snow on my back, I began to breathe deeply. I surrender to the moment. At first, I'm laughing in disbelief. I begin thinking of my friends learning about my unexpected death: *"How did he die? Was it in the war, Afghanistan? Drug overdose? Driving drunk?"* No, he died avoiding hitting a big ass moose! Then, the laughter changes to waves of tears, and more tears. It's as if the earth is my mother and I am a wounded child in need of comfort, safe to cry in her arms. Images of Mikey, the Sarge, Krissy, Francine, war, Shahzada, my family all cross my mind. So much love, there is so much love in me. I am so blessed. I don't know how to hold it in, what to do with it, or how to express it. More tears. Why am I so fucked up? A truck pulls up next to me. After a moment, I hear, "You okay?"

I lift my head slightly, with the helmet shield still closed, so they couldn't see my tears, and with the sun's glare I can't see who is asking. "Yeah, thank you, I'm just making snow angels!"

"Mind if I join you?" asks a lovely, yet strong female voice.

"Not at all!" I say, wondering who the hell is inquiring.

Towering over me, an attractive, fit, blonde woman with a tan face, and vise grips for hands, pulls me up to my feet.

"Wow, you really scared me when I came around that curve. I thought you were dead!"

"No, I am very much alive!"

"Where you from?"

"Austin, Texas... you?"

"Stockholm, Sweden, by way of India, Paris, Seattle, Taos, and presently, Datil."

"Wow, where is that?"

"You are lying on it!"

"No shit?"

"Would you like to come to my studio and have lunch, and get out of those cold wet clothes?"

"That would be fantastic, thank you so much. I will follow you, if my bike starts."

Fortunately, my bike is not mechanically damaged from the fall, and starts with no problem. We continue up the mountain and, once we reach the summit, she turns down a goat trail a short distance, to an extraordinary hillside adobe compound with sweeping views.

Upon entering the gates, I am shocked to see a courtyard full of blown glass shapes everywhere: hundreds, if not thousands of colorful, large pieces of stained glass. It is so unexpected. I am deeply intrigued.

When I get off my bike, I say, "Please excuse me. I didn't introduce myself back at the scene of the accident. I'm Dylan Griffith. Thank you so much for inviting me here. This place is amazing."

"Oh, it's my pleasure," she says. "My name is Sigrid, but my friends call me Sigi."

"Did you have something to do with all this stained glass work?"

"Yes. I am, among other things, a glassblower."

Her "social space," as she calls it, in the main house, is filled with rustic wood furniture, Saltillo tile floors, with large windows spilling into her breathtaking view. There are many Native American vessels, and one wall is filled with Kachina dolls, some standing and many hanging on the wall.

I get an overwhelming feeling that Sigi has been guided by Mikey to look after me and get me safely to Hopi, Second Mesa. As I look at the Kachinas, I find one representing an eagle, and I remember Mikey, back in Afghanistan saying, "Books, you are the eagle who brings our prayers to God."

Sigi is moving around the kitchen and says, "Are you OK?"

"Yes! I am just emotional today." I don't really want to talk about it.

"There is much more at play." Sigi says, lovingly.

She brings me a glass of water and puts it on the table beside us, and faces me, quietly looking into my eyes, and without a word reaches to hold both of my hands.

My eyes fill with tears, and so do hers.

"You don't have to tell me, Dylan. I can feel your pain. You are safe here," she whispers softly.

"I can see you have been hurt, and that you can't easily trust. I feel the injured child. The wounded warrior. I sense the need to heal ancient pain. You are safe here."

I have an overwhelming desire to see Krissy. I'm surprised that my heart leads me to Krissy in the company of this beautiful, exotic woman, but it is clear that Sigi is on a path of spiritual renewal, and has no interest in confusing why we are together. I realize that Krissy and I are supposed to be in one another's life. I know it sounds crazy, but this feeling is so strong.

Sigi puts her hands over my forehead, and begins to whisper something. At first, I think it is prayers in Swedish. Eventually I recognize that she's speaking in Hopi, just as Mikey did on the chopper when he and I first met.

Sigi gets a bundle of dried sage wrapped in purple thread and lights it. She continues praying and uses an eagle feather to wash the smoke over my body as she prays.

Her prayers stop and we both remain quiet. I realize that this is the most beautiful silence I have ever experienced.

Sigi quietly leaves me alone. I can hear her in the kitchen, but there is no sense that I'm supposed to follow. After some time, she returns with a beautiful salad on a handmade pottery plate. It has chicken that tastes like turkey, the day after Thanksgiving. I smile and say, "Wow!"

She smiles and continues to look at me. I am slightly uncomfortable and try to entertain her with witty banter. After a moment, she says, "You don't have to do that here, Dylan.

"In Sweden, I had a very happy childhood, until my father died when I was four and my mother went into a deep depression, and no longer was available for me and my sister. I felt empty and alone. I escaped in art. When I graduated from university, I went to India for a spiritual journey. I met a dashing young French journalist and moved to Paris. There I became fascinated with glassmaking, until one day I was walking down the street and was dragged into an empty hallway and raped by three Algerian guys. I felt so much hatred and pain, I had to leave the city I loved most, and I came to Seattle to study glassblowing with Dale Chihuly. That man saved my life."

"How so?" I ask.

"With sand and fire! Did you know that glass comes from sand and fire?"

"No," I say.

"For me, it was perfect. I could take my hate for those guys from the 'sand,' add my 'fire' and blow all of me into creating something beautiful from my pain. It was the perfect philosophical balance of artistic expression. Chihuly taught me how to use my feelings to create something bigger than myself, how to make those expressions more universal, and that is the project I am working on now."

I interrupt her to say, "Wow, that reminds me of a verse in the Bible from Genesis 3:19: 'For dust thou art, and unto dust shalt thou return.' What's your project about?"

Sigi stands up and walks over to the window and looks out as if she can see the entire world in front of her and continues talking. "My friend took me to visit many sacred sites. We visited the Hopi reservation and my life changed forever. I spent more and more time with the people. I learned about the Hopi way and the Katsinas. I realized that, literally from the sand, these precious people developed a highly sophisticated, spiritual identity that has kept them going for fourteen thousand years. I want to pay homage to these amazing people for the many gifts they share with the world. I am researching the more than three hundred Kachina spirits with the elders, and deconstructing those visual elements with my glass forms. When I am finished, I will create an installation at *Homolovi*, on sacred Hopi lands, to honor their ancestors. Can you imagine, three hundred glass Kachinas dancing on the landscape?"

"That is amazing, and so is this salad! Thank you so much. How did you come to New Mexico?"

Sigi walks back to the table and slips slowly into her chair. "I met a very cool artist who was visiting Seattle, living in Taos, and he invited me to come stay with him. He was a very spiritual guy, and very generous. When I got to Taos, something very special happened for me. All of my concerns about the pain of my childhood, my distrust of men, and all of that shit from my past just went away. I began to appreciate quiet. I learned how to be quiet. How to lean into what I was placed on this earth to do—love and create. After our friendship ended, I needed a quiet place to work, heal, and find my compass."

I feel that for her, the infinite reasons that we harvest pain, the specific details of who said what, or this or that happened, are all irrelevant garbage that keep one from being in one's true, and best state, of love and peace. After I finish my salad, she sweetly asks if I would enjoy looking at her glass Kachina project.

We walk slowly and quietly through her Kachina garden, as she calls it. The pieces are spectacular. She explains the process and selects key pieces to illuminate the unique spiritual meaning of the work, and to point out certain artistic features. She finally selects a beautiful golden pot, with sensual curves and an etching that gives the appearance of feathers.

"I want you to have this one, Dylan. This is to remind you that you have been selected to soar. You are a representative of the people to carry their prayers to God—you are the eagle."

My brief time with Sigi is intoxicating. I'm not sure I know how to think about it. More puzzling is the depth of my feelings, coupled with a sense of a deep transformation beginning to happen. It's something I can't quite describe yet. My instincts are simply to breathe, and carry on.

Sigi walks me to my bike, gives me a farewell hug and says, "Remember friend, as the Hopi say, 'Take a breath of the new dawn and make it a part of you.'"

I smile warmly, and answer, "I'll need to start waking up earlier!"

Sigi smiles, and I feel sad I'm leaving her company so soon.

• • •

By the time I get to Quemado, New Mexico, the bike is running on fumes. I've never been happier to see a gas station. I drink a couple of cups of hot coffee, and I begin to feel much better. But I'm still sore from the fall on my bike, so I buy extra-strength aspirin and hit the road.

The scenery, when I head north to St. Johns, Arizona, on Highway 191, changes to rolling hills with bushy green-mounded vegetation. Soon I reach the Petrified Forest National Park. The landscape is filled with beautiful petrified trees and a "painted desert" floor with reds, purple, gold, and white powdery hilltops.

When I get to Holbrook, I'm kind of sickened by the contrast from the recent lovely natural landscapes to the 1950s-kitsch: huge plastic replicas of dinosaurs in front of a rock shop, a Wigwam Motel, and a huge sign in the shape of a Katsina doll announcing the Pow Wow Trading Post. I was finding it hard to get my "kicks" on Route 66.

When I finally arrive at Winslow, or *Homolovi* — "Place of the little hills," the traditional name given by the Hopi — my body is stiff as a dead cat. The last 1,100 miles of bad coffee, green-chile cheeseburgers, booze, intense personalities, the freezing snow and wind, and dumping my bike, have all contributed to my fatigue. Not to mention getting hit by a grasshopper at 100 mph, which by the way, hurts like a motherfucker!

All I can think about is getting off this bike, finding a room, a meal, and a nice strong drink. I end up at the Delta Motel on the old Route 66. The young dude behind the counter takes one look at me and insists I should have his best room, the "Beatles Room" for $39 a night. He seems so starved for stimulation and customers that he's hyper-hump-your-leg enthusiastic.

"So, what brings you on the Mother Road?" he asks.

"The what?"

"Mother Road is what they called Route 66 back in the day. Because it's said that people travel on this route to 'find themselves.'"

"Well, I'm here to visit a buddy's family. By the way, how far is the Hopi Reservation Second Mesa from here?"

"The Hopi Reservation? Oh, that's only about an hour north of us. Just go back into town, and on the farthest outskirts of town, take Highway 87 North and you will run into it."

After a long hot shower, I lie down for a thirty-minute power nap. But when I wake up, everything is pitch black. The sound of the mini-fridge and an occasional truck on the highway is all I can hear. It feels eerily cold and lonely. I turn on the light beside my bed, and the yellow walls and psychedelic posters jump out at me as if I've woken up in a teenage girl's bedroom in the 1970s. I have to get out of this room fast. I brush my teeth, throw my hair in a ponytail, grab my jacket and head out.

I've been pretty frugal with money my entire life. The idea of "splurging" for me as a kid meant that I bought myself a Snickers bar instead of giving it to Daniel, or Gabby. But tonight I am going to splurge and go to the *La Posada Hotel* and dine in the Turquoise Room. Thinking of Gabby brought on an unexpected wave of concern about her. She is such a basket case because of Malcolm's abuse and now she's mixed up with a drug dealer. She's like a drowning person who wants to latch onto the first guy who can pull her out of the water. *When I get home, I am going to sort this shit out. I'm not going to let this Raven guy fuck up her life.*

The La Posada is lit up with landscape lighting. I walk through a lovely patio and garden. Entering the front door, to my right is a bookstore and to my left is the front desk and "trading post" filled with Native American jewelry, Hopi Kachinas, pottery, and other gift items. I've never been in a place with so many Native American art objects. It's so beautiful. Mikey always talked about how poor the Hopi are, yet the Hopi art is so rich.

I consider how so many things of beauty in human history have been born from the hands of the poor for the enjoyment of the rich: the blood diamonds of Africa, the sapphires of Sri Lanka, the Renaissance paintings of the masters, concertos and operas, and countless paintings, poems, and prayers.

After dinner, I ask my waiter for a nightlife recommendation. At "P.T.'s it's packed!" I decide to get a beer and play some pool. A group of local guys are cool about letting me in on a game and there are some cute girls walking around, but I stay focused on the game. Soon, a hot chick bumps into me and says, "Sorry, sweetheart, I am all boots and boobs tonight!" I quickly fire back, holding my cue stick up high: "Well, that's funny, because I seem to be all stick and balls." She laughs so hard she drops her drink. Of course, I buy her a new one, and we start joking around. She might be up for romance but she's *really* drunk.

When the bar closes, the group of guys I'm playing pool with invite me and the cute drunk girl, and some other girls over to their house for an "after-party bonfire." The cute drunk girl, Rachel, rides with me on the back of my bike to show me how to get to where the guys live. Needless to say, her legs squeezing against my butt, and her hands finding their way around my chest, stomach, and thighs, was a hell of a lot more interesting than the usual cargo on the back of my bike. Unexpectedly, it makes me think of Krissy.

The weather is super cold, but beautiful, and I can see thousands of stars overhead. They build a huge bonfire, and we all stand around and drink whiskey. Rachel goes to the bathroom, and another girl, Angel, walks straight up to me. "Why don't you show me where you are sleeping tonight?"

I just smile. "OK, but do you like the Beatles?"

She responds with, "Who's that?" and drags me away from the party.

The next morning, I feel like my bike has run over my head several times. Angel is gone. I'm not sure where she went and I see no note. My stuff is all still there. When I go to the bathroom, I see a note in red lipstick written on the small mirror. FUN. THNX—ANGEL.

Next to the "A" she drew big, exaggerated angel wings.

The Delta Motel, for all of its personality and charm, doesn't have a restaurant. I begin to feel worse. Just how *bad* I feel, is confirmed moments later when I appropriately empty the contents from last night's "Wild Platter" from the La Posada. I suppose combining tequila, mescal, wine, beer, and whiskey is not a good idea when you are already dehydrated, exhausted, and road-weary. All I can do is to lie down, drink water, and throw up. Repeat.

By the time I wake up, the sun is setting. I sure as hell can't ride out to the Hopi Reservation at night. For one thing, I don't know where I'm going, or where Mikey's family lives. Further, I don't know if non-natives are even allowed after dark, or if it is even safe. My head is still pounding, I have a slight fever, and I keep throwing up water. I have to eat something. I'm afraid to ride my bike for fear that I will pass out and crash. I walk down Route 66 and try and find a convenience store. Through the grace of God, there was a store within a three-minute walk, the Good 2 Go. Surely that is a good omen.

All I can find is two brown bananas, a package of salted almond nuts, and Pringles potato chips, which I bought in honor of "The Ripper," my Lieutenant back in Afghanistan. I bought all six bottles of lemon-lime flavored Gatorade they had in the cooler, another aspirin and some Pepto-Bismol. I am beginning to feel dizzy walking back to the motel, and I keep telling myself: *You can't die in fucking Winslow, Arizona. It's not where I want to go, even if it is mentioned in an Eagles song.* I force myself to inform the front desk dude that I am staying another night, which seems to delight him. After I eat half a banana, a handful of almonds, and a pinch of Pringles, I puke, and experience the horrible other. I throw myself on the bed for another rough-and-tumble night in the Delta Motel.

# Sipapu: Place of Emergence

I NEED TO CHECK OUT. I'm feeling slightly more alive, but still weak from getting up every few hours to vomit. Around six AM, I realize that I'm not going to die in the Delta Motel. I take a shower and head off to the reservation.

As I pass a couple of Indian trading posts on the way, I don't know why, but I start feeling nervous. I've traveled a very long way and I'm not at all sure if this is a good idea. *Maybe I should turn around and go back to Austin.* Something much higher in me is saying things like, *Stand up, man! Honor your brother, Mikey. You have to look his wife in the eyes and tell her how brave he was in action. You have to let her know how much he loved her, and his daughter. How proud he was to be a Hopi and how much he loved his grandfather.*

The landscape is beautiful as I head north on Highway 87: flat grassland as far as the eye can see. I soon pass the road to the *Homolovi* ruins, the ancient dwelling place of the Hopi, where Sigi said she would install her art to honor the Hopi. The Hopi people petitioned the state not to use the word "ruins" because for them the spirits of their ancestors are still alive. The park has more than three hundred archaeological sites that the Hopi refer to as *Hisat'sinom,* the "long-ago people." Most people today use the Navajo name given to them, the *Anasazi,* which means "enemies of our ancestors." Sadly, this sacred Hopi site is no longer on Hopi reservation land.

I continue across this radiantly gold and gray landscape and I realize that I am finally nearing the homeland soil of Mikey. I'm

filled with a deep feeling of respect. As I race to cross the Navajo
reservation imprisoning the Hopi, my heartbeat is faster and it
becomes difficult to concentrate. Soon I see the mesas faintly
rising in the offing like majestic monuments. This is precisely
where I was in my dream about Mikey back in Afghanistan.

Soon I reach the Hopi Cultural Center, a simple yet handsome
red-brown stucco, pueblo-style two-story structure. Once inside, I
check in with the shy girl at the front desk, and ask where the bar
is in the hotel. The girl behind the counter looks at me strangely
and says, "Drinking is not allowed here." Then I ask her if she
knows how I can find the home of Michael Sakiestewa. She looks
surprised and speaks over my shoulder in Hopi to a man in the
waiting area. The only word I understand is *Mikey*.

The man stands up. "You are looking for Mikey's house?"

"Yes, sir!"

"Why?"

"We served in the same squad in the army in Afghanistan,
and I'd like to pay my respect to his family."

"Why?"

I began to get frustrated by this guy's curt attitude. I tried to
respectfully answer. "Because he didn't make it back."

"Yes, I know that."

"Well, sir, I was there when he was shot on our FOB. I'm the
guy who held him and tried to save his life, and my sergeant
just told me a few days ago that he didn't make it back..." Tears
fill my eyes.

"Well, buddy, your sarge is right. My name is Gary
Tawaqueptewa and I'm his cousin, and also a member of the
Sun Forehead Clan, and Mikey and I grew up together—best
friends!"

"I'm sorry, I don't mean to be rude, but it's really important
for me to speak to his family. Do you know Mary Sakiestewa
and her daughter, Ruby?"

"Yes, she lives on Second Mesa, in Shongopovi Village."

"I think my friend's family lives in Oraibi. His grandfather was named Wilson, Jr."

The Hopi man laughs.

"Wilson, Jr. is my uncle and he is alive. His father, the Chief of Oraibi, was my father's brother. Our culture is matrilineal. When a man marries, he goes to live with the wife's family in their village. If she throws him out, he has nothing but the clothes on his back. Mikey grew up in Old Oraibi, but his wife's clan lives in Second Mesa. It's all pretty complicated if you don't grow up in our culture. Anyway, I can take you to see Mary. I don't think it is a good idea for you to be going around the villages without anyone knowing you."

"Wow, Gary, I really appreciate you helping me."

Gary says something to the girl behind the desk in Hopi, and they laugh and look at one another with that look of *Oh boy, this is going to be good!* I experienced that look many times in Afghanistan. The Afghan guys talking to one another, and then laughing.

I really didn't know what to expect. Do the Hopi live in teepees? Do they still wear traditional clothing around the house? Do they eat Big Macs? Gary and I got into his beat-up old truck and he apologizes for the window that won't roll up all the way. It is cold on the mesa and the wind is blowing about 40 mph from the southeast. As we leave the cultural center, a sign painted in fanciful script announces: SEXUAL ASSAULT IS RAPE.

This sign says it all: these people are dealing with the same shit that everyone across the country is dealing with. Mikey used to say that whatever hits the white folks, hits the Hopi ten times harder. He told me that the suicide rate is five times higher and the unemployment rate is 65 percent. I remember Mikey and Dope talking about this back in Afghanistan. The poverty is more evident as we slowly drive toward the Shongopovi Village. I see trailer homes parked in golden fields on the mesa, littered with black car tires on the roof. Gary says that's to keep the roofs on when the wind gusts up to 100 mph. I notice a couple of mustard colored temporary buildings, the "G shacks" that Mikey told me about. The vistas are breathtaking, but the homesteads are sad expressions of poverty.

Gary asks with great interest about my military service, and how I've been feeling. Normally, I would say, "Great!" but I can tell the question is from a deeper place. I give him the short answer: "Well, I've had some ups and downs..." He just smiles and looks at me with a look that implies, *Yeah, right, buddy!*

"Well, Dylan," Gary says, "I spent six years in the Marine Corps. Yes, sir, I was running around in the bushes in San Salvador. You see, we weren't supposed to be there, but we had to help out the twelve families that own the country get the 'bad guys' to calm down. One day we were out on patrol..."

Gary pauses. I can feel the depth of his pain, an ancient pain that he usually keeps buried.

"So we are in the jungle and doing intel on a small village, looking for rebels. The sweetest young girl comes into view. She's singing and skipping barefoot. I remember thinking: *my God, she looks like my little girl, Laura.* I had to stay hidden and watch her get her legs blown off by an IED. You've never heard more horrifying screams and crying in your life... I had to watch her bleed-out. There was nothing I could do. We weren't supposed to be there."

I couldn't hold back my tears as he spoke, remembering little Shazada. I wanted to protect her, and have more time to laugh, and get to know one another. This gives me a sense of *urgency* to help my sister when I get home. Gary continues:

"Man, I think I was born angry. When I came home I did so many drugs, drank myself half to death, and tried to wrestle with every fine chick this side of the Rio Grande. I put a pistol in my mouth six times. The elders said, 'Someone had to do it… someone had to protect our people!' That's why the Sun Forehead Clan was accepted into the tribe by the Hopi after the Spanish left. We are the warriors for our tribe. We protect the people. Every culture has to have warriors. We aren't crawling around the fucking bushes and riding around in the desert to protect the 'politics,' we are there to protect our people. The tough thing is when the politics no longer serve the needs of the people, or the tribe, just the few trying to profiteer. There can be no good in this."

As we approach Mary's village on Second Mesa, my heart beats faster. I'm worried about what to say to her and Ruby. I'm frozen in fear. Gary can sense my mood change. "Don't worry, Mikey's old lady is really cool. She would have to be to put up with his shit!" He laughs. "Mikey was a wild fucking Indian… he and I used to run, ride, and terrorize these parts. He loved to catch the Navajo trying to fuck up our ancient petroglyphs at *Taawaki,* or what they call Dawa Park today. That boy could fight!"

We pull up to the village and park just outside on a bumpy dirt patch overlooking the landscape. The architecture is a mix of old stacked stone, stucco, new construction, in two stories, with wooden ladders going to the roofs, built around a common courtyard where religious ceremonies and dances are performed. There are no people in sight, just a scruffy-looking dog sniffing a corncob in the plaza. Mary's family's home is in the middle of the plaza.

Gary smiles. "This is Park Avenue shit, Bro!" He knocks on the door loudly. In moments an adorable young girl with enormous brown eyes answers and screams, "Mom, it's Uncle Gary!" She runs and throws herself into his arms. "Did you bring me anything?" Gary laughs. "Yes, I brought you this *Kachada* Kachina doll, a very good friend of your daddy's. This is Dylan. He and your Dad were in the Army together in Afghanistan!"

She looks at me shyly, smiles sweetly, and throws her head into Gary's neck to hide her face.

I see Kachina dolls hanging from one of the beams. I can recognize that they are Mikey's work. The furnishings are simple. You can feel the poverty, but you can also feel the love in the air.

Gary speaks in Hopi for some time, which at one point causes Ruby to burst out laughing. Moments later, Mary appears. Gary introduces me. "Mary, this is Dylan. This is Mikey's friend from Afghanistan."

Mary starts crying, and comes over to hug me gently.

"He told me about you, Dylan. He said you were 'Jahu,' the true white brother. That is something really big for Mikey to say!"

Gary speaks again in Hopi, and then I hear the word 'Oraibi,' and I am interested in what is being said. Mary looks serious for a moment, and says, "Okay!"

Gary turns to me. "Well, Chief, I have some business. You stay and have a visit with Mary and Ruby, and I will come pick you up in a while."

I'm nervous. I don't know about Hopi customs, and I don't want to do something upsetting, so I just start talking. "I am so happy to have found you. It is a miracle that Gary was sitting in the lobby of the Cultural Center. Where is Oraibi?"

"It's on the Third Mesa," Ruby says enthusiastically.

"That is where Mikey's grandfather lives," Mary says, sweetly.

"So, he is still alive?"

"Yes, very much so." Mary says, laughing.

"I would love to meet him!"

"You will, after Gary returns."

"Today?"

"Yes, they are preparing for the Soystangwu Ceremony."

I don't know what that means, but Mikey told me that the Hopi have ceremonies every month and that all of them have deep spiritual significance.

"After the Winter Solstice, the Katsinam, or Kachinas as you say, will return to our villages."

Mary smiles because she realizes how complicated the names and rituals are to someone outside of the Hopi nation. She excuses herself to make hot tea, and she informs me that she has part of a letter from Mikey that she wants to read to me. She invites me to sit.

Ruby is running around the room, speaking in Hopi and dancing. She is doing some kind of ceremonial dance. She is adorable. After a couple of minutes, she stops and sits on the couch and stares at me. Finally, she asks, "Can you dance?"

"Not really! I kind of look like SpongeBob when I move..."

This causes Ruby to burst out laughing. Then, she screams, *"Show me!"*

Before I really have time to question how well this will work, I just stand up and start dancing like I am—in my mind—a Native American, and singing, "Haya haya haya ha ha, hoya haya ha ha..." This causes Ruby to literally scream with laughter and, as I dance, her laughter is joined by Mary's laughter. When I stop, they both applaud.

"Well, I guess I have a lot to learn!"

Mary, still laughing, suggests that I should lead the village Soystangwu ceremony. She explains that it is the first Katsina to return after sleeping in the mountains for six months and the dancing isn't too lively!

I turn red in the face, and I'm happy to sip the delicious hot tea, with honey.

I feel like Mikey is with us. I'm feeling so guilty that I'm here sharing in laughter and love with his family, and he isn't. Mary says, "I would like to read you this now, from his letter..."

*"I have made a new friend in my squad. He is a strange Kachada... he seems to actually care about human beings and to be on a higher path. Now, he holds too much pain from the past. Sound familiar? I invited him to visit Oraibi. He's the kind of guy that will actually come. If I don't make it home, please take him in as a brother and introduce him to Grandpa if he is still with us. If Grandpa is gone, please share this with Gary; he will know what to do. All my love, Mikey."*

I couldn't hold back my tears. Mikey knew me only a short time, but I feel the same way—that we are brothers, united by something much greater. I need to understand more about the Hopi, so I can better understand him. Mary smiles warmly. "Those we love are always close by, Dylan." Ruby jumps up and says, "Don't cry, you should dance some more for us... Hopi freestyle!" We are all laughing, interrupted by a loud knock on the front door. It is Gary, coming to take me to Oraibi. It's time to meet Mikey's grandfather, Willy Junior.

# Home

WHEN GARY IS DRIVING to Old Oraibi, he looks at me and says, "Mikey's family has lived in Oraibi for over eleven hundred years. His grandfather is from the Bear Clan. They were the first people to arrive here. His grandfather lives alone. He doesn't have running water or electricity, and he still lives the old Hopi way. He is a deeply religious man who has dedicated his lifetime to teaching our people the right path. We've had many challenges; especially since the United States government placed our reservation in the middle of the Navajo reservation and tried to 'modernize' Hopiland.

"Our entire spiritual lives have been built on this mesa, and with growing corn for thousands of years, we have cultivated a very complex society and spiritual practices that keep our people in balance and harmony with the natural world. It is literally like the air we breathe. Remove corn, our language, and our religion—and we die. All of this is done by oral tradition. They used to take our children away and punish them if they spoke our language, or prayed in our traditional way.

"A growing sickness enters my people, and causes us to divide. It's been slowly eroding our people for the last one hundred years. Some call it the 'Friendlies,' those in favor of the path of the white man, and the 'hostiles,' those in favor of maintaining the traditions of our people. There are also those who favor both paths. I think Willy doesn't see much good in the path of the white man.

"He has been preparing for many days for the upcoming Soyal ceremony. When I told him that you are here to pay respects to Mikey's family, he said, 'My heart is full and I must meet Mikey's brother.' I have to warn you man, Willy is deep. He will see you, more than you can see yourself."

As we pass a beautiful pastoral area, Gary says, "That's where we bury our dead. That is where Mikey is buried." There are no tombstones. When I ask him about it, he smiles. "We believe that when you die, the moisture remaining in your body, leaves, and we become clouds."

Out of the truck, the wind blows hard and cold. Clouds of dust swirl around us, and the noise from several generators makes it difficult to hear. The village housing is ancient and in some places completely abandoned and disintegrating. As we go into the center of the village, I notice that I am walking over centuries of pottery shards. Gary stops and says, "This is our Kiva." A large wooden ladder emerges from the top, and an old cement base of some kind on one side. I ask him about it and he laughs. "That is where the Spanish built their church. It's the cornerstone. They filled our kiva with virgin sand and built their church over it. When we kicked them out, we left it to remind us—never again!"

At Willy's house, Gary knocks, enters ahead of me, and tells me to follow. An old man walks over, holds my hands, and looks deeply into my eyes. At first, I feel awkward. Then I take a deep breath and surrender. He smiles and Gary speaks to him in Hopi. Willy responds, "Okay!" He tells Gary to go to the Kiva, he wants to speak to me now.

Willy asks me to sit down. He is quiet for some time before he speaks.

"Bad spirits are attached to you and have caused you great suffering. There's been great sickness around you since you were a small boy. Your mother wasn't there to comfort you with her love, or your father to teach you the path. She loves you, but she is sick. He loves you, but he is lost. This pain isn't yours to hold. Mikey says you have a good heart. He says you have the spirit of the eagle, a warrior of words. This is good — strong, and important in this fourth world. I will teach you what you need to take from this place and teach the world. I will take your sickness, remove the bad spirits, and guide you to the place of balance and peace.

"We Hopi have tried your God, medicines, education, jobs, and entertainment, now my people are divided: *Kahopi* — not Hopi! I will guide you to the path. If you decide to walk upon it, is your choice."

Willy stands and announces that we are leaving. I follow him outside. The wind is howling now, and light falling snow blows across my path. He turns to me and says, "You brought this snow... that is a good sign." I have no idea what he is talking about and keep walking. When we get to the kiva, I see smoke coming from the top and I hear the faint sound of drums. He says something in Hopi and we descend into the Kiva. It is a square with four layers. The bottom layer is the lowest and represents the Hopi place of emergence, *sipapu*. Men sit on ledges on all sides of the kiva. An elaborate altar sits in the corner, with small, carved statues and Kachina dolls. Prayers are stamped onto a cottonwood floor covering. Willy picks up a *paho*, a prayer feather, and chants. He places me on the floor and rubs cornmeal over my forehead.

I haven't had time to adjust to my surroundings, and I'm overwhelmed by the intensity of the energy around me. The drums are intoxicating as the men chant in unison. Gary sits beside me for when translation is necessary. He says, "They are offering purification prayers. You no longer hold the weight of the past. This is the time to let go, my friend. Willy will remove all negative entities attached to your spirit." Willy laid his hand on my forehead, and I can feel tremendous energy and heat flowing from his hand. I close my eyes and see bright white light wash over me. Soon the room and people disappear and I am in my spirit body. Shahzada stands before me and tears stream down my face. She says, *Dylan, I must leave you now. Let me go, and remember me as love and light...*

Moments later, my mother and father appear. Tremendous pain swirls through me and my mother is crying. She says, *I'm sorry, baby boy. Mama loves you, I just can't overcome my pain. It's not you baby.* Instead of anger, I'm filled with compassion, and I forgive her for being weak and afraid. My father doesn't speak. He looks at me and begins to cry. I forgive my father for being absent and lost. The ceremony continues for hours. I'm not asleep, but in a deep trance and meditative state. I'm not sleepy or hungry. I am vibrating with energy. The drums and chanting stops and Willy sits in front of me. He instructs Gary to translate and to speak very slowly. This must be delivered in Hopi. I close my eyes and concentrate with all my being. Gary translates:

"You are the lucky one. You are the one who came home. You are a Spirit Warrior and therefore I give you this Hopi name—*Hania,* Spirit Warrior. You've been lost, but you have come to us, in love, and with respect for one of our people, and we now accept you as a brother for the rest of your life. To understand the path of the Hopi, you must receive these words and let them grow and live within you, and you will find balance and peace:

"A Hopi is one whose lifetime quest is to gain strength and wisdom through prayer, education, and experience.

"To acquire a practical and spiritual understanding of life, and to acquire the ability to address life's circumstances, and community's needs, from an eagle's viewpoint, with a caring attitude, and humility.

"A Hopi is one who fulfills the meaning of *Geftse*, maintaining the highest degree of respect for, and obedience to, moral standards, and ethics, so as not to knowingly abuse, alter, or oppose the progressive order and cycle of nature, and the sacred manifestations of the creator's teachings.

"A Hopi is one who fulfills the meaning of *Samitnemwa*, to come together to do activities for the benefit of all, out of a compelling desire and commitment to contribute, or return something of value to the benefit of society.

"A Hopi is one who fulfills the meaning of *Nametnawa*, helping one another, or give aid, in times of need without having to be asked to do so, and without expecting compensation for the deed.

"A Hopi is one who fulfills the meaning of *Hetanema*, by having the initiative to take care of something without having to be instructed, asked, or reminded, regardless if anyone will notice your effort, but that it will make a difference.

"The Hopi is one that understands that *Bosinamwa* is to have the characteristic qualities of humility, modesty, and patience. To possess the ability to think things through carefully, and thoroughly, before reacting and voicing one's opinion on issues.

"A Hopi is one who places the society's and our community's interest and benefits ahead of individual, and personal interest, and gains.

"A Hopi is one who understands that to realize a dream, one must not only pray for their desires, but also must make a sincere commitment and work diligently to pursue that dream, or goal, until it is achieved.

"A Hopi is one that understands that the creator has provided all the necessary resources needed by all living beings to co-exist here, including the means by which the human race can achieve a happy, healthy, and self-sustaining life.

"A Hopi is one that understands that the greatest feeling of accomplishment and fulfillment is one's participation in social community functions or activities, and knowing that your contributions have resulted in the benefit of the community, and its people."

After Willy speaks, the men rise and dance counter-clockwise. Gary pulls me up by the wrist and dances beside me, until I am able to follow the rhythm and movement. The song is difficult, but I eventually find the words. I am powerfully aware of the interconnectivity to all of life. Tears cleanse me and the primordial pain that has been trapped in my gut is released. Experiencing this feeling, not as a thought, but actually, the connection is spellbinding and spiritually I feel open — beyond time and space.

At some point I have a vision. I am in Llano with Krissy. She is smiling at me with so much love and sweetness. I can see her daughter laughing happily, running in circles in the backyard. We all seem happy together. I know it is time to allow someone to love me, to let Krissy into my heart.

The ceremony continues until the morning. Gary tells me that I've been reborn as a Hopi, and must greet the sunrise. Hopi babies are kept in a dark room for twenty days, and on the final day, the mother takes the child to greet the sun, puts cornmeal into the child's mouth and says, "This is who you are."

As I emerge from the kiva, I am elated. I feel like I'm floating above my physical body. When the cold hits my face, it makes me feel alive and electric. We walk to the edge of the mesa and look out onto the beautiful sunrise and my heart is full. Willy says some prayers in Hopi and we head to Mary's house to eat. I am starving after dancing all night with no lunch or dinner. When we get to Mary's, Gary tells me to wait outside the house; he needs to make sure she is ready for us. Standing in the plaza, I notice two beautiful eagles tethered to the roof in the distance. I smile, and think: *That is you and me, Mikey!*

The drummers from the kiva have arrived with the drums. Just as I think, *Surely, they aren't going to bang the drums this early in the morning… and wake up the village,* they begin to play and sing. Soon an old man dances in the plaza. Gary tells me it is the first Katsina waking up after being asleep for the last six months. The village is beginning the sixteen-day celebration of Soyal. Soon the villagers enter the plaza: children and old ladies wrapped in blankets. Many young men climb onto the roofs to watch. A line of Kachina dancers enter the plaza, single file and slowly dance in formation. They are amazing, and I feel like I am connected to an uninterrupted spiritual link for thousands of years with every dance movement.

As the Kachina dancers move throughout the plaza, I notice a young man seated with his legs crossed on the very edge of the roof. He was laser-focused on the dancers. It is clear to me that he is feeling every drumbeat, and every step of the dance. He wears a long-sleeved, bright yellow t-shirt. He moves in rhythm with the drum, his hands and arms in unison with the dancers. I am filled with a satisfying certainty that he, among all the others, will become *Hopi*—he will continue on the straight path—and carry a fourteen-thousand-year-old dance and song in his heart.

# Epilogue

*Five Years Later*

Just when you feel like you have everything in its place and your life is how you want it, there are always unexpected events.

When Sarge told me that he learned that Dope and Kong were killed in action, it set me back. It was almost unbearable. I feel horrible that I couldn't be there to help my brothers.

Listening to the new president discuss his policies in Afghanistan, and how he will seek advice from private militia guys like Blackwater gets me so fucking angry. The bad dreams and night terrors return. I'd like to think that Kong went down in a blaze of gunfire and glory. He truly loved being a warrior. Dope's death breaks my heart, because I know that he wanted more than anything else in this world, besides meeting that Afghan dude's sister in the red sweater, to help his mother and brother get out of the South Side of Chicago. When I told Bob, my adoptive father, about Dope and his family, he offered to give them a "gift" that would ensure the ability to buy a nice place anywhere they would like to move. That made my heart happy. And I bet it made yours too, Dope. Am I right?

I'm not sure what I would do without my wife, Krissy, and our daughter, Katie. Krissy has such depth, and the ability to truly see me. She doesn't try to change me or ask me to be something other than who I really am. The sound of little Katie's laughter lights me up like a Christmas tree every day. I get such joy being her "love daddy" and I try to give her all the best of me, and teach her how to live the Hopi way, on the straight path. She loves her stepsister Ruby, and her Aunt Mary on Second Mesa.

I suppose that losing Mikey, Kong, and Dope is the main reason I'm now trying to help other vets. I work for a nonprofit that offers counseling, education, and benefit resources designed to help vets who have been incarcerated. We try to help them get their feet back on the ground and to prepare them to get out and have productive and happy lives.

It drives a stake into my heart a little deeper every time I read or hear that twenty-two American vets a day take their own lives: fathers, brothers, wives, husbands, friends, lovers, and fellow citizens.

I'm blessed to have my brother Daniel doing so well, and a part of our lives. He has become such a wonderful and talented young man, with such depth and heart. Daniel loves little Katie, and they do elaborate art projects in the backyard when he visits. Because of Bob and Janie's generous financial gift to us both, he's been able to attend art school at Yale University, and he is creatively unstoppable. He even got an internship with the genius glassblower Dale Chihuly, thanks to my pal Sigi. When I took him to Arizona to visit Mary and Ruby, he became enchanted with the amazing colors and landscapes of the region, and we stopped for a visit with Sigi. He did an art installation in Sedona with Sigi, with giant blown glass with wonderful colors and shapes to relate to the intensity of the energy vortex and the surrounding red-rock formations. It was a big success.

Bob and Janie continue to be wonderful adoptive parents for us. They didn't seem to mind when I sold the Barn Swallow house to move to Llano to be with Krissy and Katie. We were able to make greatly needed improvements to the bakery, and to build an art studio in the back for Krissy. They visit us every once in a while, and sometimes bring Charlie and Natalie. At first, Charlie and Natalie seemed really bummed that I was sell-ing the place and moving to Llano — that is, until Bob and Janie bought the house back from me, and gave it to them! So far, Charlie hasn't burnt the house down making bacon or "magic brownies," and Natalie has become less randomly "boy crazy." She has actually found a nice guy who she calls her "temporary permanent!"

I don't see the Sarge much. He has been living in New Orleans, booking exotic travel for gay tours: Jerusalem, Thailand, Greece, Japan, and Hopi-land. He calls the tours to Hopi-land, "The Two Spirits adventure!" His visits to Llano are happy, fun occasions. Katie calls him "Uncle Sarge" and she adores him because he brings her amazingly exotic gifts from his world travels. We've never really discussed our drunken evening with Natalie. I think we all realize that it was just a drunken libertine moment that left us all with Mona Lisa smiles.

Mom and Malcolm are still deeply embroiled in their addic-tions and show no signs of changing. They are only about forty minutes from our house, and I try to stop by and visit the other kids from time to time, or bring them to our house to play with Katie. It is still a Charlie Foxtrot, and painful every time I see them. I guess some things will always hurt, but now, I know how to honor the pain by seeing what's behind it.

It took me a couple of years, but I've finally been able to get Gabby in a rehab program because of my connections at work. She didn't really appreciate it when I invited Raven out for a drink and hogtied him, and suspended him off the bridge over Lake Marble Falls. I think I said something poetic like, "If you get within five feet of my sister, I will come back, and next time I will cut the rope." Gabby is beginning to realize that her old lifestyle is not where she wants to be, and Raven can't give her what she needs. When she gets out, she is going to live at Barn Swallow and go to Austin Community College. Charlie says he can get her a job at the coffee shop.

I am so grateful for my blessings, but I always feel a slight anxiety about the events going on around me in the world. The news is often upsetting. Karl Marx said, *"Religion is the opium of the people."* I think now, news is the opium of the people! I try to identify news that feels important and relevant, and then within days it's covered up by the weight of more news. The news-blizzard effect is causing our democracy to suffer because the citizens are not informed of the facts.

For most, the subject of war in the news is unsavory. An unfortunate evil to keep democracy afloat, protect our freedoms and rights, but like so many aspects of our culture, it's better not to discuss it socially. For me, it is an essential topic to discuss, to consider, and to have an opinion. Twenty-two vets per day stick a gun in their mouths, drink themselves to death, overdose, or drive-off a cliff because they can't stand the pain, the lies, and the divide.

But, I don't get as angry as I used to about this shit. I stopped putting my fist through the walls. It got expensive, and it really upsets Krissy. With that said, it has caused me to get very involved in my daughter's education, and I stay frosty when it's time to vote.

I guess after this long away from war, I've begun to see the beauty in life again. It hits me when I least expect it: the sweet smile of an innocent child, a fascinating scientific discovery, a new archaeological find, a beautiful work of art, or hearing Americans sing and shine. We do like to shine!

These days, I just try and keep my path straight, and focus on telling the truth. I'm dedicated to sharing as much love as my heart will produce. I feel that if I am sharing love, I am a valuable resource on the planet. I follow the Hopi way, the credo that Willy shared with me during my healing ceremony. I have good days and bad. Letting Krissy love me is the best and most difficult thing I've done in my life.

One of the truly great joys in my life is returning to Hopi-land to see Mary and Ruby. Willy died last year, but Gary is doing well as a Hopi tour guide. He was even featured in *The New York Times*. When we go to Second Mesa, I always look up in the sky for clouds, because I know Mikey and Grandpa Willy will be there to welcome us, and lately I swear I can see Shahzada, Tacos, Dope and Kong.

The land on the reservation may look barren and uninhabitable to some. But to me, the pale cerulean blue sky, the brightness of the sun and the cool windy air, the soaring mesas, the dry landscape with all her various colors and hues, golden yellow grasses, and the almost overwhelming sense of calm one feels being there... these things feel like home.

● ● ●

# About the author

LANE ROCKFORD ORSAK began his creative life in children's theater, with a mother who was the first woman on television for ABC in Houston, Texas (*Kitirik,* 1954–1971). He studied acting and the Liberal Arts at Lon Morris College and graduated from the University of Texas, where he danced two seasons in the Austin Ballet Theatre.

His musical *Mr. Hanks* was accepted to audition at the prestigious BMI Lehman Engel Musical Theater Workshop in New York City, and his young adult *Keiko the Fairy* book series was accepted by the president of Paramount Pictures Animation in Los Angeles for consideration.

For more information visit:

www.laneorsak.com

THIS BOOK was written after meeting a young man who served in Afghanistan. He shared with me his personal struggles to heal, and his philosophical divide regarding his involvement. He now works for the Samaritan Center as a Peer Navigator, and passionately tries to help other vets in the prison system get their lives back on track.

If you want to make a difference in the life of a veteran, visit:

www.samaritan-center.org

•  ●  •